# THE PALE SORCERESS

## Book Four of the Chronicles of Ilseador

### (the Prydeen Prophecy Cycle)

## MANGALA McNAMARA

Also available in eBook and hardcover editions.
McNamara, Mangala
The Pale Sorcered/ by Mangala McNamara Indiana: Rising Dragon Books, 2024
166 pages, 2 maps
(McNamara, Mangala. Chronicles of Ilseador; bk. 4)
Summary: Damien sacrificed himself to save his ice-bound city from pirates and sorcery. Now he must endure captivity and learn the sorcery he lacks in order to win free and get back to his wife, his unborn child, his friends… and his Realm that is still facing an unknown threat.
ISBN 978-1-960160-47-8 (pbk)
1. Kings and rulers - Fiction. 2. Wizards and Magic - Fiction
ISBN 978-1-960160-48-5 (hc); ISBN 978-1-960160-46-1 (eBook)



ISBN: 978-1-960160-47-8
First Print Edition: August 2024
10 9 8 7 6 5 4 3 2 1

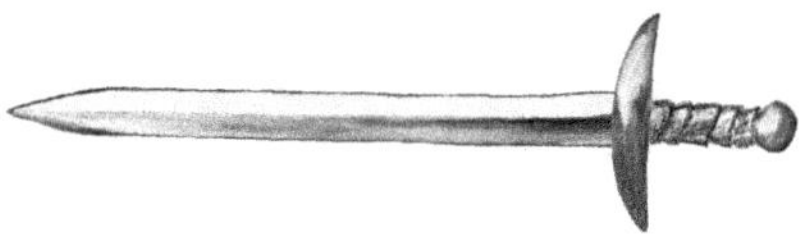

## *"You'll do."*

A smile that Damien was all too familiar with curled Azella's lips. "You'll more than do, in fact. My sources hadn't told me how handsome you are. I shall quite enjoy this, I think."

Damien tried not to roll his eyes.

"This beard..." She stroked his chin. "I assume you usually keep it a bit more trim. I usually prefer my bedmates to be cleanshaven. But then, they are usually too young to grow a proper beard. Perhaps I shall make an exception."

"Perhaps you are making an assumption, lady sorceress," Damien said dryly.

"No," she said calmly. "You are no innocent child, Damien. You know full well the Power that is raised through sex. You will be my Apprentice. You will share my bed. And you will do whatever else I require of you."

He looked back at Azella just as calmly. "I have sworn to my wife that I would touch no other woman in that way. And since I also know that the Power raised is proportional to the joy found in the doing, it won't do you much good to compel me."

Those blue-grey eyes sparkled. It wasn't – quite – anger. Nor amusement. It was... challenge. Damien suspected that the sorceress rarely found something she wanted that she could not immediately bend to her will.

He suspected that was why she had wanted him in the first place.

**"Oh, I won't have to force you to make love to me, Damien. You'll soon be begging to do so."**

For everyone who is forced
to place the means before the ends – and then deal with
the consequences

*A note to sensitive souls:*

*Damien has given himself up as a captive to an Evil Wizard - Azella the Unpitying - to save Ilseador and the people he loves.*

*He spent his youth hiding from his grandfather and Lord Prydeen's (and Prince Oskar's) Evil Wizardery - and he was sheltered from it as much as possible by his friends.*

*He's feared that by using any of his own magick he's getting too close to following in his grandfather's footsteps. Despit ethe reassurances of Adam, Genevieve, and the rest, he hasn't felt he could trust himself. That lack of confidence kept him from developing the skills he needed to fend off Azella.*

*Now, Damien is going to come face to face with what it means to be tempted  by a true master of the craft of Evil Wizardery...*

*Proceed with caution...*

# CONTENTS

*Excerpt from*
*Book One: The Rebel Duchess*

# Chapter ONE

# *Captured!*

DAMIEN WAS LIMPING WITHIN MOMENTS of exiting the market square, his barely-healed, frostbitten feet aching and burning with each step.

But he dared not stop. Dared not let the sorceress who led him with barely a touch of her hand think that he showed the slightest hesitation, lest she loose her deadly salamanders upon his vulnerable, ice-bound city.

Salamanders... Fire-elementals. Creatures of legend as unlike the gentle amphibians of his own Realm as dragons resembled lizards. They could set fire to *stone,* for all he knew – despite a purported distaste for water, he'd already seen that they had shown no hesitation at melting either the ice that clogged his harbor or a path up from that self-same harbor for the mob of pirates she had brought here. Or perhaps that *was* a demonstration of their dislike of water. It was one of so many – *too* many – things Damien's self-education in magick had not covered.

And then there was that self-same mob of pirates led by his long-vanished cousin – who claimed Damien's throne as his own.

The sorceress cared nothing it seemed, for such mortal disputes. She had come to take the Sorcerer-King of Ilseador for her own – he knew not why – and had abandoned her pirate-allies when Damien agreed to yield himself if she would withdraw rather than loose her salamanders.

If she would withdraw rather than loose *herself* on his poor, ice-bound city.

The silence behind him was almost deafening. He longed to know what was happening – were the pirates standing down in the face of a city they could no longer burn and ravage without their pet sorceress?

Was the Pirate-King, Evan Alsterling, Damien's long-lost and deeply embittered cousin content with stealing away Megan Solway, the woman he had loved since he was fifteen – thirty-five years ago? Was he trying to make peace with his son, Damien's oldest friend and mentor and now also his Heir to the Realm? Jason... just moments before revealed as Megan's secret son, and *not* her much-younger, much-reviled brother...

Was Evan Alsterling still hell-bent on taking the Crown as well, despite that it would put him inevitably into conflict with that selfsame son?

And Damien's beloved, and newly pregnant, wife and Queen... her raging, weeping voice still rang in his ears, in his heart, though the sound had long since died away.

*"Damien! I **will** find you! And I **will** free you!"*

That had been the voice of the Rebel Duchess he had married, the one who had torn the Realm apart to try save it from the evil wizard and tyrant – his grandfather. The one who had come to the city alone and in secret to see if the newly-crowned Damien would follow in those dire footsteps or be the king they hoped for – and become soul-bonded to him, to her own dismay... then finally fallen in love with him when he'd all but followed her through fire – and had *literally* followed her through stone – in order to reclaim *their* throne from the usurpation of her not-nearly-so-deceased-as-advertised former husband.

It had *also* been the voice of the Queen she had *become* – with the blood-right to rule in her own name, as a descendant of the evil wizard-king's own grandmother... The Queen that Damien hoped she could now be, since he could not be by her side.

Damien wondered if the Monarch's Blade now blazed in her hand, free from its scabbard and declaring his Genevieve the rightful Queen of the Realm, no matter what *Evan Alsterling* might claim. Or was the Sword still muffled and still held in trust by Jason, his Heir, and his beloved Genevieve still restrained by Duke Tomas Elsevier for her own protection. His beautiful love was a doughty warrior and an unparalleled strategist, but tended to hotheadedness at times...

He daren't look back to see if the coruscating rainbow light from the Sword was visible.

Nonetheless, he was distracted, and a loose cobblestone stubbed his damaged toes.

Damien stumbled, and bit off a curse.

The sorceress stopped and turned to look at him, a small smile playing on her too-young face. She looked barely more than a child, younger still with that long, pale hair, huge blue-grey eyes, and crystal-white gown. A mere waif.

*Azella the Unpitying,* she had named herself.

"We're well past those fools, and you have demonstrated yourself to be a man of your word. I don't need you to walk your feet off just to prove a point."

Instantly, they were gone from the darkened, ice-shrouded street and ensconced in a warm, well-lit room paneled entirely in wood. By the slight bob and sway, Damien ascertained that they were aboard a ship. She released his hand and indicated he was to sit in a well-padded chair. Perhaps she was not so Unpitying as all that.

If he might have begun to think so, her next words dispelled any such foolishness.

"You are a man of *honor,* Sorcerer-King," the waif said sardonically, "And you have given me your word to come away with me on pain of your city being burnt by my salamanders. This ship shall bear you to my Keep. I shall place no constraints upon your Powers for now, save for your own *conscience.*" The sardonic twist to her tone suggested she found such a restraint humorous.

Damien closed his eyes, the throbbing of his feet now that they had no pressure on them beating a counterpoint to the ache of his heart. For just an instant, he'd hoped... But no. Clearly she knew that, even though she'd withdrawn the threat, he would feel obligated to hold to his side of the agreement unless she released him.

"Until then, I leave you this toy. Do with her as you please."

He opened his eyes in confusion to see the glamour of Power fade from around the waif.

*You seem to favor redheads,* the voice said only in his head now.

The hair grew darker, redder, the eyes went from huge and blue-grey to upturned and blue-green, a spray of fine freckles across the nose... a younger – much, *much* younger – version of Genevieve stood before him. She reached up to pull a lock of hair in front of her to examine, and her expression was aggrieved. Damien recoiled in horror.

*Not to your taste, sorcerer-king? Trust me, it's not an illusion. The transformation is real. No still? Very well. The girl will do in her native form for now then.*

The red hair darkened to a rich, mahogany, the features changed again, the eyes became a light hazel-green. A stranger stood before him, neither wife nor sorceress. Thank all the Gods at once.

*Enjoy.* A sense of rippling amusement, and then the sense that she was gone. For now.

The glittering white gown had also lost its luster, and was now a simple unbleached linen gown. The girl in it stared at him.

"You're... not Azella the Unpitying," was all Damien could think to say.

The girl snorted. "My mistress go out from the Keep into danger and – worse – discomfort? Don't be ridiculous. She has better uses for her time when there are slaves to do this instead." And the worst part of it was that the girl said it entirely without irony. As if it was what she truly believed.

"Are you... her apprentice?" he asked.

"My lady does not take females for apprentices," the girl said. "It was my privilege to bear my mistress's shape and Power for some time. And now it is my privilege to serve you. I have been well-trained," she added. "And I am a virgin."

She came forwards and seated herself on his lap, twining her arms about his neck. "How should you like me, my lord?"

Damien blanched and not merely because the weight of her put renewed pressure on the soles of his abused feet.

He'd been propositioned many times. It was surprising to him, the number of nobles – both maidens and men, not to mention their ambitious relatives – who thought that the way into their king's favor was through his bedsheets.

But there were no slaves in Ilseador. Even under his grandfather's tyrannical rule that had not changed, though the way King Reginald had treated his subjects and sworn vassals, and even his scions, had left little distinction to be made.

*This,* however... *This* turned his stomach as even the baroness who had offered him a choice of her twin son and daughter had not. Well, not so badly. The expressions of avarice on said young people's faces had turned his stomach in a different way.

"I'd... just like to get some sleep, please," the king said, trying to roust the girl off his lap without forcibly dumping her on the floor.

The girl rose, and helped him over to the bed that was also in the room when it was clear that his feet hurt too much for him to stand long. She helped him remove the soft, indoor half-boots that were all he'd been able to tolerate, and that only this morning... glorified slippers, he'd joked to

Genevieve and she'd rolled her eyes at him. The thin soles were soaked through and irretrievably filthy after their unexpected exposure to city streets, the lamb's-wool interior damp and rough.

But there was only the one bed.

And he was *not* going to make the poor child sleep on the floor, or whatever she would be forced to resort to.

He removed his tunic, and she set it aside on the chair for him, neatly, then appeared to be awaiting other garments.

Damien eyed her dubiously and elected to merely loosen his shirt. He laid down, and as he had suspected she would, the girl slipped off her gown to reveal absolutely nothing underneath, and laid down next to him. At least she also pulled a heavy wool blanket over the both of them... but he felt obscurely guilty that he had the extra layer of his clothing for warmth. She also clearly had some Power of her own, for the lamps all dimmed down till the barest embers glowed from their wicks.

He trapped against his side the small hand that sought to slide under the hem of his shirt – he'd loosened, but not freed the shirt, so the attempt was bound to be unsuccessful.

"*Just* sleep," Damien told her. "It's been a very long day. And surely, after bearing the weight of all your... mistress's Power, you must be tired as well."

"That doesn't matter," the girl said. "It is my task to serve you. My mistress expects that I shall return to her well-used, and that you will have been well-entertained."

The king frowned, and raked back the errant lock of hair from his face. "I'm a soul-bonded and happily-married man."

"My mistress will solve those things for you."

She didn't seem to see any irony in referring to the best parts of his life as things to be 'solved.' It was, apparently, simply another 'fact.'

He sighed. "How old are you anyways? And do you have a name?"

"Fourteen. My mistress calls me Denisa."

Damien frowned. He was almost old enough to be her father. Definitely old enough – Evan Alsterling had been fifteen when he fathered Jason, after all. "She *re-named* you?"

"My mistress says that names are Power, and that she will keep my true-name safe for me."

Well, the first part was certainly true. Damien had seen what havoc could be wreaked when his grandfather's erstwhile apprentice had stolen the old king's name – and thereby his Power. It seemed to have been the culmination of a decades-long struggle for power – and Power – between the two evil old men.

Lord Prydeen's accomplishment had erased King Reginald's name from living memory and made it impossible to discern on documents. It had also led to the old wizard-king's death, stealing his ability to keep the damaged, angry magickal fabric of the Realm from removing what Power – and *Life* – he had left.

"She will doubtless do the same for you, now that you are hers," the girl added.

"I am not *hers,*" Damien objected. "I am merely a hostage. Not a... a slave."

**Nor** *an apprentice,* he thought. Though a part of him wondered what this sorceress could teach him. He was entirely self-taught, learning from instinct, experiment, those few books he could find... and, cringingly, from his grandfather's and Lord Prydeen's notes.

The girl's eyes gleamed in the faint light, though he couldn't make out the rest of her face. "You are here. And soon you will be at the Keep. You have chosen to come, but it was because she left you with no viable alternative."

A pretty vocabulary for a slave. Interesting.

"Please, my lord," Denisa pleaded, reverting abruptly to her previous demeanor. "Don't return me a virgin to the Keep. My lady has only one use for virgin maidens save for these rare occasions when she needs a vessel for her Power."

"And what is that?" Damien asked, dreading the answer.

"To summon demons."

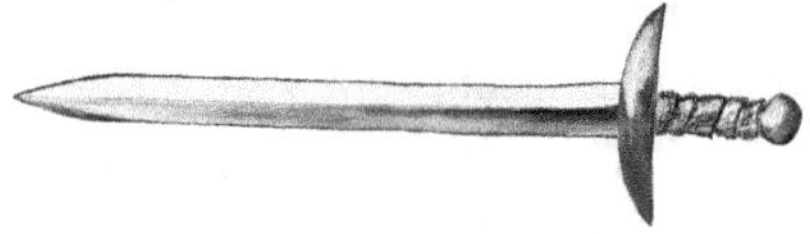

He was able to soothe the child to sleep after that... though it took a good long while of convincing her just to close her eyes and rest. Finally, he had to turn over and fake sleep himself. ignoring her until her breathing slowed and steadied.

Demons! His grandfather's notes included an extensive discussion of his researches into demonology, but he felt fairly sure that the old man's experiments had never been successful. One good thing about evil wizards was that they were not much inclined to share their discoveries, and most decent people burnt their grimoires when they were finally defeated by decadence, heroism, or personal accident.

Damien had fully intended to do just that when he had gleaned what he could – not merely regarding magick, but to fill in the lost history of the Realm, missing persons and the like. It niggled at him that he might now not be able to do so. He had, at least, bespelled the books and papers such that no one else than himself should be able to open and read them.

Once Denisa was asleep, Damien was able to reach down the soul-bond for Genevieve's reassuring presence.

*Damien!* she exclaimed, and he was surprised that her words came across so clearly.

She must be in bed and able to concentrate, perhaps even have been trying to reach him herself. Genevieve's talent for magick had far exceeded her desire to develop her abilities; while they had used the soul-bond to communicate for years, detailed discussions still required that she be touching him or meditating. Otherwise, they received only sense-impressions from each other – emotions and, occasionally, physical sensations.

He flung himself to her... wishing he dared do it physically as well. But a sorceress who wielded Elementals and *demons* as well as her own Power was not to be trifled with. They might not survive her next attack so well.

Because they *had* weathered this one well, Genevieve informed him.

Without the ability to burn and pillage, without the sorceress's backing, and faced with besieging a well-stocked force with the advantage of strong walls, not to mention the anticipated arrival of the vastly superior Army division... the pirates had begun abandoning their king like rats deserting a sinking ship. Every time Evan had turned away, another group had slipped back down the ice-free pathway to their ships.

Finally, the Pirate-King had snarled at his own crew and departed. Though he had taken Megan Solway with him.

Lord David Solway, Megan's husband, had reacted with less drama than Genevieve had expected. He was grim, but he was already making plans to rescue her. Somehow. Damien's Queen had asked that he run things by her first, but he hadn't answered and the glint in his eye suggested that she had better be sure they had spies watching his movements.

For now, however, the bereft foreign lordling seemed to be spending his time with his children, helping them to cope with the loss of their mother.

Jason... was performing his roles as Heir to the Throne and Duke of Emeralsee. He was as shutdown emotionally, Genevieve said, as she had ever seen him, and she had known him since he was thirteen.

It had been less than a week ago that Jason had learned that his father had not been the monster that his mother, the Countess Alexa Solway, had always claimed and that his conception had been ordered as part of some obscure plot by King Reginald. And that the tyrant had been his great-grandfather.

*Last* night Jason had learned that his mysterious father was still alive, indeed that he was the King of the Pirates... and that Countess Alexa was not his mother but his *grandmother.* That Megan – the woman he had always thought was his much-elder sister – had actually given birth to him.

Jason had never handled change particularly well. It had taken him days just to be able to say 'yes' to Adam's proposal of marriage – though they had been loves and lovers and completely committed to each other for over fifteen years.

Genevieve had tried to dislodge Jason's new husband, Sir Adam Loveress, from his role as her bodyguard to take care of Jason. But having so spectacularly failed to protect the king, the Champion was refusing to leave Genevieve. Although he'd at least been willing to return to Jason's side when Genevieve had herself retired for the night.

Duke Tomas Elsevier of Siovale and Sir Timothy Ancellius, Knight-Commander of the Royal Guard – and *de facto* commander of the Castle's defense in this case – had remained on the walls to monitor the pirates' retreat. It had taken the two of them, and Genevieve pretending to more exhaustion than she felt, to convince Jason to try to rest, and Adam to go with him.

The denizens of the Castle, however, had been released from the warded or secured rooms to seek more comfortable quarters now that the crisis had passed. She had hopes that they could somehow begin freeing the ice-bound residents of the city once the Army arrived.

*You should see the Army by evening tomorrow, at the latest,* Damien told his wife. And then went on to tell her where he had left certain documents and how to lift some of the spells he had used to prevent tampering – one of the warded rooms having been his personal office. She stopped his flow of information with the psychic equivalent of a kiss.

*We'll sort it all out,* Genevieve assured him. *When we get you home.*

*About that,* the king said reluctantly, and told her about the demons.

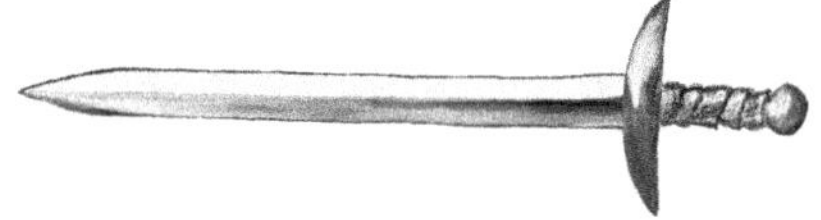

# Chapter TWO

# *Opening*

THE SHIP MUST HAVE SLIPPED its moorings while he slept, dreaming uneasily of small, pale sorceresses and murky, bloodthirsty creatures... and his beloved wife, somehow kept safe from it all. By the time he woke, the movements of the ship were so much more dramatic that Damien felt sure they must be at sea.

Denisa served him breakfast with some disgruntlement, and didn't object when he made to leave the cabin. It wasn't until the king was out into the companionway that he realized his still-bare feet barely twinged at all. After days of magickally-enhanced healing from the magickally-induced frostbite, he was *almost* back to normal. A great relief, because he felt sure that he would need all of his capabilities in top form to cope with whatever would come next.

They were, indeed, out to sea. So far out, in fact, that Damien could not guess in which direction the closest land might lie.

At least not by sight.

Damien was magickally Bound to his Realm, and so he was all too aware of where he was in relation to it. They were sailing south, into colder waters, and the coast to their right was merely just beyond visual range, perhaps due to winds and currents... perhaps out of an attempt to disorient him.

The king had never been outside of Ilseador before, never been farther from his capitol city of Emeralsee than brief visits to his vassals' lands. Given his Binding to the land, he had never thought to be *able* to travel... nor really had much desire to do so when all he loved and needed was right there. And when he – once a discarded and disregarded princeling who had hidden from his grandfather's ire in the Royal Library for nearly ten years – when he was so dearly loved and needed right where he was.

This, however...

Damien found himself unexpectedly energized by the feel of the ship cresting from wavetop to wavetop under the power of the belling sails. There was something incredibly freeing about standing at the bow of the ship filled with its silent sailors, the salt spray flying up into his face. He found himself – despite the fact that he was effectively a prisoner aboard this ship – grinning in exultation.

He was, after all, a prisoner by choice. A hostage of his conscience. He could exert his Power at any time to return himself home – if he were willing to break his word... and risk the sorceress's retaliation. Though without the pirates as her escort he suspected she would not pose quite so much of a threat.

And he had spoken to Genevieve last night and knew that all was well at home. He had even been able to sneak his Healer's sense across the bond, so he knew her pregnancy hadn't been affected by all the craziness of the previous days.

*You seem very pleased with yourself, sorcerer-king,* Azella the Unpitying's eternally amused voice inserted itself into his head as he stood in the bow, soaked to the skin and enjoying it.

*I have a name, you know,* Damien answered. *Why not just call me by it?*

*Oh, you are pleased with yourself. Enough to reply, at last!* She insinuated herself deeper into his thoughts. *I would have imagined such self-satisfaction in a male would correlate with having availed yourself of certain... opportunities, but Denisa tells me you did nothing but sleep. How odd, when you seemed so much more... **active** back in your lovely Castle.*

Damien refused to feel embarrassed. *She's just a child. I don't bed babies.*

*Hmmmn. Based on dear Evan's stories, I had the impression your people were not such sticklers.*

*He ended up exiled for that.* Damien retorted. *Effectively at least.*

*So why are you so pleased? If it's merely the cessation of paperwork – my dear, you really need to get out more! What is the use of having all the Power you do and doing nothing but shuffling papers?*

Damien realized that *was* actually a significant portion of his ebullience. There was no way to get to his desk and the reports piling up on it, therefore no guilt that he wasn't doing so. He couldn't actually remember the last time he had escaped from the paperwork for more than a day, except for his stolen week this Autumn. There had been his visit to Embervest following the reacquisition of Minglemere – two years ago. And his nearly biannual visits to Elaarwen. And even then, the paper had followed him.

He remembered that Genevieve had said early on that she went hunting to get away from it all. But Damien didn't hunt and had no desire to learn – not when he could feel the death of every animal in the Realm as it was. He had hated the idea of killing things even before he was Bound to the Realm.

But how wonderful it had felt to ride out with Jason earlier this Autumn, simply to be away...

He needed to think about something else. He didn't *really* want to be gone from Ilseador – his *wife,* the baby to come... His goal should be to negotiate a way to return as soon as possible...

*Do you really look like that?* He found himself asking her as a distraction. *All pale hair and big blue eyes? And looking like a child?*

*You'll see soon enough,* came the reply. Phantom fingers ran down his skin in very... intimate ways, and he couldn't suppress a shiver that had nothing to do with his sea-spray-soaked clothing. *I don't think you'll be... disappointed, shall we say. For now, however, it seems you have some contact still with Ilseador. And with your Queen. We can't be having that, now can we? That clever, hotheaded wife of yours might be tempted to come after you if she could sense where you were... and that wouldn't end well. For her.*

*You could let me go back,* Damien suggested.

*After all the trouble I went to just to acquire you? Don't be silly. You should be honored, sorcerer-king. I haven't seen a reason to deal with those howling sea-rats for any lesser purpose. Now... about these troublesome Bindings...*

Damien gasped, and fell to his knees clutching the ship's rail as his sense of his Realm... vanished. The Binding that had begun when he wore the great, grey pearl of the Heir's Ring, continued with his Crowning and Anointing, taken a deeper aspect when he'd accepted the Sword from the stone statue of his ancestress – and nearly eaten him alive when he'd subsequently sat upon his Throne...

...he could no longer *feel* it.

And even with the Realm in Winter-slumber, he was now cut off from the greater source of his Power.

A moment later, the sharp, white *feeling* of blankness where he'd had the constant reassuring sense of Genevieve for over five years nearly made his heart stop. He hadn't even noticed that he *felt* her breath, her pulse, tasted the low level of her mental state – last he knew, mild exasperation and irritation – until it was suddenly cut-off.

A soul-bond was supposed to be a gift of the Gods...

"*Why...?*" he gasped it aloud, fighting for breath. "What use can I possibly *be* to you with the bulk of my magick taken away?"

*You underestimate yourself, Damien. Though **I** do not. You are a much* **safer** *acquisition now, and it behooves me to blunt your teeth and claws before allowing you access to my person, does it not?*

"*Now* you're willing to use my name?"

**Now** *you're not so much a king, are you? With your Realm reft away?*

Oh, that horrible ripple of amusement...

*And as to whether you are actually worth the title of 'sorcerer'... You are half-trained at best, a glorified Apprentice at worst,* **boy**. *With all the Power of your Realm,* **you** *should have had no trouble repelling me, salamanders and all. But you don't know* **how** *– neither how to use your Power nor how to pace and ration yourself to avoid exhausting your own resources. Nor do you know where and how to seek the Greater Powers.*

**You** *are a* **child** *who has lived a life of plenty, and you squander yourself thoughtlessly and cry and give up when your wastefulness has left you with no more toys to play with.*

Damien's grey eyes blazed with offended pride. "I'd like to see *you* do better, with what I've had to learn from."

He still gripped the ship's railing with one hand; his other was now wrapped around his middle to try to contain the incipient nausea that had come upon him when she pinched off his soul-bond to Genevieve.

*You need a Master, boy,* she told him, relentlessly... unpityingly. *Or, in this case, a Mistress. I shall teach you, and you shall give me your Power in exchange. Perhaps you will even survive the process.*

"Apprentice to an evil sorceress?" He laughed, bitterly. "I've had the notes of both my grandfather and Lord Prydeen to learn from."

*Amateurs.* Azella dismissed his grandfather's eighty-three-year reign of tyranny. *And you fear to use what they learned anyways. I shall teach you not to fear your Power, Damien. I shall teach you what you need to be Great.*

"No thank you," he gritted out.

*You sound as though you have a choice, boy. You do not. While there are few – or none – as Powerful as myself, you would choose to go back to your paltry kingdom and await the next sorcerer who would take it from you? You're not such a fool.*

Damien managed to get a full breath. "You'll teach me to protect my land?"

It didn't seem like her to offer her something that would actually help him.

*What you learn from me will make you invincible should you defend your land,* she said somewhat evasively. He didn't miss that earlier she had said he might not survive her teaching.

"And if I agree to be your Apprentice?"

*You mean if you do so willingly? You are **already** my Apprentice, Damien. And this is but your first lesson. The first, but the most important: Do not think you can challenge me. Do not imagine that you can escape me. You are my **belonging** as much as that ship or my slaves that sail it – or the slave-girl I gifted you for your amusement. Do you fight me I shall enjoy breaking you to my will. And do you choose to comply without fighting, you will not lull me into any false sense of belief in your loyalty.*

*You are not a king anymore, Damien. You are my Apprentice and my chattel and what freedoms I allow you are for my amusement alone.*

The sense of her was gone, and Damien stayed crouched on the deck of the ship, recovering his breath. She had certainly made her position clear.

The bright, clear day with its blue sky and fluffy clouds seemed to have darkened, and his sea-soaked clothing suddenly chilled him to the bone.

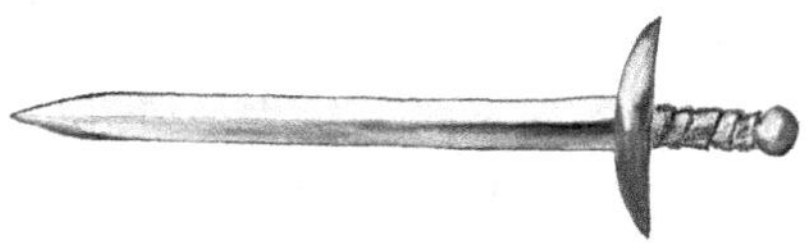

Apparently, he was still to be permitted to decide whether he would bed the child, Denisa, however. For even when she found him dry clothing – in his size exactly, and a similar style – she made no effort to seduce him again. Or perhaps she was merely awaiting the approach of night.

The dark-haired man stretched out on the bed after eating the luncheon Denisa had served him – silently, and with no indication that she knew her mistress had put him in his place. That she knew he was as much a slave as she, at least in the sorceress's mind.

Damien had never exactly felt *free* – at least not since he was eight years old and his parents had been summoned back to the city to live in his grandfather's Castle. Before that they had lived with his mother's parents and siblings and he had existed as part of a happy herd of cousins, running wild through the fields and farms and forests of Ravenscroft. There had been a herd of cousins at the Castle, too, but it was quiet, cutthroat, and as the youngest he was largely ignored.

That had turned out to be all to the good, as that herd of cousins – and the aunts and uncles that had produced them – was thinned, year by year. *Culled,* really. Accidents that weren't accidents – such as the damaged tack that had ended with his sister, Kandra's, death. Kandra, he'd discovered many years later, had been about to announce her betrothal to the son of Baron Anvliyar and then use the wedding as a way to help her parents and the then-ten-year-old Damien defect to the Rebellion.

Instead, Kandy's grand plans had been betrayed to Lord Prydeen by her fiancé's mother. She had ended up dead in a 'riding accident.' Their father, Crown Prince Eric, had confronted his own father, King Reginald, in open Court over his daughter's death and been executed right there in the Throne-room along with his lady wife for that temerity.

With his ten-year-old son watching.

Damien had fled to the Royal Library and hidden there.

He had been 'cared for' by the same woman who had betrayed his sister, the now-Dowager Baroness Theresa Anvliyar. 'Dowager' because in betraying Princess Kandra, she'd had to reveal that her husband was also party to the plan. How she'd managed to shield Raphael, her son, Damien still didn't know. For her 'service' she'd been kept as a hostage and given the title of Royal Librarian.

She'd discovered the terrified boy when she found a newly hired maid leaving baskets of food for him, reported him to the king, and ended up put in charge of Damien. Lady Theresa had made sure he was fed and relatively clean and that he showed up for the occasional 'family dinners' his grandfather would summon him to. Otherwise, she ignored both him and the Library she had also been charged with. Damien had tamed the mice with crumbs, slept hidden in corners or under couches, and read his way through much of the extensive Royal Library.

And that had been his life for four years. Alternating terror with losing himself in the stories and histories of the past. Damien had found that even reports on such plebian topics as grain production told stories that came to life in his head, and legal treatises were even better for finding stories of people who lived somewhere where there was grass and flowers and sunlight that wasn't filtered through windows.

It had gone on until Ciriis Celavell came looking for any forgotten Heirs that might not yet be corrupted. She wasn't looking for Damien, but she caught sight of the scrawny boy scrambling away into dark corners when she came looking for genealogies of the Realm, and felt bad for him. When Damien wouldn't come out at her urging, she brought her friend, the squire Adam Loveress, to help.

It was mostly for Adam's benefit, in Ciriis' eyes. Adam's beloved Jason had just been knighted and assigned as bodyguard and Champion to Prince Oskar... whose idea of a bodyguard's duties was heavy on *body*. Adam was going half-crazy watching what was going on and needed a distraction, she thought.

Adam, however, had recognized the half-feral boy as Prince Eric's vanished son.

*Recognized* him, Damien had learned only recently, through his inherited abilities as an empath and telepath.

It took them a year before Damien would even come out where he could be seen when they were present. He had almost forgotten how to speak to people by then. His interactions with people had been limited to obeying Lady Theresa's few directives and saying "yessir, nossir" to his grandfather at those rare dinners.

What finally brought him out of the Library – and started turning him back into a human, he thought wryly – was Jason. Sir Jason Solway had emerged from his time with Prince Oskar broken inside somehow. He'd mended himself by spending his infinite patience on Damien, helping the young prince heal in his own way.

Jason had become his first real friend.

Finding out over the last week that Jason was doubly his cousin – Jason's father was cousin to Damien's mother and nephew to Damien's father – had been one of the most heartwarming things that had ever happened to the king.

But it had still taken Jason *another* year to get the young prince to come out of the Library.

And another year after *that* before he'd convinced Damien that he wasn't risking his life to his grandfather's ire just to pick up a sword or ride a horse as most other young noblemen had been doing for years by that age. Princess Kandra had been noted for her skills as a warrior... and at that point Damien thought it was for possessing that skill-set that his sister had been killed.

The young prince had taken to both riding and swordsmanship naturally, but it was far too late at seventeen years of age to consider training him as a knight, even if his grandfather would have permitted it. The three conspirators – Adam, Ciriis, and Jason – had instead begun priming and preparing him to become a *king*.

By that time, the only other candidate was the on-again-off-again Crown Prince Oskar, Damien's youngest uncle – his grandfather had wed seven times and produced thirty legitimate children, but they and their own offspring had all met with 'accidents' or executions, as had all other known branches of the Alsterling family. Oskar was so perverted and self-centered that even the evil wizard-king could only tolerate him for short spans of time. Had the Ring of the Heir not been enchanted to make a nuisance of itself if it were not worn for over a year – meaning that there was no designated Heir to the Throne – Oskar would also have been disposable.

Careful planning – planning that had not included the anxious and naïve Damien – had ensured that Prince Oskar was not available when next the Ring made itself a nuisance to the king; it would fall onto his plate at dinner creating a single bell-like tone that would take longer and longer to die away each day. He'd been awarded the coronet of the Crown Prince simply to ease the king's headache.

No one had expected the 'careful plan' to fall apart in such a way that it left Prince Oskar, as well as most of the noble family of County Zialest, dead.

Oskar's demise had taken some of the pressure off of Damien, since there was no other known legitimate offspring with which to replace him. *King Reginald* had known that Jason Solway – who should properly have been named Jason *Alsterling* for his descent from the king's eldest son – was his great-grandson, but no one else had, due to the Solways having obscured Jason's father's name and origin.

There were, however, uncounted *illegitimate* offspring of the king, many of them acknowledged bastards who stood outside any chance of the line of succession as long as there were legitimate descendants. The potential for assassination by rivals or rebels had remained enough of a concern that Adam, Ciriis, and Jason had created a cadre of bodyguards for the prince.

Eleven young knights who were chosen for their loyalty and honor and cleverness... and a matching set of twelve young ladies chosen more secretly to guard the prince in more intimate settings. *Eleven* knights only, because Adam Loveress served as the twelfth and Captain, and Jason Solway as the Prince's Champion... the same role he had served for Prince Oskar.

Unbeknownst to them all, the king's dissatisfied and aging 'apprentice,' Lord Prydeen, had discovered how to steal what remained of King Reginald's Power. He siphoned off the last bits, leaving the king to be drained by the Realm and die, assuming, perhaps, that Damien would be a malleable puppet. Lord Prydeen had fallen to a back-up plan – and a back-up puppet-king – when Damien proved less malleable than the evil sorcerer had hoped... a plan which also failed and led to Prydeen's demise as well.

Fourteen years after his parents' execution, Damien had been secure on the throne... with only a Realm to Heal both magickally and politically. And a Rebellion to negotiate out of civil war. And five 'Lost Provinces' which had defected to other countries to reclaim. And a soul-bond to the most beautiful, brave, brilliant woman in the world.

He had been *safe,* but hardly *free.*

And now... he closed his eyes, reaching automatically for his links to Genevieve and to the Realm like an amputee would feel for his lost limb...

*Now,* he was more *free* in some ways than he had ever been, regardless of what the sorceress claimed. And more *safe* than he'd been for most of his life – perhaps for *all* of his life, though until Kandy had died, his parents had done the worrying and he'd been blissfully unaware.

It would be hard for this Azella to match the constant, real terror he'd lived with for so long, no matter how Unpitying.

He ignored the warm dampness making its way down the sides of his face. Genevieve was fine. Jason and Adam were fine. Ciriis, pregnant up in her mountain exile, was almost certainly fine. His other friends were fine. His Realm was... not fine, but it was in good hands to recuperate from the ice-storm Azella had called down upon it. Genevieve's among others.

He was as free and as safe as he had ever been.

The more fool he that he didn't want anything of it.

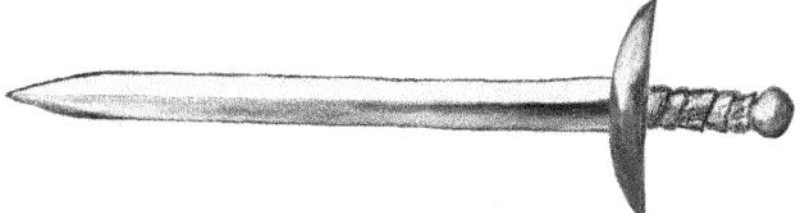

# Chapter THREE

# *Castling*

THE SHIP CAME INTO DOCK smoothly mid-day on the third of their journey.

Damien stood in the bow and watched as the sailors – as silently as ever – brought the great mass to a halt exactly beside the anchor-points. There were more silent servants standing on the pier to accept the hawsers that were tossed across and secure the vessel.

There was no one else.

Denisa came to his side and indicated that he should follow her down the gangplank onto the pier. Never garrulous, she was utterly silent now. Damien noticed that the other servants gave way before her. She might not be Azella's apprentice, but clearly that flicker of Power or her role in serving as the Mistress's surrogate in Ilseador had earned her some rank in this taciturn society.

She had begged him each night to ensure she did not return a virgin. Last night she had actually *wept*... and Damien had wished he could do something for her. He would not, he *could* not bed her.

And yet... if she died as a demonic sacrifice for the sake of his inaction...

He prayed Denisa's fears were overblown.

A part of him was woefully certain they were not.

The trail he followed her on wound slowly upwards, diverging early on from another that he could see led to a village, perhaps even a small town, shrouded in mists and nestled at the foot of a dark cliff. The cliff was a narrow promontory that rose high above the beach and the village, hundreds of feet high. A wide river joined the ocean to the left – the south – and demarcated the space beneath the cliff. The dark greens and brown beyond it suggested a broad marsh.

Damien wondered if the tide ever rose so high that it threatened the village... and what, if anything, Azella did in that happenstance. It seemed clear to him that the villagers served her needs, providing those services that one *could* have done in one's own keep but might prefer not to. Was she a good liege-lady to the people who depended on her?

His feet – encased in floppy, shapeless felted shoes that would surely be as worthless as his own indoor boots – followed the slave-girl almost automatically. Damien could detect no hint of a *compulsion* spell, but he had no desire to breakaway to explore that village or anywhere else.

His heart and soul seemed to have been wrapped in cotton roving since Azella had pinched off his bonds to Genevieve and to the Realm. And his mind seemed half-filled with the stuff, making it hard to think.

Damien hoped the effect was temporary. He knew he needed to throw it off in order to face the sorceress in the flesh. But between his internal fog and the heavy, dank mist that enshrouded these environs, it seemed a hopeless task.

At least Denisa had returned his own clothes to him, cleaned and pressed, he knew not how. It was a small thing, but it made Damien feel just a hair more confident that he would be meeting his captor in the flesh as a king – shapeless footwear notwithstanding.

There was a sense of familiarity to the entire place, though he'd never been here before. Almost, *almost* Damien could tell where he must be, but there was that mental and spiritual 'fleeciness, preventing him from making any real contact and confirming his guess.

The trail led partway up the cliff-face, then entered a tunnel.

At least he hoped it was a tunnel as he followed Denisa in.

It was, and it was lit at regular and frequent intervals as well. And had landings with seating and refreshment. Which was all to the good, since there was a seeming infinitude of stairs to be climbed.

He wondered what his would-be Mistress would have done if his feet had still been too tender to make the climb. Would she have vanished him into the upper quarters as he knew she could, or would she have made him crawl up to humble him further? These accommodations seemed too thoughtful to match her self-described appellation of 'Unpitying,' but perhaps they were relics of some earlier occupant.

Though *some*one must make certain the jugs of water were fresh at each stop.

Perhaps she merely had an excellent chatelaine.

Some of that mental fog seemed to be left behind as they climbed up above the level where the real fog outside was settled.

Eventually they reached a floor that extended beyond mere landing and into a proper vestibule, and went horizontally into a proper entry-hall. The overall feel was of gloom, with the decor in black with touches of ruby – no, he thought sardonically, *blood* – red as accents. The floor was even a black marble shot through with veins of red, limned in red marble with veins of black. There were windows in the dark granite walls, but they were tall and narrow and began at twice the height of a tall man from the floor.

The glimpses through those windows were forbidding – apparently the sky had filled with dark clouds while he climbed the stairs in the cliff. Not, Damien had to admit, that it had been a clear and sunny day to begin with.

He felt much closer to clear-headed now, more capable of mentally girding himself to face his captor.

Denisa led him past the entry-hall into... a throne-room was the only word for it, complete with a throne that was styled like some giant terrifying beast with ruby eyes the size of fists. Here there was more red, and the accents were of gold, but the black marble continued its march.

The throne-room was empty.

They went on, up a level, then another. The walls began to look less like they had been carved from the cliff itself and more as if they had been laid by the hands of men and women.

Damien did not try to pretend to himself that his calves and thighs were not burning from the unexpected exercise, that his feet were not feeling worn despite the healing they had completed. He hadn't walked this much in... years. Perhaps not since he and Genevieve had walked back from their secret grotto to his city of Emeralsee, there to re-take the Castle that the husband she had thought long-dead had come to usurp from Damien.

The memory lifted the last of his lingering despondency. He had been in hopeless situations before and boldly ventured deeper in pursuit of a greater prize, after all – and won! He wasn't blind to the idea that this was an entirely different situation, that he had no one to back him up this time as he'd had Genevieve before, or Adam and Jason once he'd emerged from the Library.

But he wasn't a child anymore either. Nor a half-grown boy nor an uncertain newly-crowned princeling trying to be a king. He was a man grown, a husband and soon to be a father. He had reclaimed two of the Lost Provinces, and was slowly but surely rebuilding his Realm from the inside and out.

He *was* the Sorcerer-King of Ilseador, dammit, no matter what this evil sorceress said!

At last, Denisa came to a closed door – one of many – and knocked.

Damien's directional sense suggested to him that they were close to the point of the promontory, and indeed when the door swung open, he could see the ocean through the huge picture windows at the far side of the room. On *both* far sides of the room – this was the very tip of the Keep.

The ocean in all its majesty, however, could not retain his attention compared to the figure that stood between those massive windows. Silhouetted mostly, in this light.

"You may go, Denisa."

The voice was that same honey-silk that he remembered from the night she had abducted him. That she had caressed his mind with – and then ripped out part of his soul, all uncaring.

Or rather, *Unpitying*.

Denisa was gone and the doors closed behind him before Damien had time to register the instruction.

"Not even a commendation for a job well done?" he asked. "Surely she deserves that much."

"She lives. For now. There is her reward."

The woman who came towards him was taller than her handmaiden, though barely of average height. The long, pale hair and huge, vividly blue-grey eyes were familiar, but the features were a bit finer, with a bit more maturity in them. The gown she wore – heavy velvet of a dark red with a hem and drooping sleeves that did not merely sweep, but trailed on the floor – did not bespeak any pretense of innocence, and the sway of her hips and the confidence of her movements gave him to understand that this was a woman grown. One who knew her desires and made her own path in the world.

But her slender build, and even the shape of her face made her look far younger. Had he seen her unmoving, he would have guessed her to be no more than eighteen. Perhaps a couple of years younger even than that.

"So, you are here, Damien, my would-be sorcerer-king," Azella purred.

He set his feet in a parade-rest, folded his arms and inclined his head. Would-be indeed!

She came close – not strutting or swaying. Her movements somehow conveyed that if there was to be that sort of thing in her house it would be *for* her benefit, not done *by* her.

One delicate finger reached out, the nail long but not overlong, and painted a shimmery pearly grey in contrast to the red and black and gold that was everywhere else. The finger traced along his forearm, then up to his shoulder as she circled him. Down his back, and up to trace his other arm.

It wasn't even a *possessive* touch, he realized with some bemusement. Possessiveness intimated that there was the possibility that some other might have a claim on the thing possessed. This... was simply *ownership.*

It might have bothered Damien more if he had not effectively been a *possession* for most of his life. Of his grandfather, King Reginald. Of the Realm and his people. Even of his wife – for a soul-bond was not a choice that was made but a set of requirements passed down from on high.

Genevieve's love... was a different story.

He fancied that Azella's amused eyes as he looked down at her from his few inches advantage – he wasn't a tall man – hid some bafflement at his lack of concern or embarrassment.

If there was, she hid it well, stepping back from him.

"You'll do." A smile that he was all too familiar with curled her lips. "You'll more than do, in fact. My sources hadn't told me how *handsome* you are. I shall quite enjoy this, I think."

Damien tried not to roll his eyes.

"This beard..." She stroked his chin. "I assume you usually keep it a bit more trim. I usually prefer my bedmates to be cleanshaven. But then, they are usually too young to grow a proper beard. Perhaps I shall make an exception."

"Perhaps you are making an *assumption,* lady sorceress," Damien said dryly.

"No," she said calmly. "You are no innocent child, Damien. You know full well the Power that is raised through sex. You will be my Apprentice. You will share my bed. And you will do whatever else I require of you."

He looked back at her just as calmly. "I have sworn to my wife that I would touch no other woman in that way. And since I *also* know that the Power raised is proportional to the joy found in the doing, it won't do you much good to compel me."

Those blue-grey eyes sparkled. It wasn't – quite – anger. Nor amusement. It was... challenge. Damien suspected that she rarely found something she wanted that she could not immediately bend to her will.

He suspected that was why she had wanted *him* in the first place.

"Oh, I won't have to *force* you to make love to me, Damien. You'll soon be *begging* to do so."

Damien gave her a tolerant look, and hid a secret grin when he saw just a trace of irritation flicker across the back of her eyes.

It would be a contest of wills, then. He wondered if she had as much patience as his beloved Jason – a solid year it had taken to woo him to talk to the tall blonde knight. Another year before he would consider leaving the library and start to learn the skills Jason and the others had felt were necessary for a king.

A full *four* years from Jason's first efforts – or *five* from the day that Adam and Ciriis found him – before Damien had been willing to take quarters elsewhere in the Castle.

Of course, the sorceress had a few other tools than his oldest friend.

She might not be able to make him do *all* of what she wanted, but she cast a simple *compulsion* spell on Damien. He decided not to spend his now-meager stores of Power resisting the spell for now.

Not surprisingly, her spell required him to disrobe and get into her massive bed.

The bed – with sheets and draperies of that ubiquitous red and black – was located in a room adjacent to the one that faced the ocean like the prow of a ship. This room was to the southern side of the promontory keep and would surely be dark for most of the day. The evil sorceress was not fond of the dawn, it seemed.

The dark-haired man sat naked on the bed as the *compulsion* spell dissipated, and gave Azella another tolerant look. *And...?*

"Is there any chance of eating dinner?" he asked mildly. "Walking up all those stairs used up a lot of energy."

He didn't mention that he'd been surreptitiously using his own Healing magick to ease his tired muscles. Healing himself didn't work very well, but he could speed things up a little. It still cost energy, however, and that meant food.

She surveyed him with that look of *ownership* again, and nodded sharply. It was wise, Damien assumed wryly, to feed and water one's pets. Especially the expensive ones, or the ones from which one anticipated getting some special use.

Azella vanished into another room, returning just as there was a knock on the door.

She was now dressed in a negligée of black silk that Damien had to admit *was* rather interesting. It revealed more than it concealed, but that made what little was concealed all the more alluring. He wondered if someday he could convince Genevieve to wear something like that... not in black, though, greens and blues were more her color...

Azella apparently did not notice that Damien was daydreaming about his wife as she permitted a striking young man to enter the bedchamber carrying a tray of food. His hair was a particularly sunshiny golden, over skin the color of mahogany wood, and his eyes were as blue as the sky. His muscles were well-defined, if not those of a swordsman, and he was dressed only in a brief kilt of pleated fabric with sandals that laced up his calves. A wide, collar-like necklace covered part of his chest and shoulders.

The young man instantly went to one knee, offering the tray as he bowed his head. But the bow was only momentary, and his head came back up to issue Damien a challenging glare.

"Mistress," he complained, "Who is this old man?"

Damien raised an eyebrow at that description. He wasn't vain about his looks – Genevieve would have tweaked his nose and told him he didn't need to be, with everyone fawning over him all the time – but he *was* rather pleased with the muscle he had managed to put on despite his late start.

Giving credit where it was due, fencing regularly with the three best swordsmen in the Realm made sure he stayed fit. He had recovered most of the strength and stamina he had lost while fighting the soul-bond and the Realm last Autumn, and even if he still couldn't beat Adam or Jason – or Genevieve – at swordplay, he had been consistently demolishing his Royal Guards again. The younger knights had started to have a look of dawning realization that the lack of a shield didn't always correlate with a lack of skills... and to wear a rather satisfying expression of trepidation when he was ready to spar.

His stomach was flat and there were no more strands of silver in his black hair now than there had been at eighteen. Which age this boy had probably yet to see.

"Variety is the spice of life, Mikhail," Azella replied. Her glance at Damien assured him that *she* did not consider him *old*. If he should happen to care what the sorceress thought.

"But you only ever take your Apprentices to your bed, Mistress. And *I'm* your Apprentice." Damien had to admire the boy's ability to say it without whining. Presumably Azella did not reward whining.

"Not anymore, Mikhail," she said dismissively. "Place the tray on the bed and then go."

The boy's face paled, but he did as she told him. "Will I... have another chance, Mistress?" he asked quietly.

She surveyed him as she had Damien. His *owner*. The look clearly bothered the young man – though whether it was because she was kicking him out of her bed or his ambitions were being decimated... or because he didn't appreciate being a *thing* for her to own, the dark-haired man could not tell.

"Perhaps," she answered. "It depends how well this new Apprentice does."

Which meant, Damien supposed, how long before she tired of having a sorcerer-king in her bed. He gave the boy a wry look, but received only a downcast gaze. Masking fury, Damien guessed, and wondered wearily if he needed to test his food for poison after this.

The boy said no more, but exited straight away. Testing the patience of the sorceress was apparently not a likely pursuit for *former* favorites.

Damien was about to reach for the silver bell-shaped cover when the *compulsion* spell kicked in again and halted his hand. He looked questioningly at the sorceress.

Azella smiled smugly. "You will eat only from my hand, Damien."

He raised an eyebrow at that, too, but shrugged.

"This is going to get old for you rather quickly," he predicted. He also wondered if this particular injunction would apply only to meals taken in bed, or to every meal. Or maybe it was just this meal. Surely the woman had other things to do than spend every moment with him.

Though... *Jason* had more or less done that when Damien was fifteen.

But Jason's motivation had been compassion. And curiosity – the man was as curious as any cat. And – be honest – patriotism.

Damien could not suppress a flush on remembering to what lengths Jason's sense of *patriotism* had taken him most recently on his young king's behalf. The sorceress looked approvingly at his reddened skin. He guessed she was assuming it had something to do with this meal.

Azella did all the things that one might suspect could be done to make the meal of finger-foods an erotic feast for the senses.

She fed him bite after bite by hand.

She required him to take tidbits from her lips with his own, or from other parts of her body.

And on and on.

Damien played along – he was hungry, after all – but without the reactions she was aiming for. He'd played these games before after all... and they were much more enjoyable when he wasn't half-starved... or when they were played with someone he loved.

As he had guessed, she tired of the effort before his hunger ebbed. Unfortunately, that didn't mean she gave him free rein on the remaining foods. Instead, she vanished away the tray with a slight display of irritation, and turned to regard him.

Damien gave her the mild expression which he had used to hide all other feelings for nearly as long as he could remember. He let his eyes flicker to the windows, where darkness had fallen during the very extended meal.

"Do you play chess?" he asked. What, after all, did one say to an evil sorceress?

She frowned at him. "What?"

Her thoughts must have been following a different track entirely. What that track might have been, he might guess, based on where her eyes had been.

"Do you play chess?" he asked again.

"Not... in some time," Azella replied, still slightly caught off guard. She recollected herself. "It is a game for kings and warriors. There is little use in such things for a sorcerer."

"I disagree," Damien told her earnestly. "Chess trains the mind to think logically, explore alternative routes to an ultimate goal, and be alert to changing conditions. Those all seem relevant to sorcery."

The sorceress glared at him. "Men often say such things."

Now he had to chuckle. "Genevieve, my wife, is the premier chess player in Ilseador as far as I know. Of course," he added thoughtfully, *"she* likens it to swordplay, at which she also excels."

"Your *wife* hardly seems a *woman*," the sorceress bit out.

Damien knew his expression had softened and gone dreamy – enough people had told him over the years that any mention of Genevieve did that to him. Ciriis had finally admitted that he had done so long before the soul-bond, when the Rebel Duchess of Elaarwen had been little more than a name and memory of her twelve-year-old self.

"My beautiful love is *all* woman," he murmured.

He re-focused on the sorceress. "My pardon," he said mildly. "It is ill-done to praise one woman when in another's bed."

Damien hid his amusement at her reaction. His admission had neatly skewered the point she had wanted to make, he was sure. Though his words underscored that while he was *in* her bed, that was *all*.

He laid back on the pillows and laced his fingers behind his head. If she wanted to look at him, let her look. The contrast between his own swordsman's muscles and her usual lovers – if that slender boy was anything to judge by – might distract her enough to let him extract some information.

While he had tried to build his own Court around a different *modus operandi,* Damien had been a member of his grandfather's Court for more than half his life and a mere five years had not been enough to completely change how his nobles behaved. He knew very well that an attractive face and body was merely one more weapon in the deadly game of politics.

"You know everything about *me* it seems, Azella," he said as convincingly as he could. She certainly did *not* and her little omissions gave him hope. "But I know almost nothing about *you*. How is it that I had never heard of the most Powerful sorceress in the world?"

Clearly, she also knew that knowledge was power... and she found it unnerving for someone to attempt to use *her* attraction to their body to angle for information.

"You know all you need to know," she said, and abandoned him in the bedchamber, stalking off to the next room, though she refrained from slamming the door.

As a last twist, every lamp was doused as the door closed, and the room was plunged into darkness.

Damien chuckled to himself as he moved himself under the silken sheets. She'd given away more than she might realize by her actions.

Azella was clearly Powerful – perhaps even as Powerful as she claimed. And she wasn't as young as she looked. But she wasn't all *that* much older, either. Damien had been a young and unsure ruler not all that long ago himself, and he recognized the signs.

The sorceress was still consolidating her power. She hadn't yet made her mark upon the world because she hadn't yet had time to do so.

She had this Keep, however, both intimidating and luxurious, and the village below. That suggested that this facility had been here prior to her tenure as resident sorceress. How had she come to possess it?

The décor... and as he sent his magickal senses creeping delicately around the Keep, probing, testing, he could *feel* that there were many places he did *not* want to explore further... the Keep itself practically screamed that it had been constructed long ago for the purposes of a truly evil sorcerer.

For Azella to rule here – and he had not the slightest impression that there was any question or challenge to her rule – she must have defeated the previous tenant.

And for there to be no evidence of a battle – no craters, burn marks, or the like – suggested that she had done it in some subtle fashion. Perhaps... perhaps she had even served as Apprentice herself to the former Master of this Keep.

That... felt right. It fit all the facts that he had been given so far. Surely no one could have delved so deep into the darker aspects of magick to have learned to halt her own aging at the tender age Azella seemed to be. Perhaps there were ways to reverse aging – or simply alter the form as one chose – but that would take even more Power than simply halting the aging process. A Master wishing to enjoy his Apprentice-chattel's... services... for longer might place such a spell from his own reserves and make up the losses from the Power raised with her thereafter. And once she had learnt what she would and disposed of her former Master, why not keep the spell going, after all?

And yet... this all pointed to her being very young, very ruthless... and very Powerful to have defeated the evil sorcerer who had trained her. Whom, it might be guessed had been in the prime of his Power.

Young, ruthless, Powerful.

Unsure of herself for all her confident behavior...

*Dangerous.*

Dangerous to him... *and* to Ilseador.

Damien needed to know more. More about Azella, and more about *magick*. He needed to know everything he could persuade her to teach him if he was to have any hope not merely of escape, but of protecting his Realm.

*Genevieve...* The aching emptiness of the soul-bond. How had *she* coped with the sudden severance? And the Realm? Had it Bound her the more fiercely as its sovereign Queen, now that he was gone?

He rolled onto his side and breathed deep and slow to put himself to sleep.

It took a very long time.

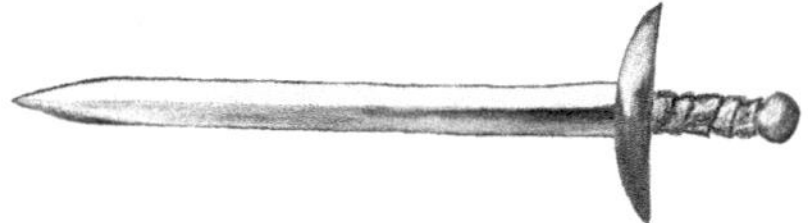

# Chapter FOUR

# *Advance a Pawn*

HE WOKE TO THE FEEL of cool, though not chill, hands sliding along his warm skin.

And smooth, warm skin pressed along his back.

She might have sent another one of her *belongings* to this work rather than risk what he was sure she felt was another humiliation... but Damien *knew* it was Azella touching him. Caressing him with that proprietary sense of *ownership*. Kissing his neck, and... oh, yes, *nibbling*.

The girl hadn't tried this sort of thing aboard the ship, thank the Gods. Of course, little Denisa hadn't the ability to force him to remove his clothes and sleep bare. Hadn't had the moxy to keep trying to seduce him when he'd continued to treat her as a little sister or child of his own.

Azella... had no reason to constrain herself. And every reason not to.

Damien kept his body relaxed, his breathing slow, as if in sleep. He let his Healer's sense seep into himself and keep his heartbeat slow... and prevented the other, even more obvious reaction to her touch. He couldn't do this for long... but it just had to be long enough to bore her.

She was... persistent. And completely lacking in shyness.

He decided that the only way to outlast her was to pretend to be even more deeply asleep. He stretched slightly and rolled fully onto his stomach. Away from her and her clever fingers, but even more importantly to make it seem that he really was still fast asleep. He was all too aware that her seeking touch could still find other avenues... and that his ability to suppress his very male response was waning rapidly. The middle of the night was not ideal for exercises in self-denial.

It was a near thing... but she gave up for now.

He didn't dare breathe a sigh of relief.

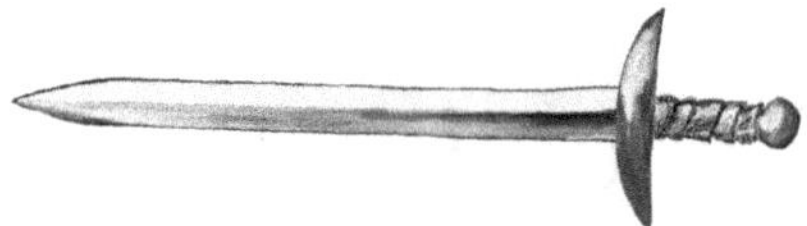

The morning brought a fresh challenge.

Somehow Azella had ended up in Damien's arms while they slept: he woke to find himself wrapped around her, vaguely recalled dreams of Genevieve fading rapidly as the strangeness of the location impinged upon his consciousness. He wasn't really surprised in one sense – Genevieve had been gone so much while she served as chief negotiator for the restoration of the Lost Provinces, and he'd spent so many long nights missing her. In his sleeping state, he would have assumed that the warm body beside him was the one he so badly longed for.

Unfortunately, this played right into the sorceress's plans, and it was impossible for him to hide his body's reaction to hers since it had begun while he was still deeply asleep. Azella rotated in his arms as soon as she noticed he was awake, an expression of smug superiority in those vivid blue-grey eyes.

She reached an arm up and pulled him into a kiss, pressing the length of her naked body against his.

Damien didn't resist, but he didn't respond. His focus was on reclaiming control over himself, using his magick and willpower to overcome the arousal. It was... slower work than he would have liked, but effective.

Azella swore when she realized he had lost his erection and pulled herself out of the bed to storm off again.

Breakfast arrived – another silent servant, a boy attractive enough that Damien wondered if he, too, had shared the Mistress's bed – and he discovered that the *compulsion* spell was still in effect. He'd used enough magick through the night and morning that he was starving again, and his nose informed him most frustratingly that bacon and melted butter and cinnamon were all involved in whatever was hidden under the covered dishes on the tray.

Azella returned – dressed in a silky black gown that fastened behind her neck and left her shoulders and most of her back bare – to find him glaring at the unseen food.

She smirked at him, then dismissed him to use the washroom while she opened up the covers. Which was another urgent need she had stymied; he had discovered that stepping off the bed was impossible.

Breakfast was also too meager to satisfy Damien's hunger, as Azella grew bored with feeding him by hand, but refused to relinquish the *compulsion* and let him feed himself. She offered him opportunities to 'earn' more bites of food by touching her more than was necessary to claim the various morsels.

Damien declined. He might reach that level of starvation eventually, but he wasn't there yet.

He didn't let the sorceress know, of course, but Damien knew he had to yield to her blandishments eventually. Not merely because of her effect on his body, though he suspected that his willpower would diminish rapidly as this continued, especially if she denied him sufficient food to replenish the magickal reservoirs he was using to suppress his very *male* reactions. But also, because he was sure she would not be willing to teach him until he yielded to her in bed.

And he *had* to learn whatever he could.

This time she left the tray on the end of the bed – within reach, but frustratingly out of touch.

"You've found the one thing you can do to frustrate my plans," she said, and her tone was amused again, and somehow ancient. He wondered what she had been through to obtain that sense of immense age, when he was sure she couldn't be far past his own age of twenty-nine... and might even be slightly younger.

Damien inclined his head, a king's acknowledgment to a lesser noble. "One does one's best."

The flash of her eyes told him that she had not missed the implication in his motion.

"How do you keep this place so warm?" he asked, changing the subject to distract her. "I noticed that the breeze that sailed us up here was warmer than I would have expected, but it explained the fog at the base of the cliff. Up here atop the cliff the winds should be colder and steal away the heat. I'd think it wouldn't be worth spending the magick to heat this hulk of a Keep, but..." He gestured to her thin garment.

She gave him a long look. "It will do you no particular good to know it, but there are hotsprings within the cliff. They provide sufficient non-magickal heat for comfort."

"And I suppose you cool the place off in Summer with all the windows," Damien added thoughtfully. "But surely it isn't natural to have hotsprings in a cliff-promontory like this. I know that one can reach hot flows of rock if one goes down deep enough anywhere, and presumably running water down to such a flow would create a hotspring. But that seems like it would be an incredible feat in and of itself."

"My M–" she cut herself off. "The builder of this Keep was well-versed in the uses of Elemental spirits. It is likely he made use of their talents rather than expending his own resources."

"Ah," Damien sighed with disappointment, hiding his attention to her near-slip of the tongue. "It was done before your time here then. I suppose you wouldn't know how to accomplish such things yourself?"

Just the right touch of disbelief and hopefulness... had he gotten the mix right?

She narrowed her eyes at him. "Of course I could. There's no reason to do so, however, since it has already been done. *My* interests lie elsewhere."

He gave her a lazy grin. "In taming kings?"

Azella resisted lifting her chin in defiance of his sally. "It is not for an Apprentice to question his Mistress's means or goals."

"But then," Damien's grin grew wicked. "You're not my *mistress* yet, are you, Azella?"

He let the word be suggestive in his tone.

It wasn't his imagination that she breathed a little harder at that. "I don't encourage pertness from my Apprentices any more than I do from my other chattels, *Damien.* You would do well to remember that."

He leaned back against the headboard, stretching his legs out and crossing them at the ankles, his hands laced behind his head once again. "I think, *Mistress,* that you are used to dealing with little *boys,* not grown *men.*"

She raised an eyebrow. "Think well of yourself, I see."

Damien shrugged and gave her his mild smile. "I've done a few things. They mostly turned out well."

"Until you faced *me,*" she retorted.

"Until I faced you, your salamanders, nearly a thousand pirates, and an ice-storm that battered my Realm and sealed my subjects and my Army away," he answered her, still keeping tone and expression mild... then added the tidbit that he suspected she didn't know that he knew. "An ice-storm that you *summoned,* but that your allies in Deltheren *sent.*"

Her Master could not have been too harsh with her, evil sorcerer though he must have been. Her expressions were controlled, but not enough to prevent Damien from reading them.

That slight widening of the eyes? She definitely had not expected him to know that.

She'd never had to learn to hide herself behind a mask for the merest chance at staying alive. Never had to learn to read minute changes of expression in hopes of blunting the misery before it rained down.

There was a bitterness in her eyes – or perhaps he merely *felt* it the way his friend Adam absorbed the emotions of others – but she didn't bear the same kinds of calluses on her soul as Damien did.

"I didn't think evil sorcerers collaborated," he finished.

Azella made a dismissive gesture. "Occasionally interests coincide."

"Best beware enemies made allies from common cause," he commented. "When one player is destroyed, all of his pieces leave the board and you are vulnerable in ways you may not have foreseen."

"What *are* you talking about?" she demanded, though again, he saw a flicker of understanding.

"Four-person chess," Damien said easily. "I've had few opportunities to play, but the dynamic is completely changed."

Azella scowled. "Does *everything* come down to chess with you?"

He tilted his head thoughtfully. "I hadn't considered it that way before. Perhaps it does."

The pale-haired sorceress stood up, shaking out her long locks. "The spell will allow you to use the washroom. Other than that," she smirked at him. "You'll just have to stay there and look sexy, since clothing is *not* permitted."

Damien grinned back at her. "I can do that."

Clearly *not* the response she was looking for, but did she really expect him to react like her cowed little slave-boys? Apparently so, considering the slight frustration she betrayed as she stepped out of the room and shut the door.

*And what will you be doing?* He sent the thought after her, and felt a start of surprise.

Apparently, her *other* Apprentices hadn't known how to do *that* either... But then her other Apprentices likely had not had someone else living in their thoughts day and night for five years.

*I have many other projects,* Azella replied too quickly, making him suspect that he was her only *current* 'project.' *But don't worry little sorcerer-king. I'll send you some entertainment.*

Amusement and vast self-satisfaction in that mental tone.

*Good books?* he suggested hopefully, and received only the fading impression of laughter.

A half-hour later the door opened, and the striking boy, Mikhail, entered. Carrying a chess set and bearing a bemused expression.

"The Mistress would have you teach me to play this game," he said, clearly baffled by the instruction.

Damien, however, was neither baffled nor fooled. Azella would subsequently have Mikhail teach *her* the game. She would then come to him thinking she knew what she was doing. It would take... subtlety. Demolishing her without half-trying was a given. Making it *look* like he'd had to try... that would take work.

Or, perhaps she merely meant to listen in to their thoughts while they played. That might do her more good, if she could sort through Damien's to understand how the strategy worked.

"Her voice is beautiful," he said noncommittally, testing one of his hypotheses. "Especially when she speaks inside my head."

The boy gave him another baffled look. "What are we supposed to do with this game?"

"Set it here." Damien showed him how to set it up and began explaining how the pieces moved.

So, Mikhail had never heard Azella's voice-without-words. But Denisa clearly must have to follow her orders at such a distance. Why accept the boy as an Apprentice, but not the girl?

And why choose Damien to fill the same role? Why not simply conquer and eliminate him if he was a threat or a potential rival? Why bother to abduct and attempt to co-opt him?

Teaching the moves and playing against such a raw beginner took barely any concentration at all, leaving his mind free to consider other things. Although he did find himself considerably distracted by the boy's snacking on the remains of breakfast... which he was himself forbidden to touch.

After the third or fourth dip into the tray, Mikhail's intense attention to the game somehow snagged on Damien's frustrated hunger. The boy gave his teacher a guilty look.

"She's forbidden you to eat on your own, hasn't she? I'm sorry, I'll stop... though I daren't cover the dishes, since she left it like this..."

Damien waved this attempted kindness off. "Go ahead and eat. I remember being hungry all the time when I was your age." He paused. "How old are you, anyways?"

"Seventeen," Mikhail answered. He looked a little sideways at Damien. "And... you?"

The man grinned at him. "Twenty-nine. Which would only be *old* if I couldn't outfight *and* outride belted knights ten years younger than me." He snickered, remembering Sir Drake's expression the first time he'd demonstrated *that* a few weeks earlier.

Mikhail gave him a wide-eyed look. "I didn't think Power-slaves were allowed to learn to use a sword."

"I'm a king, not a slave, regardless of what *she* thinks," Damien said casually, jerking a thumb towards the closed door and noticing the look of fear the boy followed it with. "What's a Power-slave? And where are you from, anyways? I've never seen anyone with your coloring before."

Mikhail lowered his eyes. "I'm from a long line of Power-slaves. We've been bred for our looks and to do what Power-slaves do." He looked helplessly at Damien as if he'd never had to explain it before. "We... have some trace of Talent for magick. Not enough to be useful, but enough to raise and hold Power for a real sorcerer. Or sorceress. When she bought me, the Mistress thought I might have more Talent than was advertised, so she took me for her Apprentice." He cast his eyes down to the chessboard. "I suppose it wasn't enough."

Damien's stomach turned at the thought of humans being *bred* for exotic looks and talents. He had known such things *happened* beyond the borders of Ilseador. But... entire families, *generations* of them?

"Is... Denisa the same?" he asked after a moment.

Mikhail shrugged, still not looking up. "Me, Denisa, all of us who serve up here. The guards and cooks and such live down below. They're freeborn."

"Are... Power-slaves ever freed?"

"No," Mikhail shook his head and those impossibly golden locks rearranged themselves, almost sweeping the tops of the chess pieces as his head bent lower. "But we never know want, either. And live in luxury. Until..."

Damien's heart contracted. "Until?'

"Until we are sent back to be bred – few owners want to run their own breeding programs – or until the owner decides to... use us up."

Damien didn't need to guess what that meant.

"I thought I might have another path," Mikhail admitted quietly. "When the Mistress chose me for her Apprentice – first at the auction in the Bazaar, and then again here from among the other boys – I imagined that *I* could be an evil wizard myself. Or at least a warlock."

What an ambition. And yet... compared to the alternatives...

"But she's chosen you over me. So, I suppose you have more... more magick or more sex appeal or something. I'd hoped to keep her attention long enough to learn some *real* magick, maybe even enough that she'd consider keeping me as a servant when I'm too old to want in her bed."

Damien reached across the chessboard and lifted the striking boy's chin, testing for that spark of magick as he looked into the startlingly blue eyes. As he suspected, all that breeding had resulted in more than a mere 'trace.'

"You have more magick than most freeborn people who make their living with their talents, Mikhail. And what your Mistress sees in me is a *challenge*. It's no lack in *you*." He sucked in his breath. Azella's efforts throughout the night had not left him as unaffected as he pretended – Mikhail was very *striking* indeed, and at this close range... It was simply that he wasn't dangerous like his Mistress, Damien told himself.

"It's definitely no lack in *you*," he repeated somewhat lamely.

He let go of the boy's chin and started to draw back, but Mikhail caught his hand in a stronger grip than he would have guessed.

"You're... different," the boy said. "You meant that, didn't you? Are you really a king and not a slave?"

Damien nodded. "In my Realm there *are* no slaves. And no evil wizards either," he added dryly, "Not since my grandfather died and I defeated the Apprentice who killed him."

Mikhail's eyes grew wide again. "You... you're a *hero*."

"I don't know that I'd go that far..." Damien said uncomfortably.

It had just been what he had to do to survive and protect the people he cared about. He hadn't sought out the task for some greater purpose. Though that greater purpose had come seeking *him* when the Realm claimed him as its own and Bound him...

"We were *warned* about ones like you," Mikhail continued. "That it was our duty to adhere to our owner regardless of what a *hero* told us we could do to change our fate."

Oh. That wasn't a compliment.

"They said *heroes* might pretend to help us. Might pretend to kindness. But in the end, all they would want to do was to kill our owners. And since we were to be Bound, killing the owner kills her Power-slaves." Mikhail's eyes were pleading. "You're not going to kill the Mistress, are you? I don't want to die. Not yet anyways."

Damien shook his head. "I haven't any plan to do that."

It was true. Although hearing about these slaves made him want to go on a crusade and end all of this... Realistically, he knew he too was Bound and the best he could do was to keep Ilseador as a haven where slavery was banned and where escaped slaves might go to be free.

Perhaps he could strengthen the moral backbone of his neighboring monarchs regarding this issue. Always assuming he made it back alive in the first place...

*"Thank you,"* Mikhail said fervently, then pulled the startled Damien closer into a kiss.

It was an... *expert* kiss.

*'I've been well-trained,'* Denisa had told him on the ship. Clearly Mikhail was as well. He wasn't a child either – fifteen was considered marriageable in Ilseador, though still unusually young. This boy... this *young man* had been sharing the sorceress's bed for some time and knew what he wanted, apparently.

He was a slave... but he wasn't *Damien's* slave. If he bought Azella's assertion that he belonged to her now, then Damien was as much enslaved as Mikhail.

It was all excuses.

Gently, he pushed the young man away, trying to reassure him with a smile. "You're welcome... and that has to be the most sincere 'thank you' I've ever received for something I haven't done," he joked.

Damien began to straighten and reset the chessboard. A good excuse to avoid the younger man's eyes.

"You... sir..." Mikhail seemed at a loss for how to address him.

"My name is Damien," Damien said, adding dryly, "Though where I'm from, 'Your Majesty' is more popular."

The sharply indrawn breath made him look up. "You'd give *me* your true-name?"

Damien raised an eyebrow. "Does that matter?"

"I *knew* your name," Mikhail whispered, "I heard the Mistress use it. But you have *given* it to me..."

Damien began to wonder if he'd made a serious mistake. He realized suddenly that although Azella had been *using* his name, he hadn't actually *told* it to her – *given* it to her as Mikhail described it. He'd simply assumed she knew it, since she knew most of the other public details of his life.

Had she been trying to taunt him into *giving* it to her by calling him 'sorcerer-king' and even 'would-be sorcerer-king'?

"What... will you do with it?" Damien asked uneasily.

Mikhail glared at him with offended innocence. "I will treasure it as the precious gift it is. But," he added seriously, "There are others who would use it to control you. You should ask the Mistress to give you a call-name."

"'Mikhail' is a call-name, then?" Damien asked, and the young man nodded. "And Azella knows your true-name?"

Another nod. "It is in the papers, when we are sold." Mikhail's head dropped down. "The Mistress has been very careful with our true names. She has been kind. I heard stories in the Bazaar of other evil wizards who delight in using their slaves' names – even those who are not Power-slaves – to control their emotions. Make them laugh, cry, love, hate..."

"Feel aroused?" Damien said dryly.

Mikhail shrugged. "That, of course. It's barely even an emotion. More like a bodily reaction. But there are stories of evil wizards who use the true-name to make the slave lust after them while on the rack itself, cry out with desire while being branded... or worse."

Damien's eyes closed and he shuddered.

"The Mistress will give you a call-name if you ask," Mikhail assured him earnestly. "Damien," he added shyly, saying the name as if it were a precious jewel.

Damien opened his eyes and smiled a bit weakly at him. "Somehow... I don't think she'll give me a new one unless I give her this one first."

No, he was absolutely sure of it.

Mikhail's eyes widened again. "She doesn't have your name? You truly *aren't* a slave!"

"Mmmn," Damien scratched his beard, eyeing the young man dubiously. There had to be another solution to this... or other problems. "Are *you* able to give my name to her now?"

"No!" Mikhail exclaimed, then stopped. "I... don't actually know. I've never known anyone else's true-name. And no one but my owners has known mine. The first thing we're supposed to do after we're bought is give our true-name to our new owner." And it was recorded in the paperwork transferred with the sale, he'd said, so there was no way to give a false name instead of the true.

But something else caught Damien's attention and he looked at the young man sharply. "What about your parents? Your brothers and sisters? Wouldn't they know your true-name?"

Mikhail gave him an odd look. "I was given to a wet-nurse when I was born, as we all are. The slave-breeder named me. I don't have 'parents' or 'brothers' or 'sisters' that I know of, although I'm sure they are out there. I was told that my dam and sire were both much in demand as breeding stock."

Damien's heart turned over. "Your wet-nurse, then. She must have known your true-name," he persisted.

Mikhail shook his head. "No. She gave me a call-name to be used until I was old enough to be sold to a trainer. The trainer gave me a different one." He paused. "I'm lucky. This is only the third name I've had to learn to answer to. The Mistress purchased me in my first auction, when I was thirteen."

"She's been bedding you since you were *thirteen?*"

The young man shook his head again. "No, though if she had chosen me as her Apprentice then, perhaps I would know enough now that..." He broke off, giving Damien an apologetic look. "I have been so privileged only this last year. I have heard it rumored..." He leaned forward and his voice went low. Damien had to lean closer to hear him. "That the Mistress *herself* was once a Power-slave, though she was freeborn. And that she was auctioned at age fifteen to become her Master's Apprentice. And supposedly *that* is why–"

Mikhail's voice choked off as if he suddenly had no air, his back arching in agony.

It lasted only a moment, but long enough for his rich, mahogany skin to go slightly grey.

Then he was gasping for breath again, waving off Damien's alarmed attempt to help.

"I should have known better than to gossip about the Mistress," Mikhail said ruefully as he regained his breath, but seemingly without either shock or rancor. "Especially here in her own bedchamber and to her new Apprentice. It was only a matter of time before she noticed." He paused. "It was kind of her to let me have my air back so quickly. Not everyone has been so lucky."

His eyes sickened Damien – instead of hatred or fear, the young man... the *boy* felt hope. *Hope* that this small dose of mercy might suggest she still had a use for him.

The man swallowed hard and looked down at the chessboard. "I... didn't sleep well. I'd like to take a nap, I think. If you understand how the game works well enough to... to meet her requirement."

Mikhail looked surprised, but nodded understandingly... even somewhat jealously.

"The first few days take some getting used to." He paused. "I think I understand. But it's clear that there is much more to this than just how the pieces move. If the Mistress permits, would you show me more? Tomorrow?"

"Of course." Damien couldn't tell that eager, puppy-dog expression 'no.'

The boy collected the board and pieces and departed. He paused just before opening the door. "Damien," he said again, with a smile that made it clear he saw the name as a great gift.

The dark-haired man put his head in his hands.

The little game of wills he had embarked on with Azella suddenly seemed far more dangerous. He had somehow talked himself into believing she was nearly harmless. Or... not *harmless*... but manipulable. In Damien's experience, those who tried to use sex to manipulate others were often themselves capable of being so manipulated.

But Azella's demonstration of her power over 'Mikhail' had been a stark reminder that he was playing with fire to try this, as surely as if he attempted to juggle her salamanders.

*What* had he gotten himself into?

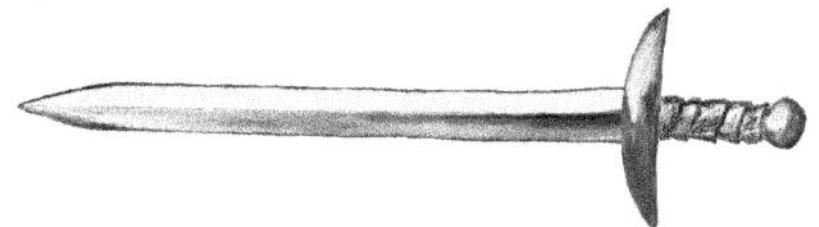

# Chapter FIVE

# *En Passant*

THE NEXT FEW DAYS FOLLOWED a similar pattern. Azella attempted to seduce Damien, Mikhail stopped by to play chess, and he never got enough food to eat or enough sleep. He knew he was reaching the end of his ability to play this game of wills when he actually began wondering why she didn't just put some powerful aphrodisiac in his food to overcome his resistance – and rather wishing she would, just to get it over with. He had already discovered that her *compulsion* spell prevented him from easing his own discomfort from her nightly attempts to importune him.

Mikhail's visits were pleasant breaks. The young man was intelligent and picked up strategy quickly. It would be some time before he could provide Damien with a challenge, but the man enjoyed watching him improve. Teaching was more satisfying than he'd realized, never having had the opportunity to teach anyone anything before.

The young man's exotic beauty continued to work on Damien, and to an extent that he wondered if the controlled breeding Mikhail had described included something that triggered sexual interest in those he met. Damien had learned, from being embedded in his Realm's magickal fabric, that most animals from insects up through horses identified possible mates by scent.

While he hadn't found any scents that humans released, his Courtiers certainly attempted to rectify that lack with various perfumes and colognes – sometimes to the point where he'd found it headache-inducing. And he had to admit that the scent of Genevieve's... *hair* had always driven *him* delightfully wild.

After four long days and longer nights, Mikhail arrived to find Damien half-asleep, no longer even bothering to wistfully regard the untouchable remains of breakfast. The young man quietly set the chess supplies down on a side-table and climbed up to lie down beside him.

"Why are you making this so hard on yourself?" he asked, honestly baffled. "Is what the Mistress is asking of you really so repugnant to you?"

Damien rubbed his eyes with one hand. "No. It's not. And that's the problem."

"I don't understand," Mikhail confessed.

Damien sighed. He'd tried to explain before. "I made a promise. A vow. I can't just break that without breaking a part of *me.*"

Slaves, Mikhail had told him, made no promises.

"This person you made the promise to, your 'wife'," the golden-haired young man said, and Damien could almost hear the quotation marks he put around the word. Family relationships were utterly alien to the young man, it seemed. "Would she be pleased that you are holding to it, or displeased that you are making yourself sick?"

Damien winced. "She'd probably tell me I'm being an idiot."

Indeed, Genevieve's recent soul-bond with their dear friend Jason was hopefully what had sustained her when Azella pinched off Damien's own bond to his wife.

He didn't want to think about that, grateful though he was to know she was probably all right. None of the three of them – nor Adam – had ever heard of a second soul-bond forming. They hadn't had time to determine if – no, *how* – it would change their relationships before Damien had given himself up to the sorceress in hopes of saving them and the rest of the city. The new soul-bond hadn't seemed as overpowering as the first one had been – but Damien could all too easily imagine Jason and Genevieve being lost in each other to the point where they barely noticed *he* was missing at all.

Damien buried his face in the mattress.

"I just want to go *home,*" he mumbled miserably.

"You are too hungry to think straight," Mikhail declared. 'Home' was another concept that didn't resonate with him. "It is one of the Mistress's most effective tools. Never so little food that you are in real danger of starving, but never enough to feel quite right. Once you do her bidding, she will allow you more."

Damien had figured that out.

"I *must* be hungry," he tried to joke, "because *you* look delicious!"

Mikhail gave him a curious look. "You pushed me away before. Does that mean you will not do so now?"

Before Damien could respond, the young man gave him another *expert* kiss.

It was more than merely expert this time, though. They had tentatively become friends these past few days. This kiss had *compassion*.

Damien had thought he had managed to forget what it felt like to be so alone, so hungry, so – well, in the Royal Library he had never exactly been *bored*.

The loneliness was the hardest. Genevieve's long absences for her work as negotiator – with the Army behind her – had made him all too aware of how much he relied on other people's presence. When she was gone, he'd practically clung to Adam, in his role as Captain of Damien's Royal Guards, to keep at bay that feeling of being abandoned and forgotten.

Abandoned.

Forgotten.

And now also *trapped...*

This place was too close to all the things that threw him back into that dark time when he knew, *knew* that his grandfather would summon him at any instant and have him killed as his parents had been. Or that Lord Prydeen would decide to take him for those 'experiments' in the dungeons that no one dared speak of, but everyone knew to fear.

Damien had desperately needed a friend right here and now.

And the line between *friend* and *lover* had always been blurry for him.

He couldn't help responding to the young man's touch. A friend's touch... a lover's touch... not the proprietary *ownership* with which Azella caressed him deep in the night. Damien melted into it with no further objections, letting Mikhail do as he would with him and enjoying every moment of human connection.

Well, almost every moment. Azella's *compulsion* spell still held, and since he'd released the spells he'd held on *himself* the result had been... quite nearly painful. Apparently only *her* touch would be permitted to give him that release. As usual, his own Healing magick worked but slowly on himself.

Mikhail, at least, had not been surprised. Nor had Damien, upon annoyed reflection. Yet another trick she had used on others, it appeared.

"How is *this* any different than what the Mistress wants of you?" Mikhail asked, his head pillowed on Damien's shoulder.

The older man sighed. "I could answer that it's because you're not a woman... but that would just be parsing legalities. Really... it's because this wasn't a forced choice." He turned his head to kiss Mikhail's golden curls. "Just something really nice between friends."

Mikhail tensed.

"Is something wrong? Damien asked him.

"You... *do* know I asked the Mistress's permission, don't you?"

Damien smiled slightly. "Good. I'm glad this won't get you in trouble." He winced, though he knew Mikhail couldn't see it. "You were right about my not being able to think clearly before. It didn't even occur to me that you could suffer for what we were doing until it was... well, a little late."

"You're thinking more clearly now?" Mikhail said.

"Some. I'm still very, very hungry."

The golden-haired young man hesitated again. "The Mistress said I might feed you some if we..." He stopped and Damien wondered if he'd be able to detect a blush against that mahogany skin if he could see the lad's face.

He chuckled. "May I guess Her Royal Highness's language was a trifle... blunt? I've heard worse, I'm sure, my friend. Now you said something about food?"

It was still a cumbersome way to eat, though Mikhail didn't make a great production out of it. He simply selected the most nutrient dense foods and methodically fed the hungry man, bite by bite until the tray abruptly would not allow him to take anymore. Damien sighed with something between contentment and disappointment.

"Thank you," he told the young man earnestly. "For everything."

"It's... good to have a friend," Mikhail said shyly.

He'd already explained to Damien – a day? two days ago? – that there was too much competition among Azella's Power-slaves to allow for friendship. He'd had a friend or two in the crèche where he'd been placed after his wet-nurse weaned him, and friendly acquaintances in the training facility where he had learned his bedroom skills.

But as Azella's favorite, no one *here* had been willing to befriend him, even the girls.

"You *will*... do the Mistress's bidding now, Damien?" Mikhail asked anxiously. "If you will only go back to injuring yourself further..."

Damien looked up at the heavy velvet canopy over the bed. "Yes. But on *my* terms, not hers." He said firmly, then his tone went very dry. "Insofar as that's possible."

# Chapter SIX

# *King's Gambit*

EVENING FOUND DAMIEN PERCHED AT the edge of the bed, looking at the spread of books on a nearby table. He could make out the titles from here, but that was all.

*Salamandres & Sea-Nymphs.*

*A Beginner's Grimoire of Fire Elementals: Salamanders.*

*Salamanders: care and feeding.*

*Raziel's Guide to Salamandres and Other Fire Sorcery.*

*A Historie of Mythical Beastes of Fyre.*

There were several more along the same lines.

Azella had brought them in the day before to see if books might seduce him better than kisses after he had told her a little of his personal history. He'd been so worn by the near constant drain of his magick and insufficient food that he'd barely noticed them. Or her.

Perhaps that was why she had permitted Mikhail...

Damien snorted to himself. 'Permitted,' hah!

She'd set them up as sweetly as a knight-fork in chess might set up for a checkmate.

Had it even been the young man that asked, or had it been Azella who gave him instructions? He didn't want to know and didn't really care.

It had been a respite he needed, either way. And the bit of extra food had given him the remainder of what he needed to clear his head.

The sorceress entered the room, and smirked at him. "Interesting day?"

Damien did what he'd been avoiding doing since he'd arrived, and gave her his full attention. Most of the people he knew – other than Genevieve – found his silver-grey gaze disconcerting when entirely focused on them, though *why* he'd never been sure. But it was a tool, a weapon, like any other, and he'd use it for its effect.

"You needn't pretend that you don't know everything that happens in this Keep."

Her smirk grew wider, and she came closer in the gliding walk that suggested a noblebirth for her – only women who wore floor-length gowns from an early age ever really mastered how to move in them. "Did you find Mikhail as delightful as I have?"

Damien gave her a wry grin, but didn't answer.

"I should have guessed you'd cave for a handsome *boy*. After all, it was your princely lover that I found you roaming your city with in magickal form."

"We *were* doing work," he said mildly, but didn't deny her description of Jason.

It was true, after all. Friend, mentor, swordmaster, Heir, lover...

"Ah, yes. Saving your poor, iced-in people. You know, I could have had my salamanders evaporate all the ice in the city in a few hours?" She leaned 'coincidentally' against the table scattered with books.

Azella was very beautiful this evening, Damien admitted to himself. She'd put up her long, moon-pale hair to bare her long, slender neck, and the very slight golden-peach blush of her skin was set off against a blood-red gown that concealed – for once – more than it revealed.

Since he'd seen her entirely bare on more than one occasion already, the gown served to force his imagination to fill in... always more riveting than what was actually seen.

"As if you would have helped my poor people," he scoffed. "Without your salamanders setting the whole city afire and doing the pirates' work for them."

"As if I would do anything extra for those filthy scoundrels," the sorceress retorted. She drifted forwards, and ran the back of her hand along the side of his face. "I might have done. For a kiss. Right there, in front of everyone, to let even that hotheaded wife of yours know that you were *mine*."

He closed his eyes and leaned in to her touch, trying to put aside the thought of what that would have done to Genevieve. And to himself.

Not tonight.

Tonight, he had to be... pragmatic, as Adam had often accused him of being.

Damien's eyes opened, and met the sorceress's again. Faint startlement in hers that he was doing more than accepting her caress with resignation.

Startlement, then sardonic humor, as she clearly decided that this was Mikhail's doing.

He shook his head slightly, giving Azella his usual half-smile, catching her hand as she started to withdraw it, turning it to place a kiss in her palm.

"You'd rather I had kissed Denisa wearing your semblance than... saved my kisses for the *real* you?" He touched the center of her palm with the tip of his tongue.

She wouldn't have been a woman if she didn't shiver with that, he reflected, and his smile grew a little more... predatory, he suspected was the right word. It was appropriate. If he wanted to survive here, he'd need to match her, after all.

This young sorceress, who wanted him to imagine that she was ancient beyond his reckoning, had been dealing with trained boys. Boys grown into young men, but boys nonetheless. Doubtless there were things they knew that he didn't. But there was always a difference between learning a thing and practicing it.

He pulled her in close, but didn't kiss her.

Instead, he explored the long curve of her neck, taking his time and letting his tongue flicker against the depression at the base of her throat all the way up to that spot behind the ear that was sensitive for almost everyone he'd ever made love to. It worked as well on the pale sorceress as on anyone else.

"I should have turned Mikhail loose on you sooner," she murmured.

"You should have given me enough to *eat* sooner," he corrected, turning her in his arms to access the nape of her neck, "I was too hungry for food to realize all I had to do to sate my *other* hunger was *this.*"

He bit right where her neck met her shoulder – harder than she might have guessed he'd dare. He might well leave a bruise on that fair skin. Since he had to hold her as her knees buckled and she gasped, he knew she wouldn't mind... though it was better than even odds that she'd leave some marks on him before they were done.

"You said I needed to *earn* my right to read those books over there," Damien murmured into her ear, making sure each breath elicited new shivers.

His hands were exploring her breasts through the fabric of her dress, seeking lower, and lower... He lifted them up and caressed her shoulders, and she almost moaned with disappointment.

"Shall we see if I can *earn* everything you know about Fire Elementals more generally? Not just salamanders?" He purred it into her ear, his hands going back to her breasts for round two.

Let the sorceress believe that it was the books on the table and his own desire to *know* that had driven his decision to acquiesce – not merely the weakness of his body.

It was true enough. Hopefully she had no idea of how closely he had come to caving in to her demands with no more of a bribe than a satisfying meal... or simply to sate that other hunger she had so successfully stirred.

"Oh, I *very* much doubt you can manage *that,*" Azella replied, though the way she arched her back and pressed against him gave the lie to her words.

The very fact that she'd left those books *almost* within reach suggested that salamanders were nothing more than the merest edge of the topic. He *needed* this information, and everything else he could eke out of her, or his people would never be safe.

From her kind.

From her.

His people. His friends. His Genevieve.

His *daughter,* waiting to be born.

"You claimed you were looking forward to the challenge I would pose you," Damien told her. "You're not the only one who enjoys a challenge." Let her take that as he intended and not question what else underlay that statement. "But we need some way to determine whether I've *earned* that knowledge or not. Something incontrovertible."

Something that she couldn't turn around and claim wasn't real as soon as she recovered herself.

"A Binding contract as it were?" Azella's voice was still controlled, still filled with that facade of ancient humor. This might be more work than he'd thought. "I follow my agreements to the letter. As you know."

Damien chuckled into her neck, and was himself amused to feel her fingers digging into his thighs for support. "Let's say the books are mine to read for agreeing to this as you already promised that. But if I can make you *beg*... then you teach me everything you know about Fire Elementals."

She shivered with anticipation when he said the word, and he smiled to himself.

"Deal. In fact," she twisted around to face him, the full skirt wrapping her legs tightly. "I'll even extend it to *whenever* you manage that feat. But not *until* then."

Damien had not spent half his youth reading legal treatises for nothing. "And we add another Element and its Powers *every* time?"

"There are only five. How sure are you of yourself?" she had access to *his* body now, and was making good use of her hands. "And what do *I* get out of this deal, if you *don't* succeed?"

"Oh, that should be *very* obvious, my lady."

"I have an entire stable of handsome young men down below if *that* is all I want," she disagreed.

Damien held her away from him for a moment. "Beardless boys. You said it yourself. You wanted a man, grown, and with true Power of his own. A challenge."

A fit *mate,* he suddenly realized, and the shock was almost enough to make him drop her.

She wanted more than a source to tap for more Power... more than a Realm to rule and subjects to wait on her command. She could have all of those things already, did she but stretch out her hand for them.

No, she wanted *him.*

*Damien.*

But she wanted him tamed, muted... *safe.*

How long had she been watching him and his soul-bonded wife? Watching and waiting and biding her time? Growing more jealous of their simple happiness day by passing day...

Was she possibly even *responsible* for the string of miscarriages – ten in five short years – that had nearly claimed his love's life? And his own, as her soul-bond?

Genevieve, he realized was in *more* danger the longer and the better he played this game, not *less.*

But there was no going back now...

"I'm offering you that challenge, milady," Damien went on, hoping his pause hadn't lasted for long as he feared. "And what Power we raise this way. I think that's a fair deal."

Apparently, she hadn't noticed. "All good contracts have time-limits, Your Majesty. *Damien.* Say a year. If you haven't won the right to learn about Fire, Earth, Air, Water, Aether, *and* the raising of Demons by then, you're mine to keep."

A year... he planned to be gone long before a year was out. His baby daughter would be born in less than a year. He'd only been gone a week so far – and it had undone him already.

"Demons don't interest me," he argued to buy time to think. To wrap his mind around the idea of a *year*.

"Demons should *interest* every magick-wielder," she said, dropping the humor and utterly serious for once. "Whether you choose to summon them or to banish them."

Damien couldn't disagree with that.

"I should think," he said teasingly, to pull her back to the mood he wanted her in and away from the sobering topic of demons, "that if it takes me so long, you wouldn't want me to stay. And what if instead, I *earn* my right to the knowledge in *less* than a year?"

"Why then," she met his eyes, and the ancient humor was back, but somehow, she didn't seem as sincere about mocking him. "You would be free to leave. But I should think – if it takes you so little time – that you wouldn't want to go."

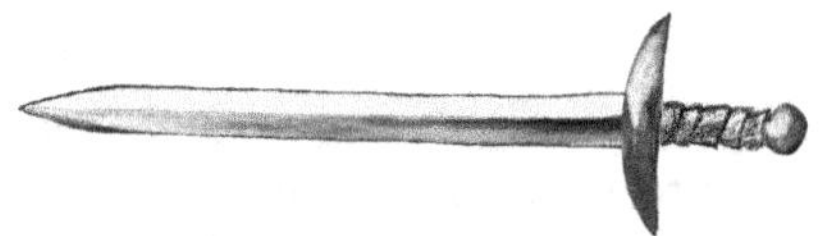

By morning, Damien was ready to learn about Fire Elementals.

He couldn't tell if Azella was more pleased... or more disgruntled that he had won his first lessons so *quickly*. On the whole, he suspected, *pleased* won out.

She'd snuggled into his arms, after.

Damien had lain awake for a long while, thinking.

When the late-morning sun finally reached these southern windows enough to wake the pale sorceress, the king had been up for several hours. It was probably a sign of his recovery that he was oblivious to the rhythms of light and dark, Damien thought wryly. Adam had always blamed his king's unconstrained youth in the Library for why he 'couldn't sleep at night like decent folks.'

He lifted his head at the little noise Azella had made on realizing she was alone in the wide bed, and closed the book he had been reading to come back to her. He'd been delighted to discover that – now that he had met his end of the bargain – he had been able to leave the bed to reach the selection of books on salamanders.

"Good morning, milady," he smiled, leaning down over her. How much would be too much before she decided he was pandering?

Apparently not a kiss, because Azella reached up and pulled him into one. At least not too much from *her* perspective. Damien's own line to walk was a good deal narrower.

After several moments, he pulled away. "Breakfast is in order, don't you think? And a *real* breakfast, if you please."

He thought for a moment that she would pout... but instead she almost visibly decided that it was below her dignity as an evil sorceress.

"What were you doing before?" she asked. *Instead of staying by my side...* she added soundlessly, the whole thing interspersed with images and sensations of where she would have ensured that led.

"Reading. I've never slept well at night. It drives my Guards crazy to have to follow me all over the Castle at odd hours of the night." He smiled again. "Those books were interesting – though they cover a lot of the same material, as I suspected they would."

Azella frowned, and sat up so she wasn't looking up at him. Damien had been careful to half-recline so that she could look down at him when she sat. It was a little thing... but he felt some of the tension go out of her, and he knew he'd made the right choice. His life was going to be made up of such little things for the foreseeable future.

"What do you mean the books *'were'* interesting?"

Damien shrugged. "I finished them."

Somewhat aghast, she looked at the five slender volumes and two rather thicker ones that were now neatly stacked on the table. "You can't have. How long were you up anyways?"

"I'm a fast reader."

He didn't bother to mention that he remembered everything he read, or heard, or witnessed... or felt... in detail.

It had startled Damien to discover that other people couldn't do that. And it had startled him all over again to find that the few others who *could* remember everything often remembered things they heard, but not what they saw, and so on. And he had yet to find anyone who could take all those pieces of information and cross-correlate them to see the bigger picture. Genevieve did some of it, as a strategist; but again, her field of operations was much narrower.

Azella was unlikely to believe him if he tried to explain.

She frowned more deeply and repeated, "You *can't* have read all of them."

She slipped out of the bed and picked up the thickest volume – *Raziel's Guide* – which just happened to be the last but one he had read and therefore second from the top of the pile. She flipped to a random page and skimmed quickly down the text. Looking for some unique piece of information, doubtless, upon which she would test him.

He'd been through some variation of this with most of his close friends.

His vassals and Royal Councilors – not having the same opportunity to quiz their monarch – had finally just come to expect that the king knew every random fact, so long as it had shown up in a report at some point in time. Damien remembered with amused satisfaction the look on the irritable face of young Quillian Mirion, newly-made Duke of Reyensweir, when the king had given him a run-down of every harvest in Reyensweir for the last hundred years, comparing it to the other duchies, and noting trends. From memory.

Of course, the downside was that he never knew what pieces of information he was *missing*. Occasionally he could see the shape of what he hadn't been told, but there were surely things he was still missing...

And to that point...

He wondered if Genevieve had ever figured out what the 'missing piece' of the strategic situation was. His brilliant wife had seen that something wasn't adding up the day before the pirates attacked – Damien had had his hands full with his own efforts in the battle and hadn't followed up.

And now he was *here*...

"Here," Azella announced. "This book has some details on the mating habits of salamanders not found in any of the others. Tell me what it says."

Damien leaned back with a sigh and stared up at the canopy. "That's page one hundred and eight. It's not so much about mating habits as about subspecies. Most salamanders find a mate of the opposite gender, but there is a small group of them that reproduce parthenogenetically – that is, there are no males. However, the females produce more offspring if they mate with each other." He rolled up onto one elbow to look at her. "The author doesn't say where to find them. I think she was trying to protect them from curiosity seekers. I rather liked her style. She seemed to really care about fire creatures."

"Of course she did," Azella bit out, "Raziel-Mizriel was the pre-eminent Fire sorceress of her time." She glared at him. "What spell are you using to do that? I've never heard of such a thing."

Damien gave her his mild smile and shook his head. "It's no spell, Azella. Just me. It's just the way my mind works." He gave her a raised eyebrow. "*Raziel's Guide* claims that behavior is unique to salamanders, but *Erezeth's Compendium* describes fire-sylphs as doing much the same thing. The difference, of course, being that fire-sylphs seem to be an off-shoot of air-sylphs, who are actually reproductively compatible with humans. And elves."

54

She dropped the *Guide* with a thump that made Damien, who loved all written material, wince, and snatched at the *Compendium*.

"Pages fifty-three, and then ninety-six through ninety-eight," he told her helpfully. "Though about halfway down page ninety-seven the author goes off on a tangent about the connection of air-sylphs to mist-maidens to the royalty of Pathremir and their Silver Dragon goddess." He shook his head disapprovingly. "Making connections is all well and good, but disorganized writing is a bane."

The sorceress's bemused expression told him she believed him now.

"Breakfast?" he said hopefully, as she sat down slowly on the edge of the bed.

"You don't have any idea how Powerful this could make you, do you?" Azella asked him slowly.

Damien sighed. "It kept me on my throne for five years. That's power enough, I think. And all the power in the world won't help if I starve to death right here and now."

"Damien," she said seriously, turning and taking his face in her hands, "This is *important*."

"So is breakfast," he told her.

She rolled her eyes. Such a human gesture, so unplanned and uncalculated. Perhaps there was more to her after all than sheer ambition and a need for control.

"Keeping track of knowledge is one of the hardest things for a sorcerer to do. Spells must be memorized and practiced – but not to completion – lest the sorcerer forget some small detail. And since nothing is ever practiced to completion, those last few details are always in danger of getting away from us. But you..." her vivid, blue-grey eyes seemed to glow with enthusiasm, "*you* simply need to read the spell or try it once. And you'll always know where to find it again – or do you forget things eventually?"

"If it's important enough, I usually go back to the original source to be sure." Damien admitted. He sighed. "Sort of like going down to the *kitchens* to get *breakfast*."

She laughed. "When they say men have one-track minds, I'm fairly sure they usually mean something else. You can eat *later*."

Damien ran a hand up her arm and down her bare side. "We should eat now. And something else *later*."

Azella shivered in delight, then gave him a fond look. "Men. Always thinking with something other than your brain. Breakfast will be up momentarily. And," she assured him. "You can eat as much as you like. Though I'd hate to see that impressive physique run to fat."

She padded off to the washroom, leaving Damien to wonder how she'd react to seeing Jason's chest if she thought *his* muscles were impressive. Did these slave-markets she apparently frequented not sell warriors as well? Surely, she must have *some* warriors Bound to her, for appearances, if not because she actually needed them.

He contemplated the mystery that was still the pale sorceress as yet another handsome youth brought in the breakfast tray.

Freeborn, Mikhail had said, but sold as a Power-slave when she was only fifteen herself. Nobly-born, he'd determined for himself, from the quality of her movements and her ability to instantly tell when he condescended to her ever-so-slightly. And from the way she preened slightly every time he called her 'my lady' – as if feeling vindicated by his words.

What tragedy could have caused a nobly-born girl to end up auctioned to the highest bidder? Damien could imagine a number of situations with that result, but none at all where the girl in question had the talent to be a Powerful sorceress. No invader or usurper would dare leaving such an asset where it might come back to punish them later – unless they were foolish or unaware. Had she perhaps been turned out into a regular slave-market by some such ignorant captor – though he winced at the thought that such things existed – and been found by a speculator searching for hidden treasures? That seemed the most likely scenario, based on what he knew so far.

He wondered if she had yet taken her revenge on those who had taken her from her life of ease.

More interesting to the captive king was that notion that Azella – whatever her real name was – was likely a precious and pampered child who had been thrust into a world of unspeakable horrors. And – perhaps – rescued by her unknown Master. An evil sorcerer who had created his rival... and most probably his destroyer... by teaching her.

Damien wondered if that man had also been seeking to create an ideal mate. A gently-reared young lady of immense potential, ready to fall in love with her rescuer... The dark-haired man's mouth twisted in self-deprecating humor.

Yes, he resembled that remark all too closely himself. His heart ached for Jason to rescue him again... but he was a man grown now and had gotten himself into this. He'd have to get himself out.

What had changed? Had the ancient evil man finally simply died? No, for she had none of the signs of a broken heart. Instead Azella seemed caught between throwing herself at Damien and needing to control his every movement and make him *safe*.

*Safe* in the sense of safe for her to love, unable to betray her.

The captive king had been entirely unprepared for how *eager* she had been last night. He'd assumed that while she was leaving *him* to suffer the effects of, ah, unrequited love, that she had been easing her own needs elsewhere, perhaps even with the beautiful Mikhail. But her reactions last night had suggested otherwise, as well as some of the things she had murmured to him. Clearly, she had been *waiting* for him.

The pale sorceress was returning, her gown today a lighter shade – shimmery silver silk.

He turned to look at her, and her pale skin took on a roseate hue. She twirled, and the skirt flew out.

"See anything you like?" she asked, then raised an eyebrow as she realized he hadn't touched the food. "I gave you permission to eat."

Damien smiled at her. "It would have been rude to begin without you."

He lifted the first lid and offered, "May I serve you?"

Her blush deepened at his courtesies, and she nodded.

He didn't do anything exotic with the simple breakfast items – though he was tempted to get some of his own back after the last several days. He simply put together a plate of eggs and bacon and toast and handed it to her, before preparing a plate of the same for himself.

A pot of oat porridge alongside nuts and honey and sliced apples called to him, but she had promised he could eat as much as he liked today... and he had too many tender memories involving porridge. Hopefully, she would hurry off to her 'other projects' again and leave him to salt his porridge with tears out of her sight.

"I suppose you will want to begin learning about Fire Elementals immediately," Azella said, patting her linen napkin elegantly to the corners of her mouth as she laid down her utensils just so. Now that Damien was alert again, her every littlest mannerism bespoke her birth.

Her tone was reluctant... and possibly unprepared. Their deal last night had been a surprise he sprung upon her, and she had signed onto it assuming that he could not live up to his end. If he pressed her now, she might seem clumsy and that would annoy her and would set his plans back instead of progressing them. Time to ease off.

Damien leaned back on one elbow. "Perhaps not yet, milady. I should probably take a few days to recover my full strength before beginning as arduous a magickal endeavor as that. My full *physical* strength," he emphasized, letting his gaze roam boldly down her body.

"Oh. Yes, that makes sense," the sorceress agreed almost too quickly.

Her own gaze traced Damien's chest and down...

"You're not going to keep me in here anymore, are you?" he asked, and her eyes came up suddenly and suspiciously to meet his. "Now that I have everything to stay for, after all?"

Afraid he was layering it on too thickly, the captive king nonetheless reached forwards to capture her hand and brought it to his lips, keeping his intense silver-grey gaze on hers the whole time.

"Everything..." she breathed. "Oh. You mean your lessons."

Azella visibly pulled herself together and gave him her old, amused look.

"Yes. You definitely have reasons for staying." She smiled smugly. "Not that you could go very far anyways. I collected a great deal of Power last night and my shields are all at full charge."

Interesting. She had shields to prevent people – or was it just him? – from leaving. Presumably in addition to whatever she had for defense against incursions.

Damien smiled. "Excellent. Then you can send someone to bring me fresh clothes and real boots now that my feet are healed – and find me a sword and someone to practice against." He paused, scratching his beard. "And a barber. I could use a trim, as you said."

She frowned. "A sword?"

Damien gave her a 'what can you do?' gesture. "You said you liked my physique, milady sorceress. To maintain it I need to exercise. I'm a swordsman, so that's what I need to do."

He paused. "Surely a sorceress of your Power and prestige has some men-at-arms or Bound warriors you could lend to such a purpose. Not that you *need* anything other than your magick –" though she'd never have abducted him from Emeralsee without the aid of the pirates, "– but for appearances. Or to handle those things that aren't worth spending magick on, such as guarding caravans of goods and supplies to maintain this Keep.

"Those caravans must range rather widely," he added casually. "Farivera has never been known for its sophistication, after all."

Azella had begun to relax, clearly distracted by a vision of him practicing with a sword that he had carefully been sliding across mentally in bits and pieces. At this last statement, however, she sat bolt upright.

"How did you know we're in Farivera?" she demanded. "I'll flay alive the person who told you!"

He had no doubt in that instant that she meant that literally. Luckily, Damien had an answer that didn't implicate her unfortunate slaves and servants.

The captive king laughed, his entire posture carefully relaxed.

"I've been the *Bound King* of Ilseador for five years, Azella. Farivera may have defected from my grandfather's reign even before I was born, but my Realm knows its own. I've known where I was since I first stepped off your ship."

And before that, really, since his Realm had *called* to him across the intervening stretch of water, the ship never having gone much beyond the edge of the continental shelf.

Damien tilted his head and gave her a genuinely amused smile. "You didn't *honestly* think that my connection to Ilseador could be so easily ended, did you? You've managed to cutoff any *communication* across that Binding, but I doubt the Binding itself could be removed short of my death."

Well, not *removed,* but she had certainly done some serious damage to both that Binding and his soul-bond to Genevieve. He'd been *aware* of being on and within his own home-ground when Denisa had led him up from the quay via that stone tunnel through the cliff – but he had felt oddly *numb* and *muffled.* Reaching out to try to stabilize his connection with the Realm had been beyond him.

*Shock,* he now guessed it had been. As a Healer, he knew that the body could only process so many insults to its systems before it walled everything off in a desperate – and frequently unhelpful – attempt to prevent further damage from being inflicted.

In this case it would have been more useful – and Healing – to make that contact with Farivera… Though after so long a time of isolation, Gods alone knew if the Lost Province would have had more demands of him than he could have handled in that state.

She glowered at him suspiciously. "I *ended* that Bond. And I could *feel* that there was nothing left."

Damien shrugged. "I thought it was gone, too, at first. But that was aboard a ship and beyond the coastal waters that the Realm considers its own."

He looked at her, as if noticing her irritation for the first time. "My lady, I have sworn to stay here as your student – even your Apprentice. And to… ah, *raise Power* with you in exchange for my lessons. You cannot imagine I would renege on that deal simply because we stand at the farthest possible point of the province which has longest considered itself independent of my throne?"

He snorted.

"Give me better credit as a strategist – as a *chess-player* – than that. If *that* were my plan, I'd have done better to conceal my knowledge from you. Instead, sweet lady," and he picked up the silver platter with the last strip of bacon lying on it and offered it to her. "Instead, I offer to you what I know, upon a silver plate."

She looked at it scornfully. "What you *know* is a piece of bacon?"

Damien gave her his mildest expression. "Surely you don't think there is anything that can lure me from your... *lessons.*"

Azella's eyes were still narrowed, and he could see that she was well aware of just what – or *who* – might lure him home... but to admit it would weaken her hold upon him. Or at least her perception of that hold. He was tempted – so tempted – to prod a little more, but his instincts told him to let her walk down the pathway his words had carved on her own.

"Lessons..." the pale sorceress said at last, and disappointment seethed beneath her words. "Well, we shall certainly have to see you are not deprived of *those.*"

She stormed out of the room.

Damien sighed, and sat himself back up to prepare a bowl of porridge.

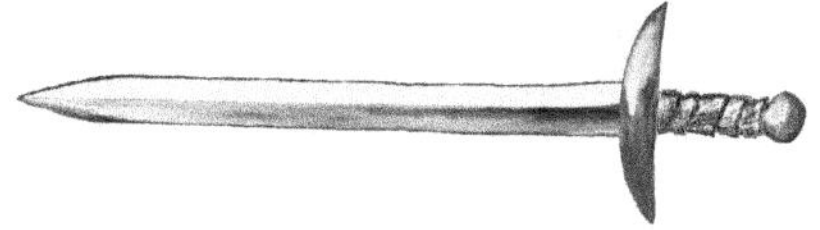

# Chapter SEVEN

# *J'adoube*

DAMIEN SPENT MUCH OF THAT day gazing out the windows. It was such a relief to be well-fed and out of that bed. He'd finally been able to engage in some proper exercises and use up some of the low-level of frenetic energy that always built up inside him during even short periods of inactivity. Not being permitted to so much as *pace* had worn on him almost as badly as... everything else.

Gazing out of these south-facing windows created its own set of frustrations, however.

They were high enough up that he couldn't see the branch of the Tree of Life River that he had noted as Denisa led him up to the Keep. The river marked the boundary of Farivera with the neighboring kingdom Sindala – the name stemming from the broad river delta with which it joined the sea. The Winter-brown marshes between the branches of the delta had never clearly been claimed by either Realm when Farivera formally gave its allegiance to Ilseador, and now they belonged to Sindala.

Thus, he could not see even the smallest part of his Realm and it *itched* at him to be so close and yet unable to reach. If he could just get outside... though he had small hope Azella would allow that. Perhaps... perhaps he could persuade her to allow him to move about *within* the Keep. If he could get down below this built-section where the stones were so long disconnected from the rock that gave them birth, if he could make it down to the levels that were carved from the still living rock... *that* was still Farivera.

A pity that he'd been in shock from Azella's assault on his Bindings when Denisa had led him up through that stairway carved into the very rock of the promontory itself. If he'd been more mentally put-together *then*, he could have reconnected with Farivera and the Realm the first time he set his hand on the stone wall of the passage.

Unless, of course, Azella had thought of *that*, as she seemed to have done everything else with regards to his capture. Perhaps... perhaps he *hadn't* been numb to the touch of his Realm so much as that the sorceress had layered an insulating spell over those stone walls and floors and he'd never *really* have been able to touch anything connected to the Realm after all.

Dismissing the question as irrelevant at this point, Damien looked back out of his windows. *Her* windows. This was *her* bedchamber, he needed to be careful to remember, not *his*.

It was darker than it would have been on the north side of the Keep. The sun would never shine directly into these windows, regardless of their impressive size, and the grey overcast sky did not help.

But still, it was *beyond this room.*

Damien hadn't tried the door yet. His entire plan depended on getting Azella to trust him, so he would not impinge on that burgeoning trust in any way he could avoid.

He wondered how long it would take her to *believe* that Damien had told her he knew they were in Farivera in order to demonstrate that he was holding nothing back. To convince herself that it would have been easy for him to simply refrain from mentioning it, and that surely, he would have done just that *if* he had some deeper laid plan of escape.

He wondered whether whichever Court she had been raised in could possibly have elevated subterfuge to the artform it had become under his grandfather's rule.

*Trust...* The captive king mocked his own thoughts.

It wasn't *trust* Damien was hoping to elicit from the pale sorceress. He should be honest with himself, if no other. He was trying to make her *fall in love* with him so that she would teach him her magick.

And the worst part of it was that the poor girl seemed to be trying – in her own, weird, evil sorceress way – to woo *him*. As if she was already more than half in love with the *idea* of him.

The whole thing made him feel sick to his stomach, but he could see no other way out.

Damien wondered bitterly if he was any better a man than the evil sorcerer whom he guessed had trained her. In magick, as in life, the ends could not justify the means.

Simply because he was prostituting himself – why mince words? – for the protection of the two million people he was responsible for in Ilseador; for the Realm itself so damaged by the tenure of the evil wizard-king, his grandfather Reginald; for his loved ones...

Simply because the target of his plot was herself an evil sorceress...

None of that made what he was doing *right*.

Would he ever be able to look little Giendra Marlerite – his daughter, conceived just days before Azella abducted him – in the eye?

For a moment he was able to escape the Keep, if only in his imagination. His daughter – sired by his Heir and cousin, but *his* nonetheless. He had no doubt of what she would look like: golden hair with just a hint of red, eyes as blue as the sky itself with just enough green for mystery, tall and fair.

She'd look a proper Alsterling, not dark and barely above average height, like him. Damien took after his mother's family, the Eldridges, with black hair and eyes as grey as... well, as that overcast sky outside.

The captive king sighed pensively, staring blindly out across the marshes and the leaden sea once more.

Mikhail never came with his chessboard.

True to her word not to starve him any further, another handsome boy arrived with lunch. He took away the demolished breakfast tray and spoke not one word.

By mid-afternoon, Damien had experimented with reading the salamander books upside-down and backwards. There was nothing to write or draw with – the hot springs warming the Keep were apparently so effective that there was not even a fireplace. His studies had suggested that fireplaces – and their attendant chimneys – were as likely to chill a room as warm it, so he admired the efficiency and mourned the lack of ashes and half-burned kindling that he might have at least used to write on the tiled floor.

By late afternoon, he was frustrated enough to try the door, despite his best intentions.

It opened at his touch.

Which left a different problem.

Damien wasn't particularly body-shy, but he had not so much as a thread of clothing, and no idea who might be out there in the rest of the sorceress's personal suite. Wrapping himself up in a sheet from the bed would be almost as ridiculous as seeing if one of the sorceress' frilly, feminine robes would fit him.

Best to brazen it out?

He peered carefully out at the room he had been ushered into some five days earlier. It was no less grand than his first impression – sweeping windows scarcely darkened by heavy velvet drapes secured with golden-tasseled pulls came to a point as if this were the prow of a ship.

The black-and-red marble was softened with accents of white here, though it was white marble shot through with veins of blood-red, lest anyone begin to forget whose space this was.

No chairs, not even a grand one for the Mistress of the Keep. The heavy, oaken double-doors that Denisa had led him through were strapped with darkened bronze and stained almost black.

The pattern worked into the marble floor – picked out in gold between the individual tiles – made an enchanted circle. It looked plain enough now, but Damien suspected that at least *some* of her greater workings were conducted in this room. He himself had only the slightest knowledge of ceremonial magick, most of which seemed to involve communicating with – or compelling – creatures from different planes of existence as best as he had been able to determine.

The salamander books had suggested that for those magick-wielders without a natural affinity for the Elementals of this plane, ceremonial magick would serve to contact them as well.

The room, however dramatic, was entirely empty.

Damien padded across it, not daring to look out the northern windows where the Realm that had Bound him lay. Even if it weren't entirely the wrong direction – given that the promontory pointed out into the open ocean – he didn't think they were close enough to see the Elaarwen mountains that marched down from Genevieve's own rocky duchy into the sea, separating Farivera from most of the rest of Ilseador save for the one narrow passage into Siovale.

Siovale... almost the last thing he had done before surrendering himself to Azella to prevent her salamanders from burning his ice-prisoned city was to commend his family to the care of the Duke of Siovale, Tomas Elsevier. Tomas had become a true friend after they had sorted out the Rebellion and the brief usurpation by what had turned out to be Tomas's *half*-brother, Harald, a cuckoo's child laid in the Elsevier family tree in one of King Reginald's more petty and convoluted schemes. Harald and Lord Prydeen had seized Tomas's mind from him by magick for two long years – he hadn't even remembered the birth of his youngest child when Damien had freed the older man from the spells of compulsion. Tomas had been second to swear the Vassal's Oath to the newly Crowned and Bound King Damien, an oath that now took on the force of a magickal geas Binding the duke to the good of his lands and people.

The first to so swear had, of course, been Genevieve Stellarine, Duchess of Elaarwen, the so-called Rebel Duchess and leader of the Rebellion since the supposed death of her father, Duke Aldred, herself the next-most likely Heir to the Throne. And Damien's soul-bonded and own truest love. His Queen, once they'd had the time and space for him to properly wed and crown her.

Damien was doubly-bound to Elaarwen – as both King and, as Genevieve's husband, as Duke-Consort. Those mountains...

There was another door, opposite the one to the bedchamber.

Damien padded over to that one and tried it. It, too, opened on silent hinges at his touch.

The room itself was a left-handed twin to the room he had been trapped in, but far brighter with its north-facing windows letting in the sun. The late afternoon rays were golden and partially blocked by an outcropping wall to the east.

This room was clearly an office... and private library. Damien's fingers itched to touch the books and – did she really have *scrolls?* – that lined the shelves.

A very private office. Azella's desk faced the glorious view of Farivera – of *Ilseador* – that the captive king dared not allow himself to look at, lest he be unable to look away. Very trusting of her to give her back to the door and not even leave a spell to alert her to an intruder.

Her long, pale hair nestled on the floor in coils and long, open curls. The shimmery silver dress pooled around her feet, but she didn't seem to have noticed Damien's entrance as she leaned over her desk in deep concentration. As he watched, she tucked a strand of hair behind one ear. It was an endearing sort of gesture, entirely private and unaffected.

And Damien suddenly realized that there was no way he could carry out his plan to learn everything he could from her without falling a bit in love with her himself.

The thought froze him in place.

The line between friends and lovers had always been blurry for him. It had been so ever since Ciriis Celavell – one of his first friends and rescuers, mentors and teachers – had taken him as a lover. Ciriis had then proceeded to fill his bed with emotionally and physically abused young ladies who had been discarded from his grandfather's clutches.

He'd never heard most of their stories, but those twelve young women had become his most fiercely loyal, if entirely secret, guards. Ciriis had intended that his very timid and appreciative self would help them to heal and that the bond they formed with him would enforce that loyalty. Her plan had worked better than she could have imagined – to this day, Damien trusted his secret guardswomen more than anyone but Genevieve, Adam, Jason, and Ciriis herself.

It ran both ways of course – Damien could no more imagine letting harm come to one of those women than they would have let down their Prince.

The young king had gone for Genevieve's overly bold plan for just the two of them to re-take the Castle in no small part because of his driving need to protect those brave and loyal women, left behind in their desperate escape from Harald's usurpation. Genevieve's plan had worked spectacularly, but Damien had never fooled himself that he had gone along with it because of its strategic wisdom. He trusted his wife as the brilliant strategist she was, but the situation had been ridiculously stacked against them. He had agreed to her plan because it was his only chance to free the twelve noblewomen who formed his secret guard.

He'd never fallen completely in love with anyone except with Genevieve, but he loved his guardswomen fiercely and trusted them implicitly. He'd rejoiced for each one who found a husband and doted on the children they'd produced.

And more recently... there was Jason. And Adam.

Could he be this sorceress's lover without also loving her? Without also being her friend? Without also... seeing some Good in her?

When the time came for him to leave... could he do it, knowing that his betrayal would break her heart and harden it and turn her farther to the paths of Evil?

He'd paused for too long. Even without a spell to alert her, Azella had detected the faint sound of his breathing, or sensed his presence in some other fashion.

She turned on her swiveling chair, and her eyes lit up at the sight of him. She clearly fought the reaction in order to display what she must think was the proper look of cool amusement for an evil sorceress to wear. She really was heart-stoppingly beautiful, and somehow the captive king *knew* it was her natural form, not something magickally rebuilt by her former Master.

"So, you dared come out of your eyrie, my royal falcon."

"I missed you," Damien said, and was moderately distressed to find it was true.

Azella misconstrued the sincerity in his tone, however. "Or perhaps you merely wanted to look out over the land you still claim to be Bound to."

Damien came over to her, his eyes resolutely kept away from the windows. "The Realm can wait. I only have eyes for you."

She still looked skeptical, but he was standing close enough now for her to touch. She ran delicate fingers down his abdomen, and lower... and smirked as he shuddered and reacted to that caress. "I think I quite like you wandering around my personal quarters naked."

"Hmmn." *That* was clearly not going to get him the clothing he wanted. Damien stepped away and moved towards her shelves. "So, this is where you keep all of this–"

He reached out to touch one of the gold embossed spines and she froze him with a *compulsion* spell thrown out so quickly and automatically that he suspected she always held such things ready.

Azella glided up to him, insinuating herself between the shelf and his body. She took his hand and moved it away from the books. "I should let you try touching and suffer the consequences. But *you're* not as easily replaceable as one of my beautiful 'beardless boys'."

She had left him able to reply.

"You put traps *that* deadly on your books?"

"Apprentices will always seek more knowledge than they are ready for," she informed him. He didn't doubt that included knowledge *she* was not ready for them to have. "And actually, some of these books and scrolls protect themselves. I'd as soon not find the remains of their meal on my office floor when one of the boys has decided to disregard my warnings."

That... was an idea he'd never come across before. Damien had feared the contents of his grandfather's journals but not the books themselves. *Had King Reginald been the rank amateur this pale sorceress claimed, or had Damien simply been lucky?*

"Might I ask what *your* spell does then?" he asked with some trepidation.

She flicked a lock of her long hair over her shoulder in a movement of calculated grace and disregard. "I've no use for an Apprentice who disobeys my orders. But there are other uses for a boy with the Talent for Power. *You* wouldn't care about those," she smirked again, "being such a *good* sorcerer."

*You don't know the half of it,* the captive king thought guiltily, but hid the real reason for his discomfort by changing the subject back to her books. "This seems quite a library if these are all books on magick."

Indeed, the room was lined with shelves.

She shrugged. "These are my workaday references... and those tomes that are too valuable or too dangerous to leave in my main library." Her face twisted in a wry smile, apparently at seeing his reaction to the notion of *more* books. "I knew *that* would serve to distract you."

Azella was still holding his hand. She raised it to her lips and inserted one of his fingers into her mouth, keeping her eyes on his as she sucked and nibbled on the digit.

"*You*... are... *far* more distracting than... mere books," Damien managed.

Her eyes dropped low. "I can tell. But tell me truly, Damien, my handsome Sorcerer-King, have you ever used the phrase *'mere books'* before in your life?"

"Perhaps not." He smiled down into her blue-gray eyes.

"Not even with your *princess?*" she challenged.

"My what?" he was genuinely confused. The only princess who came to mind was his unborn daughter – unless... surely, she couldn't be referring to his sister, Kandra, dead these last nineteen years?

"Your *wife,*" Azella clarified, her face showing her displeasure.

"Genevieve?" He laughed. "She's no princess and never has been. She can out-fight, out-strategize, out-play, and out-govern me. She wasn't called the Rebel Duchess for nothing, you know."

Azella's face was looking still less happy, and he couldn't distract her by pulling her close, since she still had him frozen with that *compulsion* spell.

Words it would have to be, then.

"A fragile fairytale princess in her high tower, she is not. Genevieve," he added, and Damien made his tone as wistful as he could with a straight face, "has never needed *rescuing*. By me *or* anyone else. Rather the opposite, in fact."

This was not strictly true, and he *had* actually rescued her once from dire pain and torture. He would rather not have had to do so; he would rather she not have felt she had to walk into her ex-husband's untender clutches to save him and her father and the others they cared about.

The parallel with his current situation would be more cogent if Harald had actually intended to treat Genevieve as his Queen, rather than beat and rape her.

"A *fairytale princess?*" Azella raised a mocking eyebrow. "You're not trying to tell me that *you'd* pick such a delicate creature over your *warrior-queen.*"

Damien tilted his head since he couldn't shrug, and gave her a mild smile. "Would I dare? But we all have these fantasies that don't mirror reality."

Such as his beautiful and entirely *un*-fragile wife showing up to rescue him *right now* and hang the consequences.

"Fantasies... of fragile fairytale princesses..." the fairly fragile-seeming sorceress mused. She looked speculatively up at her captive king. "Models of chastity and innocence, I suppose?"

"Well... not *too* innocent," he suggested. "Or it wouldn't be much of a fantasy, now would it?"

"You said you spent your entire youth reading fairystories... It would only make sense..."

"Hair like spun moonbeams and eyes like pools of still water," Damien added helpfully, letting his eyes scan down the sorceress's slender self. "Skin as fair as milk, lips like rosebuds..."

No need to mention that he'd always re-written in his head the descriptions of the princesses both fair and dark to have exuberant red-gold hair and blue-green eyes. And that he'd imagined each one to be a warrior-princess like his memory of his own adored older sister.

No need to mention, either, that he'd fallen in love with Genevieve the first time he'd seen her – when he was eight and she was twelve.

"Did any of your fantasies involve your fragile, innocent princesses doing *this?*"

The sorceress sank to her knees and proceeded to demonstrate all sorts of things that should rightfully shock one of those delicate creatures. Held in place by her *compulsion* spell, Damien gave in to the sensations. She was... very clever with her mouth, after all.

She kept going until he was within just a touch or two more of demonstrating his satisfaction all over her face... and then stopped, leaving him gasping.

"Your turn," Azella told him smugly, and used the *compulsion* spell to force him to kneel before her.

"Fulfill *my* fantasy and perhaps *I'll* fulfill *yours,*" she purred, then lifted her silvery skirt and tossed it over his head, stepping close and releasing his upper body from her spell. She wasn't wearing any underthings, not even the lacy scarcely-there bits he'd seen on her before.

Odd, but Damien could play this game as well. He sneaked in his own *compulsion* spell to hold the sorceress's legs still while he began to do as she'd asked. She didn't even notice until he made her knees weak with pleasure and she discovered that she *could not* let them buckle. Damien chuckled and continued, taking her also to within a hair of satisfaction before releasing *his* spell of *compulsion* and letting her stagger slightly.

Suddenly his own legs were free, and he rose from under her skirts.

Her eyes were slightly glassy, and she boosted herself up onto her desk, clearly signaling what she wanted from him *now.*

Damien looked at the precious *books* scattered across the broad desk, the ink wells and feather pens, and hid a wince.

"Surely nothing so crude for a princess," he said firmly, and scooped her up, carrying her out of the office, across the grand ceremonial room, and into the bedchamber. She was quite nearly as slight as she looked, and though it was a strain, he was able to get her tossed into the bed without collapsing himself.

He took the time for a deep breath before following her for a rather short, but satisfying finale.

"A proper bed for my princess," he murmured a little breathlessly as he lay beside her afterwards and wasn't entirely surprised when she stiffened.

Pretense, however, was the name of the game.

Damien rolled back on top of her. "What? You don't like it when I call you 'my princess'?"

He kissed her, then made his way around her neck with more kisses. The neck of her gown restricted his access below her collarbone. "My *fairytale fantasy* princess...? Wasn't that what we were playing at?"

Azella relaxed. "Just a game... of course..."

"Or can it be," Damien purred, "that the Powerful, beautiful sorceress is *also* a princess born?"

Her vivid blue-grey eyes were wide with shock. "How can you... how did you...?"

"You have the manner-born, my sweet," he answered. "Did you think that a man who grew up in a royal Court would not recognize a true princess?"

"You can't know who I am," Azella stated, but there was a waver of uncertainty – perhaps even the edges of *panic?* – in her eyes. "Or rather – who I *was.*"

Damien shrugged, giving her his usual mild half-smile. "It makes no difference to me, lovely sorceress. It's your knowledge, not your bloodlines that I'm here for."

He let his smile grow smug, as if pleased to have found out her little secret. "If the Realm that birthed you was so foolish as to give up such Power as you possess... and you are willing to share it with *me* instead... who am I to complain? Their loss is my gain."

Avarice and ambition were two emotions Azella understood quite well, and she relaxed again. Though he thought there was a wisp of disappointment at the back of her eyes. "Indeed. And knowledge you shall have, my handsome Apprentice. Tomorrow, we'll get started."

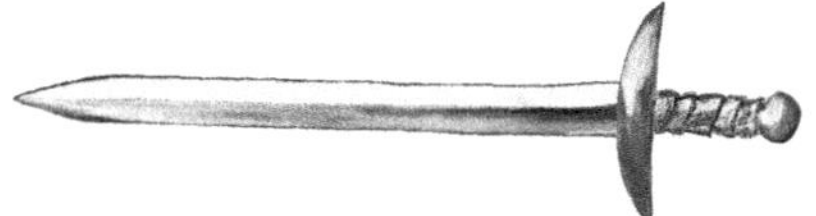

# Chapter EIGHT

# *Hanging*

D AMIEN WAS PROVIDED WITH CLOTHING the next day – rather more flamboyant than he would have chosen on his own, but it was clothing and he wasn't complaining. Even if the pants were overly-well fitted. And the shirt was lacking laces so that it hung open across his chest. And there were no boots.

It was more than Azella permitted her boy-toys, and the captive king noted looks of envy when lunch was delivered.

The sorceress's transformation from vixen to teacher was... not without its problems.

She was serious and wanted his complete attention, but her lectures were wandering and full of unneeded details. When Damien asked questions, she was either dismissive or grew frustrated. When he didn't, she was sure he wasn't paying sufficient attention.

When the sorceress's temper flared for the third time and Damien had to block using his own Power yet again, he began to wonder how many Apprentices she'd already 'gone through.' One of those pretty boys wouldn't have been able to deflect her Powers as he had. Perhaps his arrival had saved Mikhail's life – at least for now.

They were in her office, and she was pacing back and forth, expostulating. Damien was seated in her desk chair, and for once he had no desire to pace himself. Someone had to be a source of calm in this room, and it clearly wasn't going to be Azella. He leaned back, lacing his fingers together behind his head, and stretched his legs out to cross at the ankles, regarding his bare feet ruefully.

She whirled upon him, suddenly noting his relaxed – and amused – posture.

"I told you to *pay attention!*" The sorceress exclaimed.

"My dear," the captive king said, "I can repeat back every word you said. It's not just books I remember." He gave her a dry look. "Have you ever *taught* anyone before, Azella?"

She frowned fiercely. "Of course! I have had many Apprentices. None of them were satisfactory in the end." She tried to give him a winning smile. "*You* will be different."

Damien regarded her serenely. "I already am. Have any of your other 'students' ever *survived* this particular lecture?"

Azella gaped at him. She visibly had to rally herself. "I haven't had an Apprentice reach the level where they could learn about Elementals," she admitted.

"And why not?" he prodded gently.

"They failed earlier in their studies."

"Failed in what way, my princess?"

She gave him a suspicious look, but didn't argue.

"Some... attempted to read my books."

She waved at the shelves.

"Some... reached for magick they were not ready to touch and burned themselves out."

Damien cringed inside at her casual dismissal. That sounded... incredibly painful.

"And some betrayed me."

He frowned. "How *many* Apprentices have you gone through? In... is it just *five* years?"

"Two," she corrected, then looked appalled at what she had said.

Damien shook his head. "That's years, not Apprentices, isn't it? No, don't tell me. I don't need to know."

Really, he didn't *want* to know.

"Is this how *you* were taught?" He shook his head again. "It can't have been, given how Powerful and skilled you are now."

Azella lifted her chin. "My Master went through his share of Apprentices."

"But *you* were different. From the *beginning.*"

"*I* was more Powerful. He saw *my* Talent straightaway. After that, the other Apprentices were only chattel for sourcing Power. *I* was the only one he taught to *use* it." She sought to regain control of the conversation. "Just as *you* are different from the others."

Damien sighed. "Your Master saw a beautiful and gently-bred girl with great potential and *created* the circumstances for you to be more than a mere 'chattel.' I think he must have loved you very much to give you the keys to his Power."

Azella sneered at him. "Evil wizards do not *love*. We take what we want. Others are to be used and discarded – or ground underfoot and destroyed."

"Hmmmn." The captive king scratched at his beard. "What an... *interesting* set of incentives you provide, my princess."

He regarded her thoughtfully while she seethed.

"I'm a reader," he admitted as if it would be news to her. "Perhaps I should do better with the lessons if you gave me something to read so I could prepare ahead of time. I really shouldn't be wasting your time with trivialities," he added sweetly. "You have more valuable things to do than answer such minor questions as I can come up with on the fly."

Which was almost word-for-word what she had been complaining about to him, so she had no reasonable rebuttal. Azella seethed, and Damien gave her his most mild and innocent expression.

"Get out of my sight," she ordered at last.

Damien rose smoothly and gracefully. "As my lady decrees."

He stepped to the office door and opened it, then turned back with what he hoped looked like he thought she had simply forgotten his request. "And my reading material, milady?"

A half-dozen books tore themselves loose from their shelves and flew at the door. Damien ducked, snatching them from the air as best he could. He still had to rescue from the floor the couple of volumes that smacked into the doorframe before he could get his hands on them.

"Go!" Azella shouted.

Damien waited until he closed the door behind himself before letting a jaunty grin sneak onto his face. He returned to the bedchamber with his treasure-trove and curled up on the bed with the various volumes stashed around him.

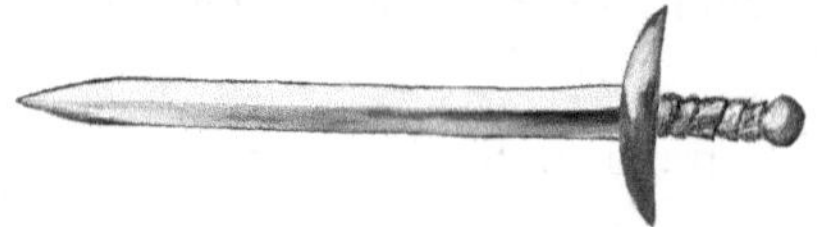

Dinner arrived, but Azella did not.

Damien read long into the night, immersing himself in the books. They dealt with multifarious aspects of the Fire Elementals, and it was fascinating reading. He only put them aside when he had trouble keeping his eyes open.

And still Azella had not come.

With a shrug, he stripped off his new-won clothes and laid them neatly aside before dimming the lanterns and climbing into bed to sleep. Damien had small doubt that she would wake him for her pleasure when she arrived.

He woke to the morning light, still alone. The other side of the bed didn't look in the least disturbed.

The captive king began, at last, to worry. Had he pushed her too far? But if she was so angry, why hadn't she exerted some punishment upon him? Instead, she had given him the very books he sought and left him free and undistracted to absorb them.

He dressed again in the previous day's garments and went back to reading. He told himself that he figured that the more familiar he was with the topic when next he saw Azella, the more pleased she would be. In truth, the opposite was more likely, but Damien could no more stop himself from reading than from breathing.

Breakfast arrived, but half the amounts, and while it was the usual boy who brought it, he sauntered in this time rather than looking appropriately cowed. Damien raised an eyebrow at the lad's saucy behavior when he flung himself on the bed to watch Damien eat and stole grapes off the tray.

"So, you're the new favorite, eh?" the boy asked boldly. "Not such a favorite today, though, are you?"

"Has your Mistress chosen another?" Damien asked politely. "You, perhaps?"

The boy scowled. "No. But she gave Mik to us and stayed to watch. All night. Didn't come in here, now did she?"

Damien chilled at his words. "What do you mean 'gave Mik to you'?"

The boy smirked. "Thought he was so high and mighty, didn't he. Not so fancy with his airs when he's getting back what he gave out. And with the Mistress filling herself up on the Power we source her through our pleasure and his pain."

"She's doing... what?" Damien was in shock.

The boy gave him a pitying look. "They don't call her Azella the Unpitying for no reason, you innocent rube." He stretched like an indolently malicious cat, and strode for the door. "This won't last long, I'm sure. It never does. But at least I was early on and Mik gave me a good ride. Some of the other boys didn't have near so much fun."

Damien stared in horror as the door closed behind him. The food was ashes in his mouth.

He sent out his Healing sense, seeking, seeking...

Oh, Gods no.

Damien leapt up and tore the door open.

He didn't see the pale, evil sorceress or her pretty, vicious boys, though he was aware they were there.

All he could see was Mikhail in the veriest center of that elaborate pattern on the floor, strapped facedown onto some sort of semi-vertical, padded support, sagging against it, the waves of pain and despair and resignation emanating with such strength that Damien barely made it to him.

The captive king knelt in front of the young man and took his limp hands in his own. Normally he didn't need to physically touch the person he was Healing, but there was a heaviness in the room that made it hard to send his Healing into the boy's body. Something was fighting him...

Enough of his magick was getting through that Mikhail roused slightly from his stupor and raised his head to the captive king, eyes glazed in pain. "

Please..." he whispered, barely a breath, almost inaudible.

Damien sent what resources he could to block the boy's suffering and found *himself* blocked.

"Azella," Damien ground out. "Let me Heal the boy. He's in pain."

The pretty, petty boys around the room snickered, as Azella's voice purred. "That's the point, Damien dear. Much Power can be raised through pain."

The captive king didn't let his attention waver from the suffering youth, seeking ways around and through the barricades the pale sorceress put up to stop him. He tried the pain centers of the brain, then the nerves at the site of the injuries. She had out-thought him and shielded both from Damien's touch.

Desperate, he sent his Healing magick into the boy's spine, blocking all sensation from below his rib-cage. Mikhail's legs went limp, pulling him harder against his wrist-restraints, but the look on his face was an intense relief.

"Clever," Azella commented. "I'll have to remember that one. For next time."

She turned on her heel and strode to her bedchamber. "Heal him if you like and come to me. You others, clean this place up. I may want Mikhail later."

The barriers were gone, and Damien flooded Mikhail's body with Healing magick. Tears poured down his face as he fixed the damage of intentional cruelty.

He may have gone a little overboard; the boy seemed to be more muscular than before. Mikhail flexed the newly-enlarged muscles with some wonder after one of the other boys came forwards with the key to the wrist-restraints and freed him.

Damien stayed kneeling on the floor, head drooped, thoroughly drained by the effort it had taken to fight Azella's spells far more than by the Healing itself. It had been a relatively minor work, for all that Mikhail had been in excruciating pain. Certain parts of the body simply had more nerves than others...

The mahogany-skinned young man squatted beside the Healer-King, regarding him calmly with those stunning blue eyes. "The Mistress said you should attend upon her, Damien. You should go."

"And you?" Damien asked, glancing around at the other boys, quietly doing as their mistress had instructed and cleaning up.

Candles and crystals on the floor, he noticed, and light-colored scrawlings in wax.

Mikhail shrugged nonchalantly... far too serene for what he had just been through.

"The Mistress said she might want me later. My status is assured once more."

He glanced up at one of the others, by chance the one who had brought Damien's breakfast. The other boy looked up, then quickly ducked his head with a shudder. Mikhail smiled with a strange satisfaction.

He stood, and offered Damien a hand, heaving him to his own feet.

"My thanks," Mikhail added. "It is clear now that the Mistress has a preference for more muscularity."

He nodded at Damien's own chest, half-visible through the unlaced shirt. "You have given me an advantage."

Mikhail strode off through the double-doors, not looking back.

He was thanking Damien for the *muscles?*

The captive king turned and regarded the door to the bedchamber without favor. Yet what other choice did he have?

Unhappily, unwillingly, he trudged back into the other room, turning to seal the door behind him before regarding its occupant.

Azella sprawled, naked, on the bed.

"Come to me, my sorcerer-king," she purred.

Damien stood still, his back bare inches from the closed door. "No."

She regarded him with amusement. "And why not? Because I decided to play with a different toy last night?"

He closed his eyes and rested the back of his head against the door.

Last night. Oh, Gods. They had been out there *all night* torturing Mikhail.

If only he had reached his Healing sense out sooner.

He'd had to learn    to do just that after Adam had yelled at him… after the third time his Royal Guards had had to carry him back unconscious from following the trail of pain down to the docks. '*You can't fix the docks one abused person at a time, you idiot,*' Adam had raged, his fear for his king all too evident. '*You need to create **policies** that make people there less likely to hurt each other.*'

But if only he'd not let himself be so *absorbed* in those *books*. Had let himself be *curious* about why Azella had not come to bed in her seemingly never-ending quest to claim him as her own. Had let himself *worry* about where her ire might fall if not on him himself.

"*Why?*" Damien breathed, tears trickling down his cheeks. "For *days* now I've given you everything you wanted. Joy and pleasure raise more Power than pain. It isn't…" He swallowed, making the argument that he hoped would sway her, repulsive as he found it himself. "It isn't a wise use of your resources."

"Perhaps I just wanted some variety." Her voice was amused.

"Mikhail is infatuated with you. You could have won more Power from *him* by pleasure than pain."

"Damien." He opened his eyes and met her amused gaze. She had sat up. "What part of 'evil sorceress' do you not understand? Last night's little exercise took no effort from me and garnered me a great deal of Power. Plenty from the other boys' pleasure, and plenty from Mikhail's pain."

She ran the tip of her tongue over her lips. "You haven't savored the taste of Power tinged with pain yet, my dear."

He looked at her blankly. "Power is all the same."

She shrugged. "Eventually, yes. When it is first generated there are different... *flavors*. And some are better for one purpose than another. Demon-summoning, for example, almost *requires* the Power generated from the death of a thinking being."

Damien swallowed. She spoke with the matter-of-fact tone of one who has accomplished the feat.

He tried to distract himself from the feel of his gorge rising in his throat by recalling how he'd explained to Adam not so very long ago about the differences in Power when it was first obtained – though his own focus had been on the nutritive value of Power raised in healthy, sustaining, Life-bolstering ways as opposed to... well, the sorts of things that Azella did and that his grandfather and Lord Prydeen had done.

Damien hated that it made the sorceress' explanation make more sense to him, but he couldn't deny a truth he'd actually discovered for himself years ago.

Azella's eyes raked him, then gave him another amused smile. "You're not laboring under the idea that you rescued an *innocent* out there, are you?"

She lay back down, fluffing her long, silky hair out to scatter across the steel-blue pillows and bedsheets like moonbeams across rippling water.

"Oh, my dear. Mikhail was my Apprentice until you arrived, and his ambitions are still to prove my worthy successor. You and I both know I shall never allow *that,* but it's amusing to watch him try."

The pale sorceress raised her eyebrows at the king's uncomprehending look. "Mikhail wants to be an *evil sorcerer,* Damien. I used him to raise Power in my bed, yes, but he has also seen my other techniques – and experienced them as well. When I did not summon him to my bed, he tried in his clumsy, novice way to experiment with raising Power for himself. Naturally, the Keep is set up to funnel all Power raised to *me,* so his efforts were useless, but he didn't know that was why, so he – as my other Apprentices have done before him – resorted to more extreme measures. I save the girls for other purposes, but the boys were at his disposal. It was hardly surprising that they truly enjoyed last night."

Damien felt frozen to the core.

Mikhail *had* told him that the other boys hated him because he was Azella's favorite...

"He... abused... *them...?*"

Azella's smug look repelled Damien. "So delicate with your language, my dear. Yes, he 'abused' the other boys. Beat them soundly beforehand also, trying to elicit some Power for himself. Took his time and enjoyed himself, too. Not that they dared fight back, lest they mar him where I might see it."

Oh, Gods. And he'd given the young man more physical strength. Unintentionally, but that didn't matter.

"Come here, Damien," Azella ordered. "Or shall I use another *compulsion* spell on you?"

He stepped forwards as woodenly as if she had, stopping at the edge of the bed, unable to stop staring in horror at the pallid, self-absorbed, inhumane... *evil sorceress*... lying there.

"Remove your clothes, Damien," she said impatiently, "or I'll have them taken away again."

It was the work of a few moments, done mechanically as he tried to *not-think* about any of this. Where he was. Who – no, *what* she was. What *he* was doing.

The only thing that was getting him through... *any* of this was *why*. He needed the things he could learn here – the magickal skills – to protect his wife, his Realm, his friends... his daughter.

"Come here," she said again, and he climbed up onto the bed, sitting beside her tailor-fashion when she patted the mattress.

Azella rolled her eyes. "Must I do *everything* today? Any one of those boys would have *happily* taken Mikhail's place if he could be where you are now. Or is it Mikhail you are wanting? I can send for him to see if he can arouse you for me."

Damien shook his head violently, and she chuckled. "Are you sure? It worked so well before."

He shook his head again.

"Then show me just how much Power and pleasure *you* can give me, my sorcerer-king. Here," she smirked, "I'll even get you started."

She ran one finger from the base of his throat, down and down... It felt like she was leaving a trail of fire along his body as she did so.

Damien caught her hand.

"Stop." he said, and his voice was gravelly as he forced it past a throat gone dry with horror and self-loathing.

The evil sorceress raised her eyebrows. "Your Mistress commands you, Apprentice."

Damien cleared his throat, trying to swallow against the dryness. "I will *never* be yours, Azella the Unpitying. Not your Apprentice, nor... anything else."

She regarded him coolly. "We shall see. I doubt your reasons for acceding to my demands have changed."

She waved a hand. "Get dressed then. But stay in the room."

Damien was dressed and standing at the window, staring at the lead-grey sea lapping against the shore, when there was a knock on the door. He looked up automatically, and was shocked to see Mikhail stride in. The boy's eyes flickered to him, but focused on his mistress in the bed.

"How may I serve you, Mistress?" Mikhail asked, his tone deeper and more... *suggestive* than Damien had ever heard it.

Azella's throaty chuckle was all the youth apparently needed for an explanation.

The bed was centered in the large open space of the bedchamber, so at least Damien could look out the windows from behind it. And do his best to close his ears. Clearly, Mikhail carried no grudges, perhaps was even grateful to have returned to the evil sorceress's favor.

Damien had been taken in by a pair of bright blue eyes and a sob-story. And his own desperate desire to believe there was goodness in *someone* here. Adam would have boxed his ears for such folly. Then run him ragged in the practice ring before giving him a lecture that would peel the paint off the walls.

He'd nearly fallen for the evil sorceress herself.

Perhaps *he* should be grateful that she had chosen to reveal her true nature before he was too far gone.

*Genevieve,* he thought achingly. *I want to come home.*

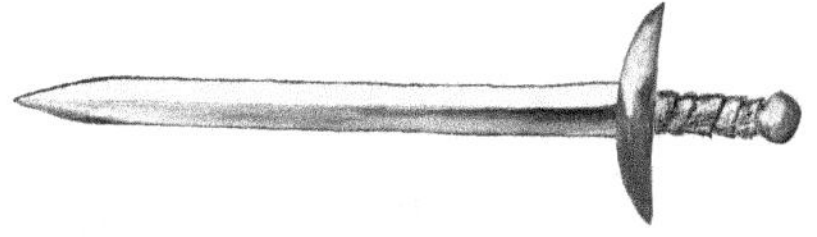

# Chapter NINE

# *Middlegame*

THE NEXT SEVERAL DAYS FELL into a pattern.

Mikhail filled Azella's bed at night – and sometimes in the day – and she usually required Damien to lie beside them in the wide bed. Sometimes she had Mikhail attempt to arouse the captive king, but he was now as repulsed by the would-be Apprentice as by his evil Mistress.

She didn't press him herself.

The three of them ate their meals together, with Damien studiously ignoring the other two as they played at being loverly. He declined Mikhail's offers to play chess.

Azella did not take away the books on Fire Elementals. Indeed, she added more as he finished them and quizzed him on their contents. At his stiff request, she provided writing materials and he began to work out some of his own ideas, based on his readings.

As always, Damien saw a larger picture. Each of the books held a piece of the puzzle – overlapping pieces, actually – about how these mysterious creatures fit into his understanding of the way the world worked. His extensive efforts with his own much-missed Realm had given the captive king a deeper understanding of the magickal fabric that underlay the world that could be seen and touched, smelled and tasted. The volumes of information about Fire Elementals added a new dimension to his understanding.

But there was too much missing.

Azella looked over his notes and drawings every day, sometimes looking amused, other times baffled, though she never commented. Damien made no attempt to hide anything from her. There was no point, after all. He had access only to the magick generated within his own body, rather than the nearly limitless Power of an entire Realm, and he was aware that his own magick was being delicately siphoned off by something. He assumed it was the Keep itself, since Azella had explained to him that all power raised here became hers.

He could not challenge her. He had nowhere near the strength of magick to do it.

At least, now, he didn't need to expend energy in not reacting to her lithe form and huge eyes. Damien could barely stand to look at her, and his skin crawled when she touched him. Mikhail was little better, and the boy dropped his mask of innocence when he realized it was doing him no good. Or perhaps when Azella gave him permission to do so.

The youth's arrogance was obvious now. He didn't dare sneer at Damien, who was still Azella's only official Apprentice, despite his denial of the term and Mikhail's efforts between the sheets. And above the sheets. And occasionally outside of the bed altogether.

Damien was still a far more Powerful sorcerer than the boy would ever hope to be without external... augmentation. He hadn't understood that, back home in Ilseador, though he suspected Adam had. No, he *knew* Adam had.

Azella might claim to be the most Powerful *evil* sorceress in the world – might even live up to that title, regardless of gender – but without the backing of her unethically raised Powers, Damien was at least her equal.

Unfortunately, she did *have* those excess Powers. And she also knew far more than he did about how to use them. How to leverage them for greater effect and how to wield them in offense and defense against other sorcerers.

Just past the Winter Solstice, when Damien had been in the Keep for something over a month, Azella sat up in the middle of the night and stood up from the bed. Damien sat up also and she spared him a glance as she quickly, but without undo haste, pulled on a simple gown.

"As you value your life, do not set foot outside this room," she told him, and glanced at her slumbering lover. "Keep him in here as well, if you can."

And she stepped out, closing the door firmly behind her.

Moments later, the Keep was rocked as if by an earthquake, and sound shattered through the empty, echoing corridors and halls as if it had also been struck by lightning.

That woke even Mikhail, who had proved a surprisingly heavy sleeper.

"A mage-battle!" he exclaimed, coming all the way awake.

"Azella said not to leave the room," Damien told him dully.

"Of course not," the boy scoffed, "I'm no fool. This room is warded. But come. Let's watch from the windows."

With all the excitement of a child, he jumped up, actually towing Damien out of bed to watch as light coruscated around the keep. It was like being in the center of their own, private lightning storm, but the lightnings were of many colors and strange shapes were to be seen as the sky lit and darkened alternately. A cloudless sky, the captive king noticed absently.

"Are the slaves' barracks similarly warded?" he managed to ask past the apathy that was that much more overwhelming in the middle of the night and while short of sleep.

"Of course," Mikhail said again. "The Mistress wards all of her valuables."

Objects of value. Of course.

"And the town?"

Mikhail shrugged. "I assume so. I have never seen it, and the townsmen will speak but little to slaves."

He pointed at a streak of eye-hurting pink that blazed across the sky, splitting into a trident... or a claw... and grasping a curl of electric blue.

"Only look! That is one of the Mistress's favorite tactics. While they are wrestling with her very obvious claw, she will do something much more subtle... there! Do you see?" He gripped Damien's arm in his enthusiasm, running a commentary over every burst of color and shape.

"We can see only a small part of what passes," Mikhail added in a brief lull in the hostilities. "The Mistress may be changing her shape or invoking demons or Elementals or any manner of excitement! If only we could see *her*... but I suppose it is fortunate that I am here at all. From the slave's quarters the view is not nearly so good and everyone would be crowding in to see it."

"Hmmmn," Damien felt a flicker of interest and tried to divorce himself from it. He didn't want to care what this horrible youth might say. Didn't want him to touch him.

And yet... it was to ward all of his Realm from such mage-battles as the one going on around him that Damien had let Azella abduct him. To *learn* how to do so. He *had* to find a way out of this sick apathy and be interested...

Mikhail continued to clutch the captive king's arm as he practically burbled with delight over the display.

Delight, and not a bit of fear.

Damien tried to ignore the grasp. It had only been a few weeks, but Gods he was starved for a human touch.

"What would happen if Azella lost?" he asked, mostly to distract himself.

Mikhail broke off his almost gloating glee and stared at the older man. "Lost? If the Mistress *lost?* It isn't possible, my friend. There is no one in the *world* with the Power to defeat Azella the Unpitying!"

Damien restrained himself from saying *I could. If I had access to my waking Realm and if she had not come in stealth and with allies.*

It made no difference. He had to learn to defeat Azella – or any other comer – no matter the time of the year and no matter what material resources they might array against his Realm. Damien was reminded that her attack had been in collaboration, however reluctant, with wizards in Deltheren, and he had no idea what had followed on the heels of the ice-storm from *that* direction.

"Humor me," he said instead. "What would happen to you and the other slaves? And me? And the town below?"

Mikhail gave him a look that said how foolish he thought it was, but shrugged. "Did her wards survive her, the victor would claim us all as spoils. Freeborn or not, we would all belong to him." He frowned. "Denisa might find that fate preferable to what the Mistress has ordained for her. So far, she has proven too valuable to the Mistress, but eventually she shall be given to a demon as a virgin sacrifice. An evil sorcerer might avail himself of her charms instead, which would ruin her for use with the demons."

Damien could not even bring himself to care that he had left the girl exposed to this fate. She was probably just as corrupt as the rest in this Keep of Horrors.

"And to take her as his Apprentice?"

Mikhail shrugged again. "Possible, but unlikely. He would probably have his own Apprentices already. And Denisa's Power is nothing special, the Mistress has told me. A new Master would be wiser to choose *me,* but most would rather have a girl. I would have sold for nearly twice the price had I been a girl," he added, "Though the Mistress paid more for *me* than for all the others combined. *Even* Denisa."

He said it as a matter of pride.

Damien decided there was no point in telling the arrogant youth that Denisa's magickal potential exceeded his own considerably. Mikhail likely wouldn't care that the *potential* Azella had chosen him for had more to do with what he could do for her in bed, so long as it gave him a greater chance to try to emulate her and inculcate himself with her evil ways.

Mikhail eyed the captive king curiously. "There are few evil sorcerers who would choose a boy to fill their bed, I am told. You will be unique, once the Mistress has trained you properly."

Damien pursed his lips and stared out at the colorful display. Almost like the fireworks the city of Emeralsee had used to celebrate his birthday. "I am not and never will be an evil sorcerer, Mikhail."

The youth laughed and it had the tone he used with Azella; deeper and more suggestive than his everyday voice.

"Do you think I cannot see that the Mistress is preparing you to be her *mate?* Perhaps even her *husband?* You can only hold out for so long. She will win in the end, as she always does. I am no longer jealous that I cannot be her Apprentice, Damien. *You* are more Powerful than I could ever be, and the fit mate that our Mistress deserves. Only..." He hesitated. "I do not want to grow old and ugly or be used up and die. Perhaps if I please you *both* enough, you will grant me eternal youth as well, that I may serve you."

His arms slid around Damien caressingly. "I have not dared speak so to the Mistress, but *you* are *kind* and will not have me punished for such temerity."

The captive king pushed the boy away. "Don't touch me, Mikhail. Watch your wizard-battle if you must. I'm going to try to get some more sleep."

He stepped back towards the bed, wishing he could sleep in his clothes. But while Azella had not taken away what he already had, she had allowed him no others. He handwashed the clothes each evening and let them hang dry overnight.

It left him all too vulnerable to the sorceress and her slave-boy, though of late they had let him be.

Now, however, Mikhail trailed him back to the bed. "The Mistress always comes back from these battles needing to replenish her Powers, Damien. She will want *you.*"

He sat on the edge of the bed beside the captive king and walked his fingers down Damien's side through the thin sheet.

Damien turned over and away. "Then she will have to go wanting."

Mikhail stretched himself out along Damien's back, sliding himself under the sheet. "She will be displeased, Damien. *You* are too valuable to her to be punished. So, she will punish *me* instead to raise the Power she needs. Would you let her punish me again, Damien? Again, because she is angry with *you?*"

Oh, but the boy knew how to play on the guilt he still felt over that night.

"You didn't seem that bothered when she called you to her that night." Damien retorted. "Rather the opposite, if anything."

He felt Mikhail shrug. "She is the Mistress. All I could do would be to invite another punishment, and perhaps one much less mild. There are... stories of what she does with *failed* Apprentices – those who challenge her or appear that they might. I was merely set aside for a time. I would much rather *this* position than *that* one."

He chuckled wickedly in Damien's ear, and kissed the older man's neck and shoulder. His fingers, still cool from pressing against the window panes, slid around to Damien's front, teasing.

There was nowhere to go to escape, and his treacherous body was responding even to this hateful touch... Even by the use of his Healing magick, Damien couldn't suppress a shiver of reaction.

Mikhail's hand came back to squeeze one buttock and then press Damien onto his stomach, rolling on top of the older man as he did so. "And I would much rather *this* position entirely," the wicked youth added.

Damien bunched his muscles to pull himself free – by the Gods, he'd sit on the bare tiles in the corner of the room if he had to – when the door opened and the evil sorceress stepped in.

Mikhail half turned to look, and Damien used the distraction to make his escape.

He was back by the windows before he turned to look.

He need not have worried. Mikhail gravitated to power, and as soon as his mistress entered the room, Damien might as well not have existed unless she ordered him to seduce the older man.

Azella looked... entirely unfazed by her recent ordeal. Not a hair out of place, her gown falling in the same perfect folds. She looked past the boy to Damien, almost questioningly, then turned her attention to Mikhail.

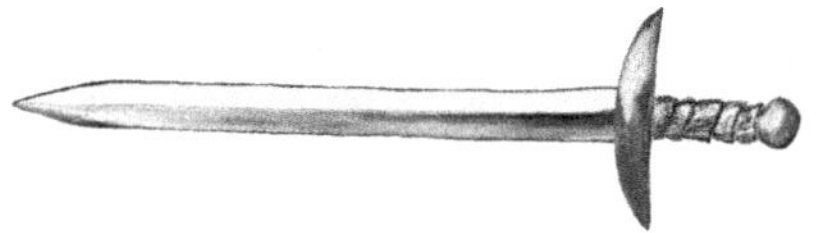

# Chapter TEN

# *Problems*

MIKHAIL WAS NOT AS WRONG as Damien could have wished, however. Azella was going to win eventually.

She was living up to the deal she had made with him and providing him with books about Fire Elementals as fast as he could read them. Faster than she liked, the captive king suspected, but she had an increasingly smug look on her face when she perused his notes. Azella knew he could tell that he was reaching the far edges of what he could learn about Fire Elementals.

The missing pieces in his picture of things were beginning to look like they needed to be filled in with other elements. And to gain access to that information... he would have to live up to *his* end of the deal.

At last, the day came when he closed the back cover of the most recent book she had given him. Somehow, she had known, and was standing beside the table where he had sat reading and drawing diagrams that made sense only to him. He knew the latter because he had seen her holding one at different angles, trying to understand it.

"I have no more books about Fire Elementals," she said coolly. "Are you ready to practice some of what you have read?"

Damien leaned back in the straight chair, stretching his legs out in front of him. He thought about stretching his arms back and up to work out some of the kinks from his hunched position, but eyed the sorceress warily and stretched them over the table instead, clasping his hands palms together, but with the right coming from the left and the left wrapping around the right. He then swung the clasped hands towards his chest to invert his elbows and stretch out his lower arms.

Azella winced, as she always did when she saw him do that, so he reversed his hands and did it again. His smile was only on the inside. There were days Damien wondered if he would ever remember how to smile again.

There were more days when he wondered if he would remember how to swing a sword should he ever get one into his hands again. No. That way lay madness. He would be gone from this foul keep and reclaim the Sword that had Bound him to his Realm; reclaim the wife who was ruling it in his place; reclaim... his life. He would. He had to.

"No." His refusal did not entirely surprise the pale sorceress, who had made the same offer several other times. Damien had not told her that his notes and diagrams were only pieces of the puzzle themselves. He was working to fit this new knowledge into not merely the entire shape of what he *knew* but into the shape of his magick.

His connection to the Realm, he suspected, was mostly Earth magick, and he also suspected that he had felt Elementals moving around in the past. But if Elementals of any ilk fit into the fabric of the Realm, he would be able to find them. And those that did not belong... he would be able to eventually repel, just as the body repelled a disease.

It wasn't as simple as that, of course. Damien had tamed the rats of Emeralsee years ago – they had agreed to leave humans and human habitations alone in return for not being trapped and poisoned as they disposed of the human-created garbage and for the king's efforts to keep them healthy. It had been to the benefit of all involved – except the rat-catchers, and Damien had made what efforts he could to find those people other work. The rats of Emeralsee now enforced the bargain amongst themselves, and Damien had one less source of disease and illness to contend with.

Unfortunately, foreign rats from the many trading vessels that frequented Emeralsee's deep and sheltered Bay tended to see the large, sleek native rats as weak and domesticated... and once they came ashore the Realm did not distinguish rats from rats. Rats were supposed to be there, it didn't matter their origins.

While the native rats tended to solve the problem within a few days by trouncing the visitors, they had been overwhelmed when a ship came in that was fine to the human eye but had all of its ship-rats practically bounding down the hawsers. The ship had sunk shortly thereafter, and the ship-rats had vanished into whatever boltholes they could find. The people of Emeralsee had been very unhappy with the newcomers, and Damien had been as hard-put to sort out the rat problem as his swearing harbormaster had been to raise the sunken vessel before it foundered other ships that attempted to dock at that pier.

Damien's eventual solution to the rats had been to gift them with sleek, golden hair and almost lambent green eyes. They looked so distinct that not only his magick, but his human citizens could distinguish between newcomers and natives. A number of Emeralsee rats had since been half-tamed by residents – much as with the feral cats that kept their numbers within reason – and ships were inviting these much more well-behaved creatures aboard to verify seaworthiness, much as miners carried canaries down into their mines.

Azella's eyes were bemused this time, however. "You look so far away," she commented. "What can you be thinking of?"

"Um... the rats in Emeralsee," he answered honestly, and she looked completely baffled.

He briefly thought about trying to explain, but such things had rarely gone well even with Genevieve.

He'd tried to avoid talking about such things with Jason before he'd Named the tall knight his Heir and had needed to teach Jason to use his untapped potential; the look of mingled awe and bafflement tinged with fear had been too hard to bear.

Adam... would roll his eyes, but would listen, and often had valuable suggestions. Gods, how he missed his cynical and insightful friend.

There was no point at all in trying to explain to *Azella*. Her interest in matters seemed to revolve entirely around what would bring her more Power. Wanting to know things purely for the joy of learning seemed... beyond her.

Genevieve, at least, loved how interested *he* was... and when she wasn't exhausted or too busy would listen and discuss anything for hours.

Almost anything. The rats had... tested her patience.

At least, his completely unexpected answer had the effect of knocking her planned conversation off its rails. Doubtless she'd had some scathing remark prepared if he had told her he was thinking about Genevieve, or home, or the Realm more generally. She still could not believe that she hadn't destroyed his Bonds, and he had no intention of reminding her, lest she try again.

"Well," Azella said after a moment, "then I have nothing left for you."

She turned away, but her steps were too slow. She was waiting... waiting for him to cave in and give her what she wanted.

Damien gritted his teeth, wrestling with himself. She was no better nor worse than when he had first arrived. He just knew now what sort of creature lay within that fair skin. If only he had something else to offer her...

But there was nothing else she wanted of him – besides his pledge to stay permanently.

"Wa–" his voice came out scratchy with tension, and the captive king cleared his throat and tried again. "Water Elementals would be next?"

She had paused at the door, and turned only her head far enough to respond. "Air, actually." She stepped through the door and was gone.

Damien stared vacantly at the pile of books on Fire Elementals and felt chilled.

# Chapter ELEVEN

# *Luft*

MIKHAIL DID NOT COME TO the bedchamber that night. Earning Damien's access to Azella's library of works on Air Elementals was... easier than he'd hoped. And more pleasurable than he wanted to admit.

"You almost make me willing to give up evil wizardry, Damien," she murmured breathlessly, pillowing her head on his shoulder.

"*Almost,*" she added after a moment, and he realized he had caught his breath at her words.

The captive king blew out his breath slowly. "Why not, Azella? You have so much Power on your own. You could do anything you wanted, *have* anything you wanted, without all... *this.*"

She rolled up onto his chest, and folded her arms under her chin to look into his eyes. Her own seemed very large, and even more vividly blue-grey than usual. "And if what I want – *who* I want – is *you?*"

Damien had no answer, and she rolled back down onto his shoulder after a moment.

"So," she said, "There's something I can't have, except as an evil sorceress."

*You can't have me either way,* he wanted to answer. Except that he was lying in her bed, having just made love to her as skillfully as he knew how. What she really wanted, though, was not just his presence – his *enthusiastic* presence – in her bed.

"Oh, my princess," he sighed. "It's not *me* you want. It's someone who will love you with all his heart and soul. As much as *I* love my wife."

Azella sniffed. "You'd be just as devoted to *me* if *she* didn't exist."

"I'd be dead," Damien said bluntly. "You can't break a soul-bond without killing both people."

She waved a hand in the air. "There's an answer. I know there is. I just have to find it. Oh, don't worry, I won't try anything until I'm sure."

She laid her arm across his chest, and snuggled contentedly closer. "I would never do anything that could risk *you.*"

So that was what she spent so much time researching. Damien felt chilled to his core.

Even if she managed to 'free' him from his bond to Genevieve, and managed to keep *Damien* alive, would *Genevieve* survive? Azella was unlikely to care enough to make sure of it.

"If you caused harm to Genevieve, I would hate you until the day I died. And through all the lives beyond," Damien breathed, shaken.

"I thought you'd say that," came the muffled voice, her face buried in his chest. "I'm taking that into account."

Which would sound *so* much more reassuring if he didn't suspect that her solution to *that* particular problem would be to cast a spell to make him forget Genevieve had ever existed. For Azella the Unpitying, the answer to any problem was always another spell. And the answer to the problems created by that spell? Yet another spell.

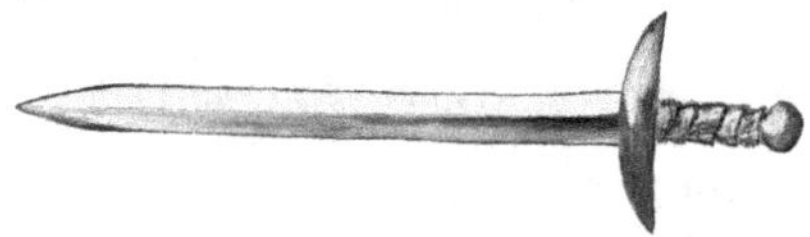

Damien flew through the tomes on Air Elementals. Now that he knew what to look for, he could *see* some of them beyond the windows of the suite. Just hints, usually, but a glimmer of giant iridescent wings or a face peeking out of the clouds.

Reading about sylphs and fairies and Cloud Maidens made him unexpectedly restless. He still refused to look out the northern windows of the suite, but he paced from bedchamber to main hall – even into Azella's office – and back to the bedchamber, often with a book in hand, and muttering to himself. He had reached the point where he was knowledgeable enough about Elementals generally to find himself disagreeing with the authors when they contradicted each other or included information that made no sense.

The day Damien wandered into Azella's office with *Wind-Deities and Their Subordinate Sprites* to argue with her – he hated to call it picking a fight, but that was really what it was – about the likely correspondences between Lord Kyo of the Muana Desert and Dawil's Lady Zephria of the Prairie Wind, was the day Azella finally lost her patience with his pacing.

"What is *wrong* with you?" she cried.

Damien paused, thoughtfully, then went back to pacing. "I've always thought better when I'm moving... but the longer I'm in one place the worse it gets. I've been in these rooms for nearly two *months.*"

It took care to say that without whining. He was *desperate* to see something besides the insides of these walls.

Azella's irritated gaze followed him as he wore a track in one of her rugs. "What do you need to settle down before you drive me completely insane?"

*That* gave him pause, and he looked at her with concern.

"Mad *and* evil?" He shuddered. "Jason and Adam would make me go riding. Or take me out to the practice ring and make me spar until I was too tired to stand up."

Damien half-smiled reminiscently, as he recalled those riding and sparring sessions. "I don't know how I managed in the Library all those years. Abject terror, I suppose."

He gave her a distracted look. "When they were busy, I would sometimes go up to the battlements. Or just wander around the Castle. I was forbidden to go out to the city when I was like this. I think they were afraid they'd lose me. I've never been quite this bad before, though. Except maybe that time we went up to Elaarwen and got trapped by a blizzard up at Cloudcroft. But then there was all the shoveling, and we saw snow leopards, and all there was to eat was pickled beets and porridge which are *much* better when not *combined,* and–"

"*Stop!*" Azella's hands were on her ears.

Damien's peripatetic wanderings stuttered to a stop with his tongue.

"Go to the bedchamber. Someone will be by with the things you need shortly." She glared and pointed towards the door of her office. "*Go.*"

Damien shrugged. "Can we talk about these gods a little later then?" he asked as he headed to the door. "I really think that the author is making some rather spurious claims about–"

"Go, *please*. Go." she begged, hands still clasped around her head, but more as if to ward off a headache than her ears, it seemed now.

He went.

Mikhail appeared a few minutes later with a set of fresh clothes "for *later*," Damien was told firmly, a pair of good boots, and a sword that looked like it might be a *shade* better than pot-metal.

The boots fit better than he'd expected until Mikhail mentioned that the cobbler had made them up off the pattern from the indoor boots Damien had arrived in. How long ago, Damien didn't want to ask.

The beautiful young man was clearly pleased that Damien had managed to get permission to leave the suite. But then, a few days ago, Mikhail had finally begged Azella that *he* be allowed to leave the suite because of Damien's incessant pacing and muttering.

The beautiful slave-boy been called back to Azella's bed after Damien showed no interest in going beyond the strictest interpretation of their agreement.

"Are we going outside?" Damien asked hopefully as he followed Mikhail through the dark-walled corridors.

The youth shuddered in his brief kilt and decorative neck torc. "Certainly not. It's chilly even in the Summer time here. Right now, ice coats the very ground and walls."

"Oh." Damien sighed in not-really-unexpected disappointment. "Where then? Does this place have an indoor fencing salle?"

Mikhail gave him a grin. "You'll see."

"I haven't seen any warriors – not that I've had much of an opportunity to look around," Damien tried again after a moment. He couldn't stop *talking* any more than *moving*. "Does Azella keep her fighters somewhere else?"

"She doesn't *really* have any fighters," Mikhail admitted. "Usually, there's just some caravan guards down the village. She doesn't really need anything more than her spells to defend us, and she doesn't seem to want to take over the country, for some reason, so she doesn't need an army."

"Wise, that," Damien commented. "I'd have known if she'd tried to take over Farivera in any material sense, and then we'd have met on *my* terms, not hers. They declared themselves independent almost half a century ago, and we've had little contact since then, but the Realm still knows its own."

Though doubtless the poison of her – and her predecessor's – mere existence must be slowly and subtly poisoning the Realm.

That would explain why Farivera seceded in the first place – like a gangrenous toe on a man fighting a gut-wound, the Realm might not have had the spare resources to even notice until then. His grandfather had been too busy raping the Land of Its Power for his own uses, and Queen Marian had never been fully and properly Bound, not being much of a mage herself...

Surely, though, there had been other Monarchs before Damien who *had* been so Bound...

Yet another mystery that someday he would unravel from the safety of the hearthfire in his sitting room beside the royal bedchamber in Emeralsee. With Genevieve at his side and Adam – and Jason – all talking through the various ramifications and possibilities.

Apparently, Mikhail did not know much about where Damien came from, or who he really was.

The beautiful youth looked confused, but plunged gamely on. "When the last supply caravans came in just before Midwinter, the Mistress hired a few mercenaries to stay on until Spring. At her order they have been living in the lower levels of the Keep instead of in the town where such types usually stay. She may be paying them extra to practice with you."

Damien snorted. "They'll probably be so grateful to have someone new to spar with they'd almost pay *her*. Especially if she's been making them stay up *here*. They have to be nearly as bored as I was."

Mikhail made a face. "Bored... and frustrated. The Mistress has had to explain to them more than once to keep their hands off of her slaves."

"Lovely," Damien muttered, wondering what sort of incorrigibles would need more than *one* 'explanation' from Azella the Unpitying.

Mikhail deposited him in a room one level down – still in the built-portion of the Keep – and took a door to the side of the one he had indicated to Damien.

Damien's door opened into an... *arena* was the only real word for it. Mikhail waved indolently from a seat in the stands, separated from the rest of the room by a stone wall with iron bars, and with the seating elevated for a good view.

The main space was empty for now.

Damien paced it out – twenty of his strides – some sixty feet across the diameter. It was well lit from windows high in the walls, but there were settings for torches as well. The floor was wood, and a few experimental jumps convinced him it was properly sprung, with a real airspace beneath for elasticity. While Damien was used to sparring on dirt or even cobblestone, a wooden floor that didn't abut directly onto stone had much to recommend it, especially, he had noticed with some dismay, as he got older.

He hadn't missed the *snick* of the lock as the door closed behind him. This was clearly a gladiator arena, and the fighters would not necessarily be volunteers, not in an evil wizard's keep.

While the walk down – and his incessant pacing – had warmed up his leg muscles, and he'd faithfully been doing what calisthenics he could every day, he knew that was nowhere near enough. Damien set down the pot-metal sword and threw himself into a fuller set of exercises than he felt comfortable doing in the confines of Azella's bedchamber. He avoided the larger, central entry hall of her suite as much as possible, unable to ignore his memories of what had happened there.

He was going through a final round of stretches, preparatory to some solo drills with the sword when three men entered from the same door that he had. Out of the corner of his eye, he noticed another too-pretty slave-boy join Mikhail in the gallery.

"We got word Her Ladyship the Sorceress wants us to try your skills with a sword," one of the swordsmen said.

They were all burly, dressed in layers of stout woolen clothing with boiled leather vambraces and shinguards. They had varying amounts of facial hair, all in a range of dull reddish-brownish. Two of them held swords similar in size to the one Damien was used to wielding, and the third had a pair of axes.

The captive king's attention perked up. He hadn't expected a chance to practice against anyone but another swordsman.

"Word is we're not supposed to let you get hurt," the other swordsman said dryly.

Damien chuckled. "I think that's *my* lookout, now, isn't it?"

The swordsmen exchanged a glance. "It speaks."

"Pretty enough to be one of her bed-boys, but not so young. And there's a few muscles on there."

Damien gave them a tolerant look. "I'm a little out of practice, but I can tell the hilt from the edge."

"Ever kill someone, eh?" the axeman asked suddenly. He was standing back from the others, arms folded.

Damien met his gaze. "Yes."

He wondered if he looked as bleak as he felt when he had to admit that.

He didn't want to add that it hadn't been with his sword. He didn't want to *think* about what he'd done to Lord Prydeen in their mage-battle or the traitors he had caused to be executed, following the traditional method required by Ilseadoran law: being nailed alive to the outside of the Castle walls, there to hang until dead and rotted. Damien had never spared himself that duty. If it had to be done and he could find no other solution, he would set the first nail. His soul would always feel ripped in two by the traitors' cries, regardless of what vileness they had wreaked upon his people and himself. Their blood was on his hands, and he thanked the Gods that some enlightened – or perhaps similarly sickened – royal ancestor had made treason the *only* crime punishable by death.

Something must have shown through. The axeman nodded and looked at the other two.

"You one of those fancy-dancy fencers?" the swordsman with the mustache asked.

The captive king shrugged. "Try me and see." He picked up the pot-metal sword and grimaced at it.

"Impressive blade," the swordsman with sideburns mocked.

"I... lost mine on the trip here. This is what Her Sorcerousness has provided me." Damien gave him a reckless grin born of the bone-deep restlessness. "Break it and maybe she'll let me have something made of decent steel."

"Not here by choice, eh?" asked the axeman from where he leaned against the sidewall.

"That's a discussion for over the ale when the sparring is done," Damien responded wryly, but all too aware that Mikhail and the other boy were here as Azella's spies as much as chaperones and guides through the Keep. If she wasn't watching for herself through her sorcery. "Are any of us here by choice?"

He looked significantly at the boys watching from the gallery, and was relieved when one of the swordsmen nodded.

"Oh, a philosopher, eh?" said the axeman.

"Occasionally," Damien admitted.

"We'll have to get that beer later," the mustached swordsman grinned, "I hear they make a decent brew down in the town. Perhaps the Lady Sorceress will *finally* allow us all a short visit to the local tavern. Men aren't meant to live so long on *water,*" he added with a look of distaste, and the other two nodded agreement.

"Not sure I have a head for the lowlands after so long up here on the heights." Damien replied, lightly, knowing that Azella would never allow *him* to go so far. "Maybe you can bring up a small keg."

He hated alcohol in any form, but he'd down a tankard if they managed to procure some and it built some camaraderie. To his relief, Azella's meal-trays included soft cider and a variety of herbal teas and even milk, in addition to *water,* but never wine or ale. It seemed she was as loathe to dull her edge with spirits as Damien was himself.

Still, it seemed oddly prissy that the sorceress would forbid her hired men their usual drink. Or perhaps spirits had been banned after one of those *corrections* that Mikhail had been mentioned.

"Och, like *she'd* let–" Sideburns stopped as Mustaches elbowed him in the side with a warning look.

"Shall we give it a go?" Damien asked. He couldn't help wondering about their infringements on Azella's 'hospitality' and employment, but it probably wasn't relevant at the moment and who knew how long he would be allowed to stay here before she summoned him – or Mikhail, who was clearly here as his keeper? "Where are you from? I don't want to cross a rule that you're accustomed to using in the practice ring."

Mustaches rattled off a list of the common rules that Damien was familiar with. "Rob and I, we're out of Sindala. Darvin is from farther west and north."

"Deltheren?" Damien suggested, knowing it wasn't true.

"Not near so far," Sideburns – Rob – laughed. "Darv is a mountain man. And you?"

"Little place no one's heard of called Ravenscroft," Damien gave them the name of his grandparents' – his *mother's* parents' – small holding. "I'm Damien."

It was a common enough name... though much more so since he'd been made Crown Prince, so most of those carrying the name in Ilseador were no more than seven years old. "It looks like we practice under the same rules, though."

"I'll go first?" Rob offered.

Damien grinned at him and made a come-hither gesture with his free hand as he sank into a deeper stance.

It was too easy.

He was much too far out of shape for it to be this easy for Damien to beat a man who earned his living with a sword. Rob – who was apparently much younger than he looked with those exuberant reddish-brown sideburns exploding out of his cheeks – barely made it a couple of passes before Damien had the pot-metal sword leveled at the other man's throat.

Rob laughed a bit awkwardly and yielded.

Damien gave him a wry look. "Thanks for going easy on me, friend."

Rob flushed and muttered something like "No problem," while Mustaches clapped him on the shoulder and hooted.

"Let's see you do better, Franz," Rob told him irritably

"Sure thing," Franz replied. "Don't mind the kid," he told Damien. "Thinks he's a big man for taking down his grandfather's sword and deciding to call himself a mercenary. I've been trying to talk him into actually learning what to do with that thing for six months. Maybe now he'll listen – *before* we run into real bandits with one of these caravans and have to do more than look pretty, eh, shieldbrother?" He tweaked Rob's sideburn and turned back to Damien with a grin. "Time to show the children how it's done, aye?"

Damien smiled, and readied his blade. "Anytime you like."

This... took a *little* bit of effort. Franz definitely knew which end of his blade was which rather better than poor Rob, but he wasn't exactly a *challenge* for Damien. The captive king had small doubt the burly man was heavier, and quite probably stronger than him after his enforced idleness, but his technique was weak, so Damien was fine so long as they didn't close.

"Looks like *I* should be asking you for lessons," Franz said ruefully. "Don't know that I've tried a blade as good as yours."

Damien held up the pot-metal blade laughingly. "Any decent swordsmith would wince to hear you say that. I've just been lucky. Good teachers."

Darvin, the mountain man, was still leaning against the wall with folded arms. "Too many of those 'good teachers' only teach a swordsman to fight 'gainst anither man wit' a sword. Do ye ken a different sort o' battle, friend Damien?"

The captive king gave him a shining smile. "I thought you'd never ask."

Darvin loosened his brace of axes, hefting one in each hand. "Hae ye fought 'gainst the doubled axes, eh?"

"No," Damien had to admit. "But I've seen it done. My wife tried her skill against the local champion. Little village up near the Endless Chasm, in the heart of the mountains."

"Did she win, eh?"

The dark-haired man chuckled. "She *always* wins."

Darvin tilted his head. "Erawan's granddaughter, she'd be?"

"Erawan the Kind Robber is a children's tale, friend," Damien said with a warning glance towards the gallery. "But I heard that there was a grand*son* not a grand*daughter.*"

"A son may have a daughter, eh." The axeman's smile was buried in his beard, but it was obvious that he had no doubts about just whom he was speaking to.

Darvin was clearly a master of those axes. Damien watched carefully as the man began swinging them around faster than the eye could follow. If he could copy Genevieve's trick from that long-ago visit to Elaarwen...

She had wanted to show him where Aldred and Harald had disappeared; the visit to the village and her fun little bout with the axe-wielder had been a spontaneous addition. It held a special place in his memories – whenever they were in Elaarwen he and Genevieve had dispensed with guards and simply ridden through the mountains just the two of them. It drove Adam and Jason – and Ciriis – absolutely wild, but his three protectors had yielded to the political necessity of showing that Damien was simply Duke-Consort of Elaarwen. And no Duke or Duchess of Elaarwen had ever taken guards to visit their mountain-folk.

Emeralsee was dear to its king's heart. It was where he'd been born, where he'd grown up, where he'd found and lost and then found again his Genevieve.

But in Elaarwen he wasn't The King, he was just Genevieve's husband. In Elaarwen, he could relax and just be *Damien.*

And Darvin was clearly from Elaarwen.

Those flailing axes could break a sword of good solid steel, let alone the pot-metal thing that he had right now.

Damien made a few feints, more because he felt Darvin expected him to than because he expected anything to come of it. Darvin gave him a fierce grin over his bushy beard, testing his own jabs to the right, the left, and underhanded – a surprise that one. Damien had expected an overhand strike.

Suddenly Damien launched himself into a roll and came up on one knee *inside* Darvin's guard and *inside* the dizzily spinning circle of his axes. His sword pointed at the other man's chin, nearly vertically in front of Darvin's chest.

The axes came to a halt.

"A good thing that pot-sticker is blunt as a fire-iron, eh?" Darvin commented, lifting his chin a tad higher. "Beard's not as thick as ye thought, I 'spect."

A single drop of blood trickled down the blade.

Damien dropped the blade instantly, and rose, offering an apologetic hand to the other man. "I should have been more careful, blunt or not."

"'Tis arms-practice, things happen, eh," Darvin answered. "Did the Lassie proud. 'Twas a *Graceful* move, eh."

He caught the captive king's eye and Damien guessed that only he could hear the capitol letters. But no one – or hardly anyone – outside of Elaarwen's mountains knew that was Genevieve's mountain nickname. And hopefully no one else caught Darvin's emphasis on the term one would normally use to address a Duke.

"That's always and ever my only goal," Damien breathed.

"Pleasure to spar wit' ye, eh," Darvin nodded. He grinned a bit. "Yer beard is comin' along jest fine, eh. Proper mountain man ye'll be when the Lassie sees ye next. Next time I'll bring a sword and we can fight like civilized men and ye won't need t' try and shave me like a lowlander, eh."

Damien laughed, and rubbed his progressively-more-scruffy beard. "I hear there's a barber down in the town. But I'm up here and he's down there. Perhaps I *will* go ahead and let it turn into a true mountain man's tangle like yours, friend."

"And maybe you'll pass on some of those lessons from those fancy teachers of yours," Franz suggested, coming forward, Rob in tow.

"I don't suppose you'd want to do that *now,*" Damien suggested. "I should probably run through drills anyways."

He was relieved when Franz's eyes lit, and even Rob looked reluctantly interested.

"No sword wit' me today," Darvin commented. "But I'll watch. Got m'own to do, too."

Again, Damien found himself in the role of teacher – and enjoying it. He gave Rob and Franz a simple pattern to work on together, demonstrating separately with each of them. It had to be closer to Rob's level, but Franz was good-natured about the whole thing.

The mercenary was almost entirely self-taught, he admitted, curling his moustaches as he spoke. He didn't have the deep foundation that Damien did, but he had traveled broadly and tried to learn at least one new thing from each swordsman he had encountered. He knew some tricks that Damien had never seen before and claimed he could hold his own in the situations he'd encountered.

Darvin had nodded at that assessment, and Damien had the greatest respect for the bearded man's skills. Their bout had been brief, mostly because Darvin hadn't expected even the Duke-Consort of Elaarwen to know how to face a mountain man's weapons. The captive king – and Duke – looked forward to seeing what Darvin could do with a sword.

Damien took some time to practice his own drills. Eventually Adam or Jason – or Genevieve – would call him out on how much skill he'd allowed himself to lose. While he looked forward to that day, he would prefer their corrections be as minimal as possible... he'd felt the flat of each of their blades often enough in the past when they felt he was slacking.

While Damien wasn't exactly *exhausted* when the mercenaries indicated they had had enough for the day, he had worn off enough of his cooped-up frenetic energy that he wasn't bouncing impatiently as Mikhail came down to unlock the door. The over-pretty slave-boy had watched with interest from the gallery the entire time, although his companion had fallen fast asleep despite the clanging of steel in the enclosed space.

"You're very good with a sword, Damien," Mikhail complimented him as he led the way back up to Azella's suite. "Very good indeed. I used to watch the warrior-slaves training and I don't think I saw any near as good as you."

The captive king shrugged. "It's not so much to my credit. I had excellent teachers, and they never let me slack off."

Except when he'd been nearly as ill as Genevieve early last Autumn. Damien could feel just how much stamina he still had to regain to return to his former level of fitness. And how much of his finer skills he'd need to rebuild.

He'd done a good deal of that rebuilding work once Genevieve had recovered enough that the Realm was no longer pulling on him quite so hard. He'd rebuilt enough so that he'd managed to shock the newer members of his Royal Guards who had never seen him at his peak and hadn't believed that a man who'd never earned his shield could out-fight a knight who was ten years his junior and at the peak of their own skills.

None of them seemed to consider that Damien's trainers from the first day he picked up a sword were the best swordsmen – and swordswoman – in the Realm, and even when he was at that severe nadir of his strength and fitness Jason and Adam had made him keep doing whatever he could manage. Not to mention working him much more intensively the last few weeks before the wedding/coronation...

Or, well, they had been up until Azella kidnapped him.

He'd been on his own to maintain his fitness since then, stuck – mostly – in that one room, with neither sword nor mats nor sparring partners. A good several days half-starved and much of the rest despondent. None of which had been helpful.

And while teaching Franz and Rob was satisfying, it wouldn't do very much for helping him keep up his training and nothing at all for rebuilding lost skills.

Still, they were what he had, and Darvin might prove a bit more of a challenge.

"You do not give yourself sufficient credit," Mikhail told him, words he was all too used to hearing from his closest friends and advisors. "You are here, alone, without your 'very good teachers' to require anything of you. Yet you have worked hard to keep your body fit and toned."

"You must be doing something the same," Damien replied, reluctantly admiring the boy's physique. "Do you have a trainer?"

"Here? No, here we have the incentive that the Mistress prefers a tight stomach and trim waist. Each of us would rather be her favorite than otherwise."

Mikhail's sharp smile reminded Damien of too many things he would rather forget.

"But I would like to go beyond that," the boy said unexpectedly. "I would like to join your lessons with the sword, if the Mistress will permit it. I have no training as a fighter," he added, as if sensing that would be the swordsman's first question, "it was not considered necessary for a Power-slave, and possibly dangerous. Yet I am lithe and agile and my body does what is willed of it."

He did not add *who* would do the 'willing,' Damien noticed.

On the one hand, he cringed at the idea of spending more time with the would-be evil wizard, of having to touch him to correct stance and guard. On the other, perhaps even still Mikhail could choose another path. Perhaps if he could be persuaded to see Damien not as a rival or a potential second evil wizard Master – perish the thought – but as a *mentor...*

It was more than likely Azella would tell him 'no.'

As Damien wrestled with himself and the silence stretched on, Mikhail added with a tone of disappointment, "It is that I am too old, is it not? The Warrior-slaves began their training as early as six or seven years of age. As did I, to source Power and give pleasure."

Damien's mind boggled and he shook his head. It was too much to imagine right now.

"I began to learn the sword at seventeen, Mikhail," he said. "If you can find more protective clothing than that kilt and another sword – and obtain Azella's permission – you may most certainly join."

He could pit Mikhail against Rob, and give Franz more advanced drills to work on...

"Thank you, Damien." Mikhail stopped suddenly and threw his arms around the older man's neck, landing an exuberant kiss.

Startled and discommoded, Damien pushed away, wincing as his neck and shoulder muscles twinged. He needed a soak in a hot bath and more stretching, if the muscles were not to seize up now that they were finally being used as intended after this long break.

The golden-haired boy looked first hurt and resigned, then noticed the wince and his weirdly-bright blue eyes went wide. "You are sore after all of that activity that your body is no longer accustomed to. I will give you a massage after you have bathed and work the knots out of your muscles. Even our trainers said I have a special gift for massage."

Damien felt himself go pale. This would just be another excuse for Mikhail to try to make love to him again. "I'll be fine on my own."

Mikhail held up his hands. "Only a massage, I promise. No matter," he looked up through his long eyelashes at Damien, "if you change your mind midway. I will not make love to you even then, I swear. You must forgive me," he added, resuming the lead and striding along the lamp-lit corridors, "for the night of the mage-battle. You are the sweetest lover I have ever had, and I longed to please you again. But I would rather have you as a friend. I miss playing chess with you."

The older man frowned, feeling like a piece on the chessboard himself. The black king, hedged about by the white queen and her pawns.

"Why not teach one of your fellows? Or are they too busy to learn?"

Mikhail snorted. "'Too busy.' Indeed. There is never enough time to hone one's muscles and the silkiness of one's hair, the smoothness of one's skin, in hopes of impressing the Mistress. Not a one of them thinks to try to impress her with his *brain*. The slave-quarters are a very dull place, friend Damien."

"Hmmn," Damien said non-committally. There was probably no reason to object to an occasional game. He had no idea how often Azella would permit him to practice swordplay, and reading those books without break was making him more antsy...

It suddenly occurred to the captive king that his excessive energy might actually correlate directly with reading about Air Elementals. Perhaps he had enough Air in his own nature that he was responding to his growing knowledge.

Had he also so reacted to the Fire Elemental readings? He remembered feeling dull and apathetic, not full of inspiration... yet he had begun building the puzzle of how this magick fit with his own. And he had been full of passion and enthusiasm the first day or two until...

Interesting.

Apathy and dullness would be the converse of fire...

If it were true that he was reacting to his readings, how then might he react to Water and Earth? Those were the two elements he already felt most familiar with, through his work with the fabric of the Realm. And then there was the fifth 'Element' Azella had mentioned as part of their bargain, and which the other books referred to somewhat elliptically.

Damien wasn't sure what 'Aether' referred to.

They entered the suite, and the pale sorceress called him immediately to attend her in her office. Mikhail, not summoned, continued on to the bedchamber.

"Come sit with me," Azella ordered him. She was curled up like a small white cat on the comfortably worn sofa. "Tell me about this practice session."

Damien gave her a disbelieving laugh. "Azella, I'm all over sweat."

She gave him a long-lashed look. "I know. Sit."

With a sigh, he thumped down beside her, setting the pot-metal sword on the floor for lack of any better option. At least it had a scabbard, nearly as battered and useless as the sword itself.

Azella curled into him until he put an arm around her, and showed him the book in her hands. It was the *Wind-Deities* treatise he had wanted to discuss earlier.

"I can see what you meant about the author's claims. It's hard to see how gods as different as Kyo and Zephria could really be aspects of the same one. And Dawil has another goddess, Sylphara of the Mountain Breezes, and worships Sifwisa of the Trade-Winds as well."

"My grandmother assured me that the accounts of the Dawilm goddesses being seen simultaneously are completely true," Damien told her.

Azella wrinkled her nose at him. "Your grandmother?"

"Queen Rena," he clarified. "King Reginald's sixth wife. She was a princess of Dawil."

The sorceress leaned her head on his shoulder. "There's so much I still don't know about you."

Damien laughed. "Most of it is probably a matter of public record. As the grandson of a king, and king in my own right, there's very little mystery left."

She gave him a skeptical look. "Is your Healing magick public knowledge then?"

He went still, remembering how she had come to learn of his ability to Heal.

"No," he said quietly.

Azella gave him an impatient look. "You're still overblowing that. Mikhail was far too expensive for me to allow him to come to any permanent harm." She snuggled in again. "I haven't before, after all."

And she thought that would make her actions less chilling. "That doesn't make what you're doing *right.*"

"Right or wrong," she said peacefully. "You're such a moral absolutist, Damien. There is no *right* or *wrong* that can be known without context. Have you asked Mikhail about it? Does *he* begrudge me the Power I sourced from him that night?"

"Mikhail," Damien said dryly, "is devoted to you beyond all sense and reason as his hope of eternal youth and Power."

She set the book on his lap and slid a hand up his chest and around Damien's neck. "And how do I persuade *you* to feel the same way?"

He moved the precious tome off his dusty, sweaty thighs.

"Azella," he said with a sigh, "I *really* need a bath."

"But I love the way you smell right now," she purred, pulling herself into his lap. "So... *masculine.* So... *sexy...*"

She was kissing his neck, and sliding her hand inside the wide vee opening of his shirt, making him again wish it had proper laces.

The captive king put his hands around the sorceress's small waist and lifted her off his lap as he stood up.

"I'm taking a bath." He strode quickly to the door, pausing only to snatch the pot-metal sword up as he went.

At the door, however, he paused. "And there *are* some things that are moral absolutes, Azella."

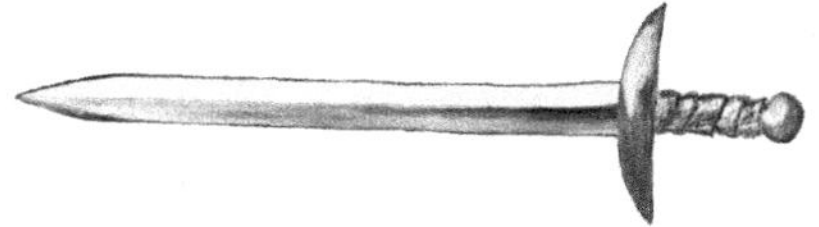

# Chapter TWELVE

## *Positional Play*

A LONG SOAK IN HOT water made him feel more like himself. Azella's questing hands combined with her willingness to actually discuss interesting questions – however distractedly – had unbalanced him. She'd managed to pique his intellectual interest as well as his physical awareness of her.

Mikhail wandered in eventually, however, to urge him out for a massage.

Damien had no end of misgivings about this, but the youth was insistent, finally pointing out that he had already sent the captive king's soiled clothing to the laundry and only he knew where the fresh set was stashed. There being a limited number of hiding places in the bedroom – or even the suite – Damien wasn't overly concerned, but he was physically tired enough to no longer desire to argue about it. He'd probably fall asleep once he was laying down anyways.

He'd reckoned without Mikhail's skill... and his own reaction to the beautiful young man's nearness. Instead of falling asleep, he found himself incredibly relaxed, but increasingly wide awake. And in more than one sense.

To his dismay, Azella came in to watch the massage, though she stayed silent and out of arm's reach.

When Mikhail tried to get him to roll over – with entirely reasonable arguments about the muscles on the front of Damien's chest – he balked, flushing bright red. Somehow, however, the youth prevailed, and the captive king could not really disagree that the muscles of his chest appreciated the attention. The pot-metal sword had terrible balance, requiring constant compensation to accomplish even the simplest drills. And, of course, the weight of a longsword itself, at even partial extension, was no mean thing.

He thought the massage was over when Mikhail laid a dry towel across his mid-section... but the youth had other plans. A few expert strokes of his hand had Damien arching and crying out with the unexpected and powerfully pleasurable sensation. Almost clinically, Mikhail used the towel to clean up, and took it away.

"Mikhail, you *lied* to me," Damien gasped breathlessly. "Only a massage... you *promised...*"

The beautiful young man gave him a curious look. "But that is all it was. I did not kiss you, nor caress you, nor offer my body for your pleasure. Are you not relaxed now, Damien?"

"That is *not* how massages are supposed to end," Damien glared, though he couldn't disagree. Every muscle in his body seemed loose and relaxed and the very idea of trying to move anywhere was beyond him.

Mikhail cocked his head. "If they do not where you are from, it must be a very tense place indeed."

"My turn, Mikhail," Azella said lazily, having stripped off her own clothes sometime earlier.

The youth's eyes lit. "Yes, Mistress," and he began laying out his oils and towels on her side of the bed.

Somewhat later, Azella drowsily dismissed Mikhail for the evening to his own pursuits and rolled close in to Damien as the door closed behind him.

"Surely you haven't anything to fear from me *right now,*" she said as he stiffened at her closeness. "If either one of us has anything left, Mikhail didn't do it right. I just... want to feel a human touch. Your arm around me... Feel *safe...*"

The sorceress was probably just playing on his protective instincts, but he couldn't bring himself to reject her request when she phrased it like that. With a sigh of emotional frustration alone, he let her wrap herself around his languid body and pillow her head on his shoulder.

"How old are you, really, Azella?" he asked after several moments. "You have the look of a girl of fifteen or sixteen, and I know you're somewhat older. Not as old as you try to give me the impression, though."

"Does it matter?" she asked in turn.

"Not really," Damien admitted. "I'm just curious. Doesn't it take a fair amount of study for an evil sorceress to be able to stop her aging? Did you somehow reverse the process?"

"My Master decided he found me fair when he bought me at the auction-house and stopped my aging almost immediately," she admitted. "I was just past fifteen."

"Poor girl," he said sympathetically.

"I'm not a *girl*," Azella said sharply.

"You were then," Damien said mildly. "You should have had years yet to grow into womanhood."

"He rescued me," she said stubbornly. "He was the greatest and most Powerful Evil Sorcerer the world has seen in a thousand years, and he chose *me* to be his Apprentice."

The captive king chuckled. "Or perhaps *you* chose *him,* my princess. I don't have much of a gift of mage-sight, but even I can see how your Power blazes. What was his name?"

*And how did I not know about this evil sorcerer living on the edges of my Realm?* he wondered.

"He no longer has one." Azella's tone was a strange combination of firm satisfaction and deepest regret and hurt. "I took it from him when he took another girl to his bed after I had loyally served as his Apprentice for ten years."

"And loved him," Damien added quietly.

She remained silent for a long moment. "*You* will not betray me thus, Damien."

He sighed. "And then you've been on your own here these last two years? So, you would be twenty-seven."

"I suppose," she said.

And "Does it matter?" she said again.

"No," he replied, then chuckled. "But your 'ancient as the hills' mask is a little less believable now that I know you're actually two years my junior."

She snorted. "Had you lived through what I have done and seen what I have seen... Consorting with demons tends to strip away one's illusions."

With the way she said it... he feared that she meant 'consorting' in its most literal sense.

However...

"That's too bad," he said lightly. "Illusions are some of the best parts of life."

He could feel her frown against his chest. "What nonsense are you talking about?"

This was probably not the time to engage her in a philosophical discourse on the ancient goddess – or idea – of Maya. That all things seen and touched and of the world were illusion was a deeper discussion than this demanded.

"Rainbows are illusions," Damien said instead. "And the pretending to not-know what your birthday present will be although you overheard someone mention it months earlier."

"Hmmn." She didn't sound impressed.

"Love is made of many illusions," Damien went on softly. "Especially in its first blush. We see the person loved through the veil of our hopes and expectations and they are more beautiful than other eyes will see them, more graceful and gracious, more – everything. It is when the illusions are stripped away that they are sometimes found wanting."

"*Sometimes* only?"

The captive king thought of his own loves.

Not merely Genevieve, but also Jason, and Adam. And even Lena, the lone unwed lady of his initial secret twelve, damaged beyond his Healing in the brief usurpation of his throne. His Realm that he loved in a different way, but just as fiercely and, in somewise, just as passionately.

"Sometimes, Azella, when the illusions are gone, the beauty remains and is only brighter and more wondrous when seen with undazzled eyes."

"That is how it will be for me with you, Damien," she said jealously, aware that his thoughts had ranged far to the north.

"Oh, my princess," Damien sighed. "I *do* believe there *is* someone for you."

*But that someone is not me,* he added silently. *And I only hope you recognize him when you find him... and will give up for him what you will not for me.*

# Chapter THIRTEEN

# *Sacrifice the Exchange*

IT HAD TAKEN DAMIEN NEARLY five weeks to burn through Azella's store of wisdom – and purported wisdom – on Fire Elementals. It took him barely a month to fly through everything she owned on Air.

It was not because her collection was more meager. Indeed, the total volume of items was slightly greater.

Nor was it because he spent more time reading. Certainly, he had progressed more slowly when sunk in apathy, but now that she permitted him to leave the suite and train with the mercenaries, he actually spent *less* time at his studies. If she had hoped the distraction would slow him down, she was disappointed – it actually cleared his head and made his thoughts flow more smoothly to be able to use his body.

For whatever reason, the day when she sorted through Damien's innumerable diagrams, looking for patterns that he was fairly sure were only apparent to him, and then admitted that she had no more books or scrolls on Air Elemental magick to provide him came sooner than she had expected. Damien had known he must be close, for he had felt the edges of the knowledge that were not in the books and scrolls.

He'd had a vague sense of nausea all the time since Midwinter that he did not dare admit. The captive king suspected that it was the little bit that was seeping through the soul-bond, and was torn between relief that he could feel *anything* from Genevieve and distress that she was going through this phase of her pregnancy without even the sense of his love and support down the bond.

At least... his explorations of pregnancy in his work with the Realm had led him to see that a moderate amount of nausea – not enough to drive a woman to being bed-ridden – actually suggested a more healthy outcome for the baby. It was as if mother and child engaged in a chess game and the harder they both fought, the longer the game would go on and the more satisfying the endgame would be.

Genevieve had sailed through the early months of her few previous pregnancies that had lasted even so long as this without the slightest discomfort. It was reassuring in an odd way that this time she was probably quite miserable.

Nearly twelve weeks that he had been gone. By Damien's count little Giendra Marlerite should stop making her mother feel ill any time now.

"Water," Azella told him, looking somewhat discommoded.

Damien gave her a wry grin. "Surely this pleases you, my princess? I thought you looked forward to these little transitions."

Her eyes lit at that comment, but her mouth was still sour.

It wasn't at all sour the next morning.

"Can you imagine a lifetime of this," Damien whispered in her ear as he curled around her back in the misty light of morning. It broke his heart to try this, but his personal happiness... even *Genevieve's* personal happiness... had to be set against the damage this one evil sorceress could do in whatever span of time she might extend her own life to live.

"A lifetime... with you?" Her breath caught, and he felt like a cad for offering himself as a lure.

"A peaceful cottage in a golden glen," Damien painted a word-picture. "You and me... waking like this every morning..."

"One room just for your books," she breathed, and his heart ached again. Apparently, she was not so self-centered as he'd thought.

Time to see if she could follow him down this 'woodland path' that he would give up everything he loved in order to tread. "Our children filling the house with wildflowers and the sounds of laughter. The sweet smell of cookies baking while we rock our grandchildren on our knees... Snuggling peacefully as we watch the sun set over the hills and grow old together."

She had gone very still. *"One* lifetime together. One *normal length* lifetime together."

"A man might father children while staying young, Azella," Damien said softly. "As my grandfather proved so well. A woman..." He trailed his fingers along her flat abdomen. "A woman who is frozen in time cannot bring a child to life."

"And..." it seemed she could hardly bring herself to say the words, "children are so very important to you?" She paused. "Your *own* children, born of your blood and your bone?"

The captive king nodded into her hair.

She blew out a long, slow breath, but did not say anything.

Damien waited, not daring to push as she struggled – perhaps – with these ideas.

Eventually however, he felt he had waited long enough.

"Will you come live with me and be my love?" he asked gently, hoping and fearing for her answer.

Could he even follow through on this if she said yes? Damien was aware that he was not just offering to stay with her... he was offering her his heart. His love, his loyalty, his unswerving affection.

Genevieve had once sacrificed herself upon the altar of marriage for the good of her lands and people. His brave, beautiful wife had suffered for eight long years in a marriage that grew from hope to indifference to a desperate facade to cover the physical and emotional abuse she was suffering within it.

She had said she never regretted doing so, for it had given the Rebellion the teeth it needed – the strength of Siovale's prosperous plains aligned with her own sturdy but sparse mountaineers. She hadn't known a soul-bonded true-love was waiting for her.

Genevieve would understand. He hoped.

Azella sat up slowly, turning to face him. She reached out and took his hand, bringing Damien's fingers to her lips. Her eyes were huge and so vivid in this morning light, their blue-grey depths seeming to hold so many things he did not yet understand.

*"One* lifetime, my love?" she said tremblingly. *"One* lifetime? When I can love you for a hundred times – a *thousand* times – that long?"

"Azella..." Damien stole back his fingers and ran them gently over her cheek. "There is only one way to sustain such a span. *I* have only one lifetime to offer you." He paused, and gave her his most intense gaze. "But I offer it with all my heart and soul."

He thought he almost saw her fold right then and capitulate to his demand.

Perhaps... perhaps if he had known the *right* words to say at that instant...

But the instant passed and she rose abruptly from the bed. "I am not ready to give up a thousand years and more. I still have three chances to persuade you to see it my way. To see that a love such as ours should not be constrained by such things as a mortal lifetime."

She padded away to the washroom, leaving Damien to flop back on the pillows and clench his fists in frustration... and open them up in deepest relief.

# Chapter FOURTEEN

# *Bind*

READING ABOUT WATER ELEMENTALS... MADE Damien very relaxed.

His students, the two mercenary swordsmen and Mikhail, all commented on it. Darvin, the axeman, who had turned out to be a more than decent swordsman as well, said nothing, but followed the new smoothness of the captive king's movements with a slightly puzzled expression when they sparred. He had grown used to Damien's more choppy and energetic style and had never seen a fighter suddenly show a completely different approach.

Mikhail was the only one who noted that the change extended to his chess game. Of course, Mikhail was the only one who *could*.

Azella simply expressed gratitude that he was no longer pacing a rut in her floors and attributed it to the increased physical activity of practicing swordsmanship. She even came down a few times to watch, but it was clearly not an interest for her. Damien suspected that if he would fence with his shirt off, she would have been glued to her seat in the gallery, but he would only do that as a last resort to keep her attention. It would be just plain embarrassing otherwise.

Water took him all of two weeks.

Earth... was different.

Damien already *knew* Earth at a deep and intrinsic level. The edges of things were fitting together so swiftly now that he barely needed to skim the pages of the books to know if there was something he needed to read in detail. He could feel his background with the fabric of his Realm knitting together the raveled edges.

He felt like he was building the solid foundation that his magick should have been structured on in the first place.

It was similar to the way he was training Franz with the sword. The mustachioed mercenary was a natural with a blade but had lacked the fundamentals to make him into a solid fighter. On the other hand, Franz was also old enough, and experienced enough, to appreciate what Damien was teaching to him. The skirmishes he had fought had worn off that adolescent arrogance that still plagued Rob, and he put his back into the endless drills that Damien assigned him. When they sparred, the difference was immediately obvious now.

Rob still complained and dragged... but Damien's first clue that this had nothing to do with his aversion to lessons came when Mikhail pulled him aside before practice one day.

It had amused Azella to let the beautiful youth learn some swordplay, so the bulk of extra muscles Damien had accidentally gifted him had become firm and well-defined. He had only a few simple patterns, but he was determined and hardworking and he had those few patterns solidly. He had similarly become a solid, if unimaginative, chess player, though his endgame was unsurprisingly weak.

"You must speak with Rob," Mikhail told Damien urgently. "He has been seen speaking *again* to Denisa. It may not go well with him if the Mistress is reminded that she has had to warn him not to make free with her possessions."

Damien frowned. "I'm sure he's bored. Azella hasn't been letting them go down to the town for some reason. What's wrong with talking to Denisa? Or anyone for that matter. He talks to you and me."

Mikhail looked frustrated. "It is beginning to go past *talking*, Damien. As it did twice before. The Mistress reprimanded them all then – Franz and Darvin as well as Rob – and punished Denisa such that she stayed herself away for this long. I did not understand then, why the Mistress was so lenient with the mercenaries, but now it is clear that she wanted them to speak no ill word of her to you when she allowed you to meet them."

That made a certain amount of sense. Azella seemed to wish to reveal to Damien her darker nature only at her own discretion.

"So, you don't think *they* realize how dangerous Azella can be?" Damien interpreted. "But Denisa should know."

Denisa should very *much* know. And Mikhail had said the girl had been punished sorely enough to warn her off for the last month or two.

Perhaps the greater question was how Azella hadn't yet noticed. Damien supposed that even an evil sorceress couldn't pay attention to *everything* – and she seemed quite absorbed lately, in her researches on how to safely sever his soul-bond.

"Franz and Darvin – they are not such fools," Mikhail said worriedly, "But the Mistress may not distinguish the innocent and guilty – as she did not before, saying that they should have enacted some restraint on their young colleague. And Denisa…"

He shook his head. "I have spoken to Rob and Denisa both, but I am well known to be the Mistress's creature. I fear they do not take my words seriously."

At Damien's blank look, he rolled his eyes, for once looking entirely the seventeen-year-old boy that he was.

"Denisa is meant to be a gift from the Mistress to her demons. For what reason I know not, but demons prize a maiden's virginity. If Rob should relieve her of it, I fear things would go badly for them both."

He paused. "And… I fear our friend Rob believes he has found his true love in Denisa, whereas *she* has merely found a fool willing to spare her from the fate she fears. At cost of his own life, most probably. She knows the Mistress is likely to spare *her* for some other use of her Talent, so any rage must be spent on some other, more convenient, object."

The captive king had seen enough of Azella's nature now to believe every word the boy said. "When is their contract with Azella up, do you know?"

Mikhail tipped his head, his long golden locks in their many tight braids – a new style he was testing out to confine it during sword-practice – shifting as he did. "I believe they were planning to leave when the first Spring caravan comes. It should be soon. It is always before the Vernal Equinox, and we are but weeks from then."

"Do Franz and Darvin know? About Rob and Denisa?"

"Since the first times they were caught, close to Midwinter, and the Mistress disciplined them all, yes," Mikhail agreed. "That the foolish pair are seeking to place them all in jeopardy *again*… I think not. They are too easy with Rob for it to be so."

Damien wondered what Azella had done to the mercenaries, but did not ask. Whatever It had been, they seemed to have retained their exuberant self-confidence; he didn't need more evidence of what she could do when 'inspired.'

And thusfar, despite her protestations of love for the captive king, Damien had not been able to convince her to forswear the unethical side of her magick.

"I'll see what I can do," he said dubiously.

In his experience, young love found itself immovable and unshakable the harder one tried to alter it. Azella being a case in point – he strongly suspected that her emotional development had been arrested along with her physical development.

Rob was barely older than Mikhail, and Denisa had yet to turn fifteen.

When Rob arrived and moped around, Damien decided not even to bother talking to the boy. He focused his attention instead on Darvin and Franz, confirming that they were planning to leave – along with Rob – on the first caravan. When he had Mikhail and Rob working together on a pattern they were both familiar enough with to need little correction, he quietly explained the situation to the two other men.

"I'd be impressed with his compassion," Damien told them, as their faces grew grim, "If not his common sense. But Mikhail is convinced that Denisa is only using him."

"Is there no way we could get the girl away?" Franz asked wistfully. "She's a sweet little thing, and whatever deep dark fate is in store for her..."

Damien had not told them about the demons, but simply that Azella was saving the girl's virginity for some dark spell that Denisa feared. It was all *he* could do not to try to spirit Denisa away himself, and he would have some small protection from his magick...

Though with her stored Power, Azella could likely overwhelm any effort Damien might currently make to hide the girl. *They* would have no chance at all.

Damien shook his head. "If I see anything I can do, I'll do it, but... The sorceress had contact with Denisa – actually worked her magick *through* her – as far away as Emeralsee in Ilseador. I don't know how far away the girl would have to go, to be beyond her reach."

He paused. "There's another thing," he added reluctantly. "I've gotten to know Mik there rather well this past Winter." He winced. "Better than I'd like, really. He seems like a goodhearted young man, but his abiding goal is to emulate the sorceress. He *wants* to be an evil sorcerer, and... he makes his own experiments on the other boys in that direction."

He hated damaging Mikhail in their eyes this way... but it was all true, and if they continued blindfolded, it would only hurt them. "I don't know Denisa very well, but it's all too likely she feels the same way. It's how they're raised..."

Franz looked repulsed, but Darvin nodded slowly. "All they know, eh? The ones with the power, to be like them. We saw that, where I come from, under the old king's reign. Most of the flatlander nobles, they went as rotten as he. Took our new king to bring honor back to our country. Very lucky we are to have such an honorable man."

He gave Damien a very direct look, and the captive king of Ilseador had to fight down a blush. Would Darvin think him so honorable if he knew what Damien traded to the sorceress for his lessons? If he knew that the Lassie – Darvin's own liege-lady – was home and with child?

"Our king's a practical one, though," Darvin went on thoughtfully, almost addressing his comments to Franz. "He went through the flatland nobility like a wildfire, but he was careful not to throw out the rotten onions with the good ones. He has some way of seeing inside a person's soul 'tis said, eh. And where there was a man or woman not rotten to the core, he turned them 'round and made them good caretakers again, magicking them to the care of their land and folk."

"Great history lesson, Darv," Franz said sourly. "But how does that help with our problem?"

Darvin regarded his friend calmly. "Friend Damien here is a good influence on yon bright-haired lad, eh. Perhaps there is still a chance his heart is true. And the same for the lass. We'll have to convince young Rob to let our friend do his best for them, eh?"

"Oh, *that's* going to go well," Franz said absently, his eyes on the battling boys.

"Aye. A challenge to get young Rob free of this place without his light-o'-love. That task be ours, eh." He looked thoughtfully at Damien, but continued to direct his words to Franz. "I've a yen to see the mountains of my home again, I think. Would ye like to join me?"

Franz jerked his eyes away from the pair of youths. "The Elaarwen mountains? Not much work there, I'd think."

"Nay," Darvin agreed. "Yet the Spring brings fur traders sending their valuable goods down to Emeralsee. Do we find one of those, our fortunes are cared for and much work there will be in the city, surely, eh."

Damien held his breath as Franz shrugged absently. "Fine by me. I've no particular yen for anywhere, and I took up this life to see the world. I've never been up in those mountains. Oh, those idiots."

Franz rolled his eyes and headed off to correct the younger men's form. The pattern they were following had gotten rather... off-kilter.

"I've... got kin at Cloudcroft, if you happen to pass that way," Damien said casually.

Darvin nodded. "Might be, might be. M'mother's kin ran with that 'children's tale,' Erawan. Think I still have cousin or two out that way, eh."

"It's easier to visit people up there in some ways than down in the cities," Damien commented. "Even Elaarwen's city is big enough to get lost in, trying to find someone."

And how much credibility could a strange mercenary have, mountain man or not?

Enough to get in to see Lord Adsel, Genevieve's Chatelaine in Elaarwen's castle? Surely not enough to see Genevieve herself down in Emeralsee... or possibly not even Sir Tim, the Captain of the Royal Guard?

But Cloudcroft was barely a manor house... more of a farmstead in an inconvenient place than anything. Darvin could get a hearing at Cloudcroft, if Damien's father-in-law exiled there by the king's own word still cared what had happened to his son-in-law.

Darvin grinned. "I've found that m'self on occasion, eh."

"I have to tell you though," Damien dropped his head. "My kin at Cloudcroft... we parted on not the best terms. I'd like them to know that I forgive them... and hope they forgive me. If they don't seem to take well to hearing my name, you might just head on down to Elaarwen's city. Fellow named Adsel is more distant kin, but he might have some work for you if you mention my name. If he doesn't have anything, he'll know who does."

'Not the best terms'... was putting it extremely mildly.

Damien had *banished* Lord Aldred – stripping the now-honorary title of 'Duke' from Genevieve's father – and exiling him to their small, ancestral holding of Cloudcroft for setting himself up to be King's Regent for a soon-to-be-born half-sibling of his daughter. The Stellarine line was as close to the Throne as Damien – Genevieve could easily be ruling in her own name. However, Aldred's yet-unborn child was going to be in direct competition with Damien and Genevieve's own... if they ever managed to produce any. Damien had been furious that the old man would set their poor land up for yet another civil war.

"Aye to that," Darvin nodded again. "'Tis friends and kin as makes the world go 'round, they do, eh."

Damien nodded ruefully. "My kinswoman up at Cloudcroft was expecting, last I knew. The babe might even be born before you get there. I know my wife would like to see it. She was sorely grieved that we'd had such harsh words."

And if any of the principals would accept this roundabout rescinding of Lord Aldred's banishment with his pregnant lover – Damien's dear friend, Ciriis Celavell – Genevieve could surely use her father's support.

Darvin chuckled. "'Tis friends and kin as make the world crash to a stop as well. I'll give them your word as I may. But mind ye. 'Tis a *gracious* long distance to travel, eh."

"And I've nothing to ease your journey... and nothing but my gratitude for the attempt." Damien met his new friend's eyes. "Though my wife would be mightily pleased to have word."

A king's gratitude, should he escape, might mean something. The *Queen's* gratitude might be more immediately meaningful, to a man bringing news of her lost husband...

But for the mercenary to leave here and go directly to Emeralsee... even if Azella was careless enough not to note their direction, it might take a while for Darvin to make it through the elegant bureaucracy of the capitol to see the Queen. Or Adam, Jason, Tim, Aryllis... Damien himself had cut through the needless layers of formality to talk directly to the people of his city and Realm, but he was well aware it was a different matter to reach up the social ladder than down.

Darvin was more than clever to have suggested the more roundabout path – and with the excellent excuse of visiting his own kin along the way. If anyone could make this work, it was likely to be him... with Franz and Rob as window-dressing for his mission as messenger.

"I will surely miss you, my friend," the captive king sighed. "It was mortally lonely here before we began these sessions."

"Well, we're not goin' anytimes soon," Darvin replied. "Caravan isn't even here yet, eh. And yon bright-haired lad will still be here."

"True." Damien sighed. "Maybe he'll even make it to where he can actually spar with Rob and not get knocked on his rear."

Darvin chuckled and clapped Damien on the shoulder. "Don' set yer hopes too high, lad. Next ye'll be thinkin' the two o' them will make it through a bout w'out losin' hold o' their blades, eh."

Damien laughed and rolled his eyes. "One more bout before we call it quits for the day, old man?" They had established at some point that Darvin was just a few months Damien's senior. The bushy mountain-style beard simply made him look older. "Perhaps today will be the day you knock me on *my* rear."

Darvin snorted. "Speakin' o' high hopes, eh."

"You never know," Damien shrugged to settle his shoulders.

Truthfully speaking, Darvin's chances were better than usual. Damien was having trouble with his balance. If Air had made him restless and energetic, and Water calm and fluid, Earth should, by rights, be making him very grounded. Instead, it appeared to be doing exactly the opposite, much as his studies of Fire had been marked by apathy as he fought a dark depression.

And, just as he'd feared, within two passes of the blades, the captive king tripped over his own feet, tumbled, and landed in an ungraceful sprawl, narrowly having avoided skewering himself on his own blunt blade.

The others all stopped practicing to stare.

Damien didn't bother trying to get up from where he'd ended at the base of one of the walls. His head was spinning and he didn't trust his sense of balance right now in the slightest.

"Damien!" It was Mikhail who was first at his side, his expression fearful and worried.

Expert fingers probed around his skull and checked limbs. Bright blue eyes, stark against that smooth, mahogany skin inspected him for a concussion.

At last, the young man sat back on his heels. "Nothing broken. What happened?"

Damien looked at him sideways, still not feeling up to rising. "I tripped."

"Not like ye, eh." Darvin said laconically, but his eyes held concern.

"My head's been a little – off – today," Damien admitted. "Perhaps I'm catching a cold."

He rolled his eyes. "Though who *from,* I can't imagine, since the only people I see are the four of you and milady sorceress. And him."

He pointed at the slave-boy peering curiously through the galleries' bars to see what the excitement was.

"Go back to your nap," Damien called. "I just tripped. I'm fine."

He waved from his prone position.

The boy waved back and vanished as he lay back in his seat again.

"Ready to get up?" Mikhail asked.

"Stop hovering like a mother-hen, Mikhail," Damien told him a trifle too sharply. "I'm fine. And you still had five repetitions left on the eighth pattern before you and Rob spar, if I'm not wrong."

"Seven," Rob called back gloomily. "Franz made us start over."

"Mik." Damien reached out a hand as the boy's eyes went shuttered with hurt at his abrupt dismissal. "I'm fine, really. I just hate a fuss when I've done something this foolish. I just need another moment to catch my breath before I stand up."

He forced a smile as the boy took his hand. "I'm grateful that you know how to check for injuries so thoroughly. It was very reassuring."

Mikhail essayed a slight smile, those bright blue eyes opening as windows to his soul again, and shrugged. "Training."

Damien gave him a wry look. "I know. Go do some of *this* training, okay? Poor Rob looks ready to call it a day if you don't get back there."

Mikhail snorted. "Poor Rob indeed."

But he squeezed Damien's hand before releasing it, and rose gracefully to go back to work. Rob heaved a very loud sigh.

Darvin and Franz waited, and Damien waved them away also, so they began a bout of their own. He knew they each had a half an eye on him, which would surely do them no good, so he pried himself up to a sitting position, leaning against the wall. He propped one knee up and draped a wrist over it, keeping the other knee half-folded flat on the ground.

This was ridiculous.

He'd been naturally graceful all his life, taken to sword and horse and dancefloor as if he'd never suffered a gap in training. When Jason or Adam – or Genevieve or his Secret Cadre of nobleborn Guardswomen – had taught him a new fighting move, he'd absorbed it with only a couple of repetitions. He'd never seemed to go through the periods of clumsiness that other boys did – though it would, admittedly, have been hard to tell while he was immured in the Royal Library. Jason and Adam had drilled him with edged steel from nearly the first days that he'd been willing to take a blade in his hand.

Damien had rarely stubbed a *toe,* let alone tripped or fallen down. Or, Gods forbid, crashed into something.

And it wasn't just *now,* either.

He'd been *tripping* all over Azella's suite for days... Until he'd begun to stay in bed as long as possible, making just a short reach to fetch his books and papers, and then staying reading in bed... Because he'd even fallen out of his *chair* a couple of times.

It had to be because of his disconnection with Earth as represented by his Realm. But Azella still would not let him leave the suite save for these short practice sessions, so he had no opportunity to rectify the matter.

He'd asked Mikhail if they could make a little detour on the way back, just for variety – just down a level or two and up again. The lowest levels, he remembered from his arrival, had been carved from native stone, rather than built by ripping the stone from its mother Earth and piling it higher with mortar and muscle.

But the boy had looked as if Damien had suggested stealing from the Royal Treasury, so apparently that, too was *forbidden.*

Likely Azella was as aware as he was himself that it wasn't in her best interests to allow Damien contact with his Realm, or even to stone that was still one with the ground beneath it. His spinning head and aching toes regretted that he hadn't somehow pressed past his physical and spiritual shock that first day and somehow remade that connection when he had the chance.

Gods. He *missed* Genevieve, but the lack of his *Realm* was like a missing *limb.* Which was moderately ironic, since separations from Genevieve – in the absence of a pregnancy – had nearly killed them both, as the soul-bond reacted badly to such things.

The smooth stone now at Damien's back was more of the built part of the Keep. Each piece smoothed and fitted together so there was not the narrowest gap. Beautiful workmanship, but it was rather lost on the captive king right now.

Idly, Damien traced a seam in the wall to his side, catching his fingernail in it and sliding down past each horizontal join. The wall extended below the sprung wooden floor, of course.

Something *zinged* sharply through him from his fingertip as he met the horizontal join that paralleled the surface of the floor. He pulled back his hand in shock.

Damien held his breath and probed again. This time it was stronger.

He didn't dare wait and think about this any longer. Damien dug both hands into the tiny gap where wall met floor, seeking the lower edge of that horizontal seam in the stone. That lower part must belong to the foundation of the Keep: the part that was carved from the living stone and still connected to the heart and soul of the land.

Yes! The Realm rushed back into his senses with wild abandon, almost as overwhelming and encompassing and, yes, *orgasmic* as the first time he had sat on the Throne after the Sword had claimed him. Damien had no doubt the Realm had been seeking *him* just as desperately as he had been seeking contact with *It*.

With *Them*.

The Realm was definitely a plural.

No doubt that It/Them loved him, wanted him, *needed* him.

Yes, the Others were caring for It/Them as best they could, but it was not the same.

The Others were still *separate*.

The Others would not let the Realm into themselves as Damien did; the Others still expected to remain distinct from the multitudinous Life that was the Realm.

The Others saw the Realm as an object, a Thing to be used or set aside as was convenient.

The Others focused their attention only on *humans*...

Damien, however, had accepted the Realm as part and parcel of his Being. He spent his attention and care as abundantly on woodlarks in Embervest and snails in Siovale as on the humans who named him King. The Realm had not had such a connection with Its/Their Monarch in a tree's age. An *oak* tree's age.

He found himself mentally caressing and soothing the Realm, as though It/They were a child or a pet dog. *Yes, I am here again. Yes, I am with you.*

He could let go of the seam of stone now. The connection was wide open again... and the Realm It/Themself was calling on some depths of knowledge even Damien didn't have access to in order to setup safeguards to prevent him from ever being blocked away again.

Almost offhandedly, It/They showed him the Others – Genevieve, Bound as Queen; Jason – Bound, he had thought, only to the Duchy of Emeralsee, but somehow in touch with the whole Realm anyways... perhaps his coronation as Heir had something to do with it; and... Adam?

Why *Adam?* He wasn't Bound to any of the land, except perhaps through Jason, his husband. He was his mother's acknowledged Heir to their tiny holding, but had not yet been Bound there in Lynncrag...

By all rights, the connection with Adam should have seemed distant and vague, but instead it almost blazed more brightly than Jason's.

*That Other takes Me/Us more seriously,* the Realm wordlessly informed Damien.

Apparently, Adam's natural gifts as an empath and the interest he had developed in the workings of magick – to support Damien initially – somehow compensated for the lack of a direct and formal Binding.

*I am home,* Damien told the Realm.

It was true. He was on – or above – Fariveran bedrock. And now that the connection was open, the feeling of homesickness was largely gone.

He still *missed* Genevieve, Jason, Adam... Emeralsee and Elaarwen... and all the other parts of the Realm that he had walked or ridden so that the land knew him personally. But it was impossible to feel *homesick.*

This was more like being in a little-used room in his own house.

The door to the arena burst inwards and Azella stormed in, energy sparking around her in her fury. Her long hair floated slightly in a crackling halo, and she looked entirely dangerous, her full-skirted black gown contrasting against skin that seemed even more pale than usual.

The other men – and boys – drew as far away as they could. They needn't have bothered. She only had eyes for Damien, and the rest might as well not have existed.

*"How did you do this?"* Azella shrieked.

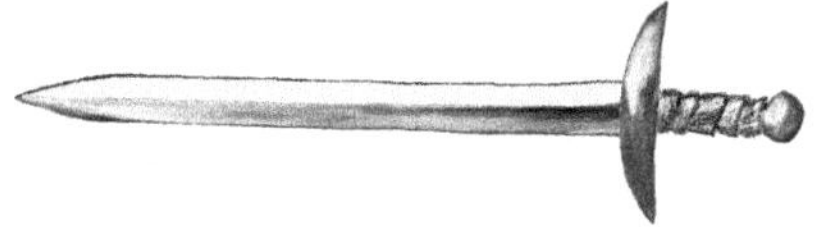

# Chapter FIFTEEN

# *Development*

THE BOUND AND CROWNED SORCERER-KING of Ilseador rose gracefully from the floor, completely balanced and comfortable once again, serene in his connection to his Realm.

He felt flooded, even *surfeited* with Power... And just as the Realm had placed safeguards around its connection to him, It/They now stopped all the little leakages that had been siphoning away his personal Power into the Keep and thence to Azella.

Damien guessed he was probably *glowing* again. The room seemed brighter anyways.

"Is this really where you want to have this conversation?" he asked politely but pointedly.

She seethed at him, but her eyes suddenly focused on her two pretty slave-boys, the three mercenaries...

Damien offered her his arm, a gentleman to a lady. Seething, she accepted it.

Without another word, they swept out.

She managed to hold onto herself until the oaken double-doors to her suite were shut behind them. At that point, Azella would have pulled her hand from his arm and turned snarling on the sorcerer-king, but he was having none of it.

"You've had a terrible shock, my dear," he said solicitously, guiding her into her office and seating her on the couch. "Have a cup of tea."

It was her own tea, sitting where she had doubtless abandoned it in her urgency to seek him out. But she stared at the delicate porcelain cup as if it was a swarm of wasps when he caused it to float over to her and into her hands.

"You're glowing," Azella said.

Damien dropped into her desk chair and stretched his legs out, crossing them at the ankle as he leaned back.

"Am I?" he asked mildly. "I've been told that's happened before, but I can never tell for myself for sure."

The pale sorceress narrowed her eyes at him. "You seem different. Not just that connection to your Realm. *You.*"

She didn't question that his Binding to the Realm had been restored, even if she still didn't know how. A very practical woman, the sorceress.

"Probably so." The king inclined his head.

It wasn't something he could explain to her – Azella's mind just worked too differently. When he re-connected with the Realm, all the pieces of things he had been studying had snapped into place.

Damien had thought he was finally comfortable in his role as king and with using the Power that the Realm gave him to mend what his grandfather had broken. He'd had little confidence in his own magick, however, and no real understanding of *how* he did what he did. A low level of anxiety had underlain every day, and he had felt like an imposter – that he was only king because of happenstance. That others, far more qualified, had been passed over and should actually be in charge.

It was actually true in some wise; the Evil Sorcerer-King, his grandfather King Reginald, had yielded not one iota of power to any of his various Heirs. He had usually had them slain, as Damien's father had been, if they even began to demonstrate any real strength.

Damien, for example, had been Duke of Emeralsee, the largest city and most populous province in Ilseador, for two years before he had become King. Yet he had never been allowed to oversee the administration of city or province, which had languished in royal disregard under the attention of a series of corrupt officials.

That sense of being unqualified had waned slightly as he learned how to actually rule.

But it had grown again as he was faced with Genevieve's string of miscarriages and his growing fear that she would die... And that they would leave the Realm with no fit Heir since as her soul-bonded he would surely follow suit.

And then as he solved *that* – however painfully and unconventionally... and finally *wonderfully* – there had come the doubled attack of the mage-driven ice-storm from the west and the pirates and sorceress from the east.

And his magickal abilities had *not* been equal to the test – much as Franz's swordskills would have failed him in any serious encounter with a swordsman who had the fundamentals down.

It had seemed that every time he met a challenge, a new one appeared just to prove how unworthy he was. Unworthy to hold his title. Unworthy of his wife. Unworthy of Jason and Adam, his closest friends and advisors, who had supported him from before the beginning, and on whom he had finally dumped all of his problems.

Unworthy of the trust of his Realm.

And the repeated assertions – of those same friends and advisors, that wonderful wife, even his subjects and vassals – that he was an excellent king... That only made Damien feel he had to work harder still to hide how very wrong they all were.

His prodigious memory helped with that, since Damien's 'solution' was to read *everything* and overwhelm his unpreparedness and lack of skill by the sheer weight of knowledge.

When Damien had given himself up to Azella, it had very nearly been with a sense of *relief* that it was no longer his problem to solve. And when she had come so close to breaking his bonds – to the Realm and to Genevieve – that, too, had very nearly been a relief, painful as it had been.

A *short-lived relief,* since he was still Bound by ethics and duty. But surely no one could expect much of him, cut off from all his supports and the main source of his Power. Elation had quickly tumbled into depression, pushed on by his realization of what it meant that his captor really *was* an evil sorceress.

And yet, somehow, this... call it what it was, this *respite* from the expectations that he felt so inadequate to meet, had somehow given him more confidence. He'd had nothing but his own wits to match against the sorceress, nothing but his own magickal Power to match against hers.

Yet he had somehow gotten her to give him exactly what he needed to build the strong foundation he had lacked.

Damien now suspected that his own Power matched Azella's closely, though it was hard to measure such things, and hers was nearly always supplemented.

He knew from his readings that he was an Elemental mage with a strong affinity for Earth, but with the ability to tap strongly into all four Elements he had studied thusfar. Adam had been telling him he was Powerful for the last several years... but he hadn't seen how the very unmagickal Adam could know... and anyhow, his abilities were so tied up with the Realm, surely that was nothing to his own credit.

Now... Damien had seen what he could do on his own, *without* the aid of the Realm. He hadn't directly tried spells or tested his Power – not wanting to reveal its extent to his captor – but he could *feel* how it was responding differently now that he had studied each aspect independently. He had been able to *feel* the shape of it as he learned what each of its component parts looked and felt like.

Damien knew, *knew* that he didn't need to read Azella's trove of literature on Aether. The wide, four-cornered base of the four 'normal' elements was already rising inside of him to complete the peak that would make it... Not a pyramid but a tetrahedron, with all the points equal and all connected.

Another ice-storm would not see him left helpless, even with the Realm's Power trapped in its Winter sleep. Another evil sorcerer would not find him – *or* his Realm – easy prey, as had Azella.

He had always hated the term 'Sorcerer-King' that his people had begun to call him. But he'd hated it as much because he didn't feel he could live up to it, as because it sounded intimidating.

Damien would still rather they adopted the nickname Adam had given him: 'Healer-King'; but he knew that was unlikely to stick. There would always be more Healing to be done, but the fewer efforts of sorcery would always be flashier.

And now...

Damien no longer feared being called 'sorcerer.'

But how to explain this internal journey to a woman who seemed to think his interest in the Elements had arisen entirely because of her attack with the salamanders? How to explain his feelings of unworthiness to someone who had always felt it was *she* being passed over, rather than the other way around? How to explain that she had given him a great gift by forcing him to realize that his inborn Power and wit and the education he had given himself were near the equal of a sorceress trained by an actual master of magick?

It was impossible.

Azella's own natural Power did not seem to touch the Elements. She seemed a natural siphon – absorbing the magick that emanated from all things.

Under normal circumstances, that would not harm anything. The fabric of Damien's Realm functioned on just that same Power, and the amount that Azella absorbed would be inconsequential compared to the total. *Was* inconsequential, as even pumping water from the ocean would be unnoticeable, and it was why he had never detected her magick before.

What Power she raised the natural ways – through joy and love and consensual sex – was hers to keep, of course. What Power she raised from crueler approaches...

Damien suspected she and her former Master had been very careful to keep it all within the built portions of the Keep and not where any part of the stone that was connected to the living Realm might give them away to Farivera's – to *Ilseador's* rightfully Bound and Crowned Monarch.

And perhaps they – or at least her former Master – had even somehow had a hand in *why* Ilseador had not had a properly and completely Bound Sorcerer-Monarch in so very long. It shouldn't be too hard to keep an eye on any potential Heirs to the Throne who had... *potential,* after all, and make sure something prevented them from ever being crowned. Damien's accession might well have been a horrible surprise from their perspective.

"You have not yet fulfilled our bargain," Azella said, and a hint of desperation was in her tone.

She had hoped for a year to wear down his resistance. A year – or a lifetime. And it had not yet been four months. Barely a turn from one season to the next.

"I don't need the literature on the last Element," Damien told her, serenely confident.

He held out one hand and a flame appeared over it, dancing. Air, Water, Earth appeared next, forming a perfect, balanced square. Then the square folded in on itself, Air linking to Earth and Fire to Water to create a tetrahedral shape rotating slowly over his palm. And within the center of the tetrahedron, a swirl of stars and burning, glowing gases formed: the Aether, birthplace of stars and all that follows from stars, re-created by the combination of the four states of matter represented by the four magickal Elements.

Azella's mouth hung open for a moment. She closed it with an almost audible snap and glared at him.

"Such Power, now that you have access to your Realm again," she said tauntingly.

The Sorcerer-King shook his head. "No, this is my own, though I was having trouble feeling the Earth when trapped so high above it for so long. The Realm... lets me use its Power, but not to play with." He gave her a half-envious smile. "Unlike you, I don't just absorb the excess magick that is everywhere."

The sorceress frowned. It apparently hadn't occurred to her that they gained and utilized magick in distinctly different ways.

"You were right," Damien told her. "On the ship, you told me I didn't know how to use my magick effectively or efficiently. It turns out that was largely because I'd had the wrong materials to learn from." He paused thoughtfully. "I wonder if that's why Grandfather aged and his spells finally failed him. It would stand to reason that he was an Elemental Mage, too."

Azella was shaking her head. "Elemental Mages have access to the Power of *one* Element. Occasionally they might have touches of one of the two others that are closest..." She eyed his tetrahedron suspiciously. "No one has the ability to work with all five Elements naturally. *I* do it," she added with some smugness, "But that's because I'm *not* an Elemental Mage."

"The Elements aren't distinct from each other," Damien tried to explain. "If an Elemental Mage can't handle all five, that's a problem with their perceptions, not their abilities. What we call the 'Elements' are simply different states of existence. Except for the Aether, of course."

Azella gave him an amused look. "And after less than a half-year of studies you know this better than all the sorcerers who have gone before you?"

Damien frowned. "It's not a matter of how long it takes to find a solution, Azella. The Truth is always there waiting for someone to notice it. It helps when someone looks at the problem with fresh eyes and few preconceptions."

Not to mention a prodigious memory and the ability to cross-correlate...

"And you're telling me that *you* can't absorb Power from the people and things around you?" she asked intently. "Because you *can* wield all five Elements."

The king nodded from side to side. "More or less. I imagine there's someone out there who can do both by nature. But as it's neither you nor me..." He paused. "Perhaps that is the distinction of a god."

The sorceress regarded him with relative calm, seeming to have set her ire aside as useless. Damien did not fool himself into thinking that she wouldn't take it out on *someone* later, unless he could distract her.

"So now I suppose you want to break our bargain, since you no longer *need* to read through my collection of volumes on the Aether."

"It's crossed my mind." He shrugged.

Azella's smile returned. "You haven't studied demons yet. Would you go home to your precious wife and the babe she's bearing – oh, yes, I know all about it – knowing that *demons* are beyond your skills... and definitely *not* beyond mine?"

Damien was sure the pale sorceress did not know *'all about'* the baby Genevieve was carrying. If she had, he had no doubt that she would have thrown it in his face that the baby hadn't been sired by him. Their secret was still safe. For now.

"You owe me *two* nights," Azella was saying. "Whether you want the books on Aether or not."

"I offered you a lifetime before." Damien reminded her.

She looked startled. "But now you have your Realm back..." Her eyes softened. "You *are* coming to care for me." Then her avarice and ambition were back. "Would you set her aside, your soul-bonded wife, bearing your child, and make *me* your Queen?"

He regarded her steadily. "I would abdicate in favor of Genevieve, for whom the Monarch's Blade has already spoken. I would divorce her and devote myself to you in our quiet cottage in a woodland glen. And *our* children."

She digested that. "And your bond to your Realm?"

"The Realm," the King of Ilseador told her, "does not care about human titles. It might release me to Bind Genevieve. Or it might keep me, and I could do my work from our cottage."

Azella the Unpitying, evil sorceress at the beginning of what could be a long and notorious career, shook her head. "I might be willing to give up the Power of an Evil Sorceress to be a Queen. But not for anything less."

Damien bowed his head, relieved more than he could say. It had been his duty to offer, as it had been his duty to give himself up to her to protect Emeralsee in the first place. But four months with this callow child had worn on him. An entire lifetime – even if only of the normal length – seemed far too long.

"Two nights, then. I will study your demons and then go home."

Azella smirked at him, and the king knew he had not won his freedom yet, regardless of what she appeared to have agreed to.

# Chapter SIXTEEN

# *Perpetual Check*

THE NEXT DAY MIKHAIL DID not appear to play chess or to escort him to the arena. The slave-boy who brought lunch was someone Damien had not taken note of before – younger and more bubbly. He was willing to gossip and confided that the Mistress had sent the mercenaries down to the town to await the first caravan, and that Mikhail and some of the other boys had been set to preparing for some large ritual magick.

The day after that, a very satisfied evil sorceress gave Damien the freedom of her keep – save for any locked rooms – and introduced him to her library. Her smug look suggested that she knew he was unlikely to explore much else, now that he had access to her full store of *books,* besides those in her office.

While he intended to prove her wrong on that count, the king had to admit that the library *was* very... alluring.

It was one room, not an entire complex, as was his own Royal Library in Emeralsee, but it was a very *large* room, with a balcony around the second story level. Personally, Damien felt they would have done better to have floored it in and used the center spaces for more shelves, but he knew that many people appreciated cavernous open spaces more than the books that might fill them.

"This section is the Elemental Magick," Azella pointed. "You've been through all of those except the Aether, of course. These here are non-magickal – histories and legends, mostly."

She turned quickly away from several shelves of newer looking volumes, and the dark-haired man thought he noticed a faint blush in her cheeks. Curious, he marked the location in his mind to examine later.

"The upper level is Demonology," the pale sorceress pointed upwards

. Two spiraling staircases that looked more ornate than safe – no outer railings at all – were the only access points.

"I've spelled the stairs to allow you to go up and down," she added, again smugly. "Don't try to have anyone else go up, though."

"Why?" he asked. Staring up at what seemed to be *hundreds* of books. "What would happen?"

"Oh, I let the stairs choose," she said flippantly. "When they're being kind, they merely turn into a slide. When they're less kind they wait till the trespasser is almost at the top, then fold flat and let them drop."

She gave him a flirtatious look from beneath her long, pale lashes. "I *have* gotten them to avoid whirling around and chopping the climber to bits. It's so *messy* to clean up, and this *is* a library after all."

As Damien struggled to contain his horror, she went on, "It's a pair of minor demons Bound into the stairs, of course."

"Of course," he echoed faintly.

"*You'll* be fine," Azella smiled wickedly at the stairs. "They know what will happen to *them* if they let anything happen to *you.*"

"Oh."

"I'll leave you to it, then," she said. "Even for you, this might take a little while. Oh, leave the books and any notes you make up there."

She pointed out a study-nook, lit by one of the clerestory windows that angled in from each corner of the roof. "We wouldn't want any of this to get into the wrong hands. Not only is the knowledge dangerous, but some of the books are a bit vicious if they are allowed to leave the pacification spell that I have up there."

Damien no longer felt so confident as she stretched up to kiss his cheek and left the room.

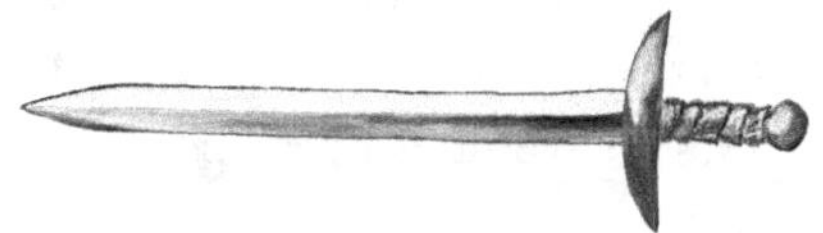

Demonology was clearly Azella's specialty, and had been her Master's before her.

The sheer number of books told Damien that, as well as the security precautions. He felt nervous every time he set foot on those open-sided spiral stairs. It didn't help that the stair-demons must have had a sense of humor and would start shaking when he was partway up.

Simply deciding where to begin was a challenge. The books were organized alphabetically, by author, with the largest single section attributable to *Anonymous*. There was no *Beginner's Guide to Demons* or anything resembling that; Damien checked, examining every single book's cover and unrolling every scroll at least a foot on the first day.

There was a completely unreasonable number of scrolls.

He tried asking Azella for advice on where to begin, but apparently this was her new delaying tactic. She agreed, but she would only suggest *one* book for each *one* more night of love-making.

He narrowed his eyes at that and turned away to her silvery laugh.

However, after three days of spot-reading and making absolutely no headway – the books all used terminology that he was unfamiliar with and never defined anything – the king was just about ready to give in.

It would take him *months* to read through all of these books... *years* even. When things didn't make sense to him, Damien had to slog through the reading like anyone else.

And there was *nothing* about Demonology that made sense to him, starting with why any rational human would attempt to summon a demon in the first place.

Some of the readings were obviously *not* written by anyone rational, which explained those at least. Some others seemed to have been written by priests interested solely in banishing the creatures.

The vast majority, however, fell somewhere in the middle. Many of the books, even the priestly ones, seemed to have been written to intentionally obfuscate their subjects, but the bits that did make sense were enough to give him nightmares.

As a last-ditch attempt, Damien settled down with something that claimed to be an *Encyclopædia of the Demonic Planes* and began to read from the first page. As claimed, it was largely a listing of 'types' that the author claimed to have either summoned or researched along with preposterous claims for the demons' strengths and abilities.

The style was dry, the tone confiding in that breathless *'aren't you just amazed at what I know'* way that he found most particularly irritating.

Damien found himself drifting off... which in and of itself was unusual when he was reading. He had once read through the entire potato breeding records of County Brindlewell – two hundred years' worth – at one sitting and never so much as felt his attention dim.

He jerked himself awake, took a brisk walk around the balcony, and tried again.

When it happened again, Damien stood up, stretched, and frowned. He wasn't actually sleepy. Not the slightest bit. And he hadn't exactly been falling *asleep*... he'd just been staring at the same page for....

He looked up at the sky visible through the four clerestory windows and was shocked to see it was coming up on evening. He had begun with the book first thing this morning – surely, he hadn't been sitting there like a gape-mouthed fool for *hours?* Had he?

Frustrated, Damien marked his place and returned the book to its spot on the shelf.

Another harrowing trip down the stairs and then the familiar trek back to Azella's suite. She had threatened to have dinner sent away if he didn't arrive at a reasonable time, and he had yet to determine where the kitchens were, despite now having the run of the place. Since he'd been missing lunch while he tried to sort through the Demonology books, he wasn't willing to lose a second meal and he trudged along resentfully, head bent and mind somewhat blank.

Abruptly the king stopped, almost frozen in place.

She had trapped him in the library almost as effectively as when she had placed compulsion spells in the beginning to keep him in her bed. Or... *just* as effectively. Had she...?

Of course she had. Damien grimaced and brushed away the cobwebs of the sorceress's compulsion spells. Suddenly the hallways off to the sides of the corridor he was walking looked brighter and more inviting rather than dark and vaguely repulsive.

To blazes with dinner. Damien was going to explore.

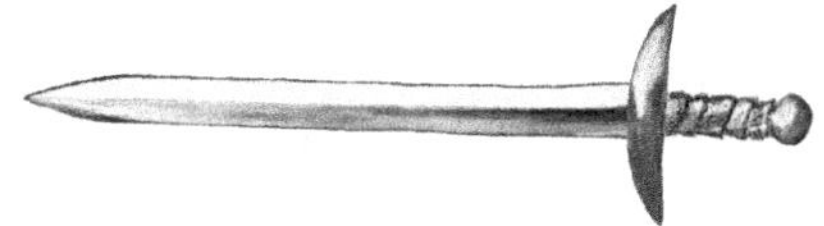

# Chapter SEVENTEEN

# *Zwischenzug*

H E RETURNED TO AZELLA'S SUITE quite late, but feeling rather self-satisfied.

One of the abilities he had just begun to discover in the last year or two was a talent for psychometry – he could sometimes gain a sense of the people who had touched an object previously, even in the distant past. Previously it had been like trying to catch whispers on a windy day and only the strongest emotions came through much at all. He'd been able to use it for research into the archives, literally reading between the lines, though it was always possible that the archivist's emotions were related to something other than the material being recorded.

Now, with his growing skills, his psychometry seemed to have been enhanced as well – he could see it as a connection between Earth and Aether, the latter of which encompassed emotions, thoughts, and soul. It turned out to be very handy in navigating this heap of stone. A brush of a hand against a corner as the owner of the hand thought about where they were headed was all the guide he needed.

He'd found the kitchens – unintentionally terrifying the cooks before he'd enchanted them with his sincere and entirely unmagickal appreciation of their art.

He'd found the slave-boys' quarters, where he was an immediate sensation as Azella's chosen Apprentice who refused to accept her as his Mistress. Damien had seen most of the older youths about the keep by now on errands, and he had small appreciation for their constant attempts at one-upmanship, and too strong a memory of their pretty, petty faces the night that Mikhail had been 'punished.'

The younger ones, however, were largely new to him, and the king was always fascinated by children. He wished there was something he could do for these boys, but they were Bound to Azella by the Power of their names.

And he'd found the slave-girls' quarters, where Denisa was the only current resident, it turned out. There had been another, she told him, prior to the attempt on Emeralsee.

The moon-dark was the best time to summon demons, and when it coincided with one of the four Quarters of the year, so much the better. There had been such a concatenation of circumstances the previous Autumn... and since then, Denisa had been the only girl. She'd apparently helped prepare for the dread event, and she gave him a rather gruesomely detailed description of both preparation and aftermath.

The girl had inadvertently given him the key he needed, however.

Azella had kept her book of spells handy during the preparations to ensure that everything was set up exactly properly. Since the ritual itself took place on the flat, open roof of the Keep, this had made things complicated because the book could not be read by sunlight. The sorceress had required a canopy to be erected and draped with heavy curtains and Denisa had been required to hold the lantern to properly illuminate the pages. One of the boys had attempted to sneak a glance when the Mistress was busy and the book was exposed to daylight – he'd promptly keeled over, fast asleep and then been whipped for laziness as well as snooping when he woke.

Needless to say, the sorceress was displeased that the king had missed dining with her and was further displeased to hear that he intended to go back to the library later.

"Why even bother come back to tell me?" Azella grumped as he leaned against the doorframe.

"I didn't want you to stay up late worrying about me," Damien told her mildly.

Actually, he had considered going straight back to the library, but he'd wanted to see how she'd react to the knowledge that he intended to read by lantern-light. It was... disappointing. Was there more to the method than just light?

The pale sorceress rolled her eyes. "I'm hardly likely to do *that*."

She seemed to realize that made her sound more uncaring than the image she was trying to portray and added belatedly, "How much trouble could you get into in the Keep after all? I've locked and warded all the truly troublesome areas."

Damien shrugged. "I was raised to use my manners." He gave her a wry grin. "Now you'll have time to summon Mikhail to fill your bed instead of languishing in hopes of my return."

She lifted her chin, eyes flashing. "Mikhail has other duties and I doubt I've ever *languished* in my life."

He had to concede her that one. "I suppose not. You're more of a doer than the sort who waits for rescue."

From him it was definitely a compliment, but as she was still sorting that out, he added, "Where is Mikhail anyways? I could use a game or two of chess – or someone to practice with – to break up the monotony of those books."

"*I* could break up that monotony for you," Azella reminded him. "And I'd even give you an idea of where to start your reading *after.*" She looked coquettishly up at him through her lashes.

"Oh, I seem to be getting that figured out," he said casually. "And you don't play chess."

"Are you indeed?" He caught a look of astonishment from the sorceress, quickly masked.

Damien shrugged. "I suppose I'll see you later then. Or tomorrow."

She waved him away.

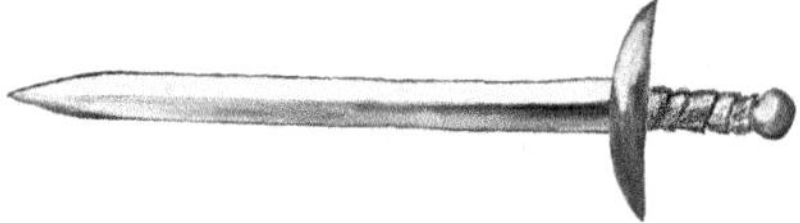

Lantern-light definitely helped. Damien wasn't falling asleep – or into a daze or whatever it had been – anymore.

Unfortunately, it wasn't *enough*.

There was still far too much to read here.

The sorcerer-king settled down in a chair and tented his hands in front of his face as he surveyed the vast quantities of books and scrolls.

There had to be a trick here. Azella was hardly the reader he was. Even with the encouragement and tutelage of her former Master and the ten years she had been his Apprentice and the two after that, Damien doubted that she had read a tenth of this.

And yet, clearly, she was a Mistress of the Art. The books he *had* read had made it clear that dabblers did not survive their first attempts.

What was he missing?

Absently, he called up the tetrahedron of Elements that he had showed Azella a week or so earlier, letting it rotate slowly on all three axes as it would.

Elements. Hah. States of Being, more like. He'd meant it when he told her that an Elemental mage should be able to touch all five States – and was limited only by their own perspective.

Which was not to say that one's perspective could not be a serious limitation. Doubtless most of them felt such a strong affinity to one State that they really could not reach out to touch another. Or not very *well*.

Earth – solids – were where his own connections began, but he could feel the change to liquid, thence gas, thence fire. There should be a better word than 'fire' for that State, but he had none to name it with.

And then the fifth State that was an evolved property of the other four – currently he was equating it with Soul or Consciousness, but as with Fire, he suspected there was a more fundamental way to look at it.

The small structure lit up the very large room with its perfection and completeness.

A solved puzzle, illuminating the entirely foggy problem of demons.

He was *missing* something.

That Azella knew what he was missing, he had no doubt.

That she would give him the answer – no matter what he did *for* her, *with* her, or *to* her, he *highly* doubted.

*This* was the core of the Power she laid claim to – not her own intrinsic ability, which she barely seemed to acknowledge, but the core knowledge that she used to maintain this keep and her position in whatever society Evil Wizards shared. And it was how she had slain her Master, who had loved her, taught her, and betrayed her.

Another mystery. Surely such a savvy creature as her former Master must have been – he'd lived over a thousand years, she'd said – could not have been so unwise as to train an Apprentice to such Power as Azella and then create a situation that would raise her ire. At least not while leaving himself vulnerable to her retaliation. Had it been some sort of misunderstanding?

Damien had seen enough of Azella's methods to guess that the extraction of Power raised from sex could segue into something much darker – draining and permanently disabling – if the evil wizard's 'partner' was unable to shield herself. Or himself.

He could also could imagine that a man who had lived so long might not realize that his Apprentice and light-o'-love and perfect mate would not have the emotional maturity to understand what he was about after ten years of close... adoration?... and having her emotional growth frozen along with her barely nubile body.

If that were the case... it would likely do the young sorceress – and the world – no good for her to know it. A sense of guilt *might* turn her from her dark path... but it would be just as likely to make her feel like there was not even the slightest bit of light left in her soul, and thereby remove whatever frail barriers of conscience remained to restrain her actions.

Damien had felt her inner turmoil when he had told her how important having children was to him. In part it was true – to be a father *was* a deep-seated need within him – but it had also been a test lure to see if he could pull her away from this path that seemed as much impressed upon her as chosen.

He couldn't read someone as clearly as Adam could, but he'd sensed – too late – that children were exactly the *wrong* lure for *her*. Azella's turmoil had been a horror of child-rearing in some visceral way... not of childbirth which so many women feared, but of the *raising* of a child.

Likely it echoed back to whatever strange situation had led a Powerfully Talented young princess to be placed in a slave auction... which suggested some dire situation in her birth-family. They had done so poorly by *her* that Azella could not trust herself to do better by any child of her own. Having her body frozen in this near-child-like state was a solution to ever having to face that question.

It was a problem that the sorcerer-king could appreciate from a personal perspective.

While his own parents had been warm and loving, they had been ripped from him at the tender age of ten. He'd arguably been more than half-feral for the next four years until Jason had tamed him, much as he himself had tamed the mice in the Royal Library. His only parental models during that period had been the hateful, cold woman who had, did he but know it, betrayed his parents and sister to their death, and his terrifying grandfather.

He'd trusted that *Genevieve* had a better place to build from, being her father's beloved only child... until he'd recently discovered that Duke Aldred had *known* what physical and emotional torture she was undergoing with her first husband. And that during that time Aldred had considered – *not* throwing Harald out – but finding a *replacement* for his own beloved and long-dead wife to sire another Heir when Genevieve didn't conceive through eight long *years* of that private hell.

As, indeed, Aldred had actually *done* when she failed to successfully carry a child to term in five years as Damien's soul-bonded Queen. It was that for which the king had stripped his father-in-law's title-by-courtesy and temporarily exiled him and Ciriis to Cloudcroft. And for all that he hoped Darvin would be able to make contact with Aldred, the situation still made Damien simmer with fury.

Suffice it to say that he was no longer certain of his wife's background as a potential parent either.

Azella's reluctance had seemed... deeper somehow, though.

He stood up and shook his head. He didn't need to solve the mystery of the sorceress' past.

He needed to understand Demonology sufficiently to meet his bargain with her – and to protect his Realm *from* her.

Damien headed back down the trembling spiral stairs, giving up for the day.

At the bottom, he remembered the shelf she had tried to divert his attention away from when she'd brought him into the library, and went over to look at what it contained.

The king was amused to see that it was romance novels – as if the fact that the sorceress yearned for romance was something that she thought she could conceal from him at this late date. He briefly considered taking a few of them up to the bedroom for light reading and to tease her... but that would be cruel after she had clearly not wanted him to see her novels.

He did sit down to skim through a few of the books anyways. There had been none of these in the Royal Library – the fairytales he had read had been shelved in the Literature and History and Mythology sections – but there had been no shelf for the fictional writing of modern authors. Genevieve had never seemed interested in fiction... if his lady Guardswomen had, they hadn't shared that with their prince or king. Neither had his male Guards, for that matter.

His face was burning within moments, but he was hooked by the story. Of course. The *story*.

Azella found him there some hours later, wandering by to taunt him, perhaps, on his lack of progress.

When she saw *what* he was reading, *her* face went crimson, and she tried to leave quietly, before he noticed her. At least none of the colors she ever wore would clash with her flush, and certainly not the white-patterned black gown she currently wore.

Her quiet escape could never have worked, since Damien noticed *everything,* and he lowered the book he was reading to smile at her. It had the effect of freezing her in place, looking rather like a startled deer.

"Are you going to laugh at me for having those?" she demanded, perhaps reading more into his gentle look than was there.

It apparently didn't occur to her to pretend that the well-thumbed books were ones she'd never touched, remnants of some previous user of the library. Although attributing their presence to her former Master might have seemed a bit ludicrous and who else would have dared cause an entire shelf to be devoted to such material?

"Laugh?" Damien tilted his head. "At you? Whyever for? Some of these are very interesting stories."

Indeed, and they were, though the dog-eared pages made it clear that the person who had read and re-read these books wasn't reading solely for the *stories.*

Azella hesitated. She'd been prepared for scorn, apparently, not to be taken seriously.

"Of course..." Damien stretched, knowing that she'd be watching... knowing what she'd be watching *for* even better after exploring her favorite reading material... "These books do set some rather... high expectations."

He gave her a wry smile. "I'm not sure if a woman who reads these things would ever be satisfied with a mere mortal lover."

That brought her receding flush back full force, and she looked away. Damien's heart clenched as her reaction confirmed that she gave *herself* as some sort of a trade to the demons she summoned. It seemed... dangerous.

"You do an excellent job of... meeting expectations," the pale young sorceress said, not meeting his eyes. *"All* expectations."

That drew a chuckle out of him. Not exactly a *surprised* chuckle, though.

"I've had lots of good teachers," he said dryly, and her eyes snapped to his in her own look of startlement.

He raised his eyebrows. "You didn't know about my other lovers?"

"Besides your wife and your... prince?" She actually looked somewhat shocked. "I would have thought you were the type to come virginal to your marriage-bed. I never could understand how you could have that connection with someone else, but it was obvious in the way your astral forms interacted with each other."

Damien laughed aloud at that. "You would be the only person who thinks so, then. Certainly, my Courtiers seem to assume I'm as randy as my grandfather and as disinclined to consider marriage-bonds as inviolable – neither theirs nor mine."

He shook his head a little wistfully. "As to the other... I wasn't really given a choice, though I suppose I *could* have said 'no'." His smile was wry again. "Not that there are many seventeen-year-old boys who would probably say 'no' to a beautiful woman whom they already respect and love seducing them."

Certainly not in the middle of an emotional upheaval when Ciriis had seemed to be one of only a couple of supports he could depend on.

Azella sat herself in another of the overstuffed chairs, pulling her knees up and wrapping her arms around them in fascination. "What happened?"

Apparently, to her, this was a romance novel in real life.

Damien weighed whether he should tell her. It was old news, after all. But if this would give her another key to twist him around... He decided to tell her, but without names.

"My... friends took me on a little trip when I was seventeen to visit the family holding of one of them. I hadn't been out of my grandfather's Castle in seven years – not since my parents had been killed. I thought... I *hoped*... that this might be a chance for me to escape for good. While we were visiting, I wrote – secretly, I thought – to my *other* grandparents, begging for sanctuary."

Ah, it still hurt...

"I should have known better. To take me in would be to defy the king, and my grandfather had already killed their daughter, my mother, simply for standing with my father. And he'd done that in open Court, before all the gathered nobility, and while my father wore the Heir's Ring. At seventeen *I* was merely a half-forgotten princeling who could do nothing but bring disaster on the rest of the family – who had somehow been spared his wrath so far.

"My other... friend, not the one whose family we were staying with. She found me crying with my grandparents' letter – telling me 'no' and not to contact them again."

Damien gave the sorceress a wry look. "She found a way to soothe me. And to completely rivet my interest. I'm told I followed her around like a puppy for the next few weeks."

He snorted. "I only discovered a few months ago that it was the friends I had traveled with who had asked my grandparents to turn me down..."

Yes, and he'd forgiven Adam. He had. Completely.

Ciriis... maybe not so much.

"Why would they do that?" Azella asked, her eyes wide.

Damien closed his. "Because they were trying to raise me to be a king. They needed me to come back to my grandfather's Castle. To be under his eye, where he would remember he had another possible Heir beyond my odious Uncle Oskar."

*There,* Jason, he thought to himself. *I've said it. Aloud, even.*

He had always been careful to refer to the corrupt and perverted youngest son of his grandfather as *'Prince* Oskar' – hating everything that the vile man had done to hurt so many of the people he loved and wanting to deny any familial relationship.

But... to Jason, Oskar had been both that awful human being and... his first love.

And Jason had *needed* for someone *else* to see that. To acknowledge it. For everything Jason had done for him... for everything Jason *was* to Damien, he had promised to try.

The pale sorceress sniffed a little disdainfully. "It doesn't sound like they were very good friends if they put their plan ahead of what was right for you."

It was... almost a startling sentiment to come from *her.* And in any other case, he would have been happy to see her able to express a truly *human* reaction. In this case, however...

Damien opened his eyes and looked at her with compassion. "They are the very best friends I could have. They taught me that what is 'right for me' is not sufficient if it harms others. It was... a very hard lesson. But in the end, it brought me everything I could ever have dreamed of wanting. And more."

She frowned. This was not a direction she would want the conversation to go in.

"So, she was your first lover then? You have had three before me, counting your wife and your... prince?"

Damien gave her a wry grin. "I have had *seventeen* lovers before you. Counting my Queen. And my Prince." Well, and Jason *was.*

Azella looked at him almost uncomprehendingly, then looked almost repulsed, and he laughed.

"Come now, you are hardly a one to complain. I've seen the stable of bed-boys you keep, and you've told me yourself you've had others still."

"They each came to *my* bed a virgin," she said somewhat primly.

"And so did your Master, I am sure," Damien chuckled again.

She glared. "He was the *Master*. It was *different*." She paused, then added, even more primly. "And as long as I was his Apprentice there was no other who touched *me*. Nor do I permit anyone to touch *my*... belongings."

Damien wondered if she realized he could tell that she had quite nearly admitted her provenance as her master's slave.

"Nor did the Master touch another woman while he had me. How many of those lovers have *you* taken since you swore your marriage vows?"

"Four, counting yourself and your pretty Mikhail," Damien answered easily. After all, those last were not of his choosing.

Not that taking Jason and Adam as lovers had exactly been by *choice* either.

It had been something they were willing to do to prevent the magick from literally tearing him apart and killing both him and Genevieve. He would be forever grateful... and he didn't regret a single glorious moment they had spent together... but he would much rather have been able to hold to his marriage vows and simply have had Genevieve and only Genevieve. Forever and always.

His beautiful, brave, brilliant *pregnant* Queen...

The renewed Bond with his Realm had not restored the soul-bond. He had some vague sense of her well-being – her *physical* well-being, and that of the child – through the Realm. But he knew nothing of how she was feeling... besides that her pregnancy-induced nausea had diminished – that being the *only* thing that had come across the soul-bond since Azella had pinched it off.

The sorceress gave him a disgruntled look. "One of the others would be that princely lover you were flying about with in astral form, I suppose. Your own Apprentice."

He hadn't thought of Jason in those particular terms, but it fit.

His Apprentice in ruling the Realm as well as in using the magicks that it lent him as Crown Prince and Duke of Emeralsee to do what must be done. He'd had little chance to teach his older friend and mentor any of it... the Realm itself had trained *him*, but Jason was not yet so closely Bound.

Perhaps the ghost of Queen Marian – their mutual ancestress – was helping Jason and Genevieve as she had helped Damien. Queen Marian had been the last properly Bound and Crowned monarch of Ilseador, the grandmother of his own grandfather, the Evil Wizard-King Reginald that Azella dismissed as an amateur despite his eighty-three-year reign of terror.

Though Marian had not herself been a sorceress.

And whatever Jason and Genevieve were doing for the Realm wasn't *enough*.

Damien was spending a part of every day making those many adjustments and changes that the Realm relied upon him for. The tasks were always innumerable in the early Spring...

"Who was the other?"

He had almost forgotten Azella, and had to recall himself to the topic of conversation. Thinking about Genevieve always made him a bit drifty, and thinking about his Realm always pulled him back to his never-ending work...

From the look on her face, the sorceress did not appreciate his distraction.

"The other? Oh. My other lover." Damien hesitated on this one. How to explain Adam...? Perhaps least complicated was... "The other friend who took me on that long ago trip when I was a boy."

She looked at him with bemusement. "Before or after you knew that he had told your grandparents not to take you?"

"After." Damien felt himself blushing, remembering both the circumstances of that revelation and when – and why and how – they had taken their relationship in this entirely unexpected direction.

"Hmmn. You may be the most... *forgiving* person I have ever met, Damien," Azella said with a shake of her head.

The Sorcerer-King of Ilseador sighed. "I haven't had a choice about that either, Azella. There were... simply too *many* people who were involved in my grandfather's reign of terror. I couldn't purge the Realm of everyone who'd caused hurt. I had to see who could be salvaged... whose souls were not so damaged as to be able to take a second chance and actually do good with it."

The pale sorceress tilted her head. "Not that. Personally. You seem not to carry a grudge for anyone who has caused you harm. You've even *loved* some of them."

There was... a strange light in her eyes.

"I wouldn't go *that* far," Damien said dryly. "Harald Elsevier – Genevieve's first husband – is someone I will *never* forgive."

Lord Aldred, despite Damien's still simmering... irritation... was still his father-in-law and second father and the man who had helped him learn to rule. Provided it was made absolutely clear that Aldred and Ciriis' child was not going to be the focus of rebels pushing a second civil war, Damien would forgive him as well.

And Ciriis. Eventually.

"He hurt *her*. Not *you*. But you seem to have forgiven your *grandfather*. And even his Apprentice."

Damien cringed internally. "My grandfather... no. I would say it's not even my *place* to do that. He hurt so many people worse than what he did to me. But I've read enough of his writings to... wonder how he ended up as a tyrant. And an evil wizard."

And to wonder how to prevent himself from traveling that same road...

"And Lord Prydeen... no. He gave me – us – a gift, or a curse, with his dying breath. But *forgive* him? No."

And there were others he could not forgive, beginning with Lady Theresa Anvliyar. And Prince Oskar – though he could try to... *accept* that Jason had somehow loved him. And Alexa Solway, who had nearly broken her own son. Or rather *grandson*.

Perhaps it was just Lady Theresa and Countess Alexa and Prince Oskar. And Lord Prydeen.

"A gift *or* a curse?" Azella asked curiously. "You don't know which?"

"He claimed the Gift he was born with was Foresight and gave us – Genevieve and me – what he *claimed* was a prediction."

And *damned* if he would tell her more than that.

She looked at him thoughtfully, then rose and went to the door. "You are... more complicated than I had realized, King Damien Alsterling." And she stepped out of the library.

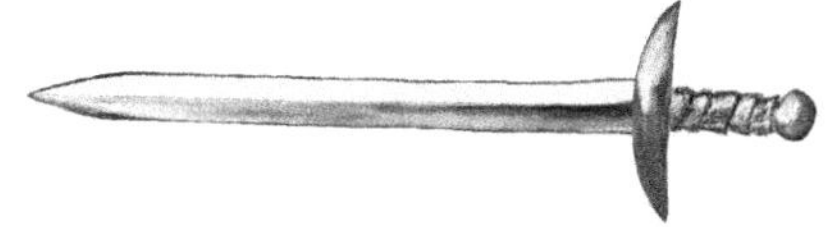

# Chapter EIGHTEEN

# *Zugzwang*

AFTER THAT STRANGE CONVERSATION, AZELLA did not importune Damien again. He caught her looking at him at odd moments, a quiet and thoughtful look on her face.

If only she was considering whether he truly believed that she deserved a second chance... If only she would take it. If only...

If only he could figure out how to deal with demons and go home. Preferably *before* he was forced to live up to that promise to *be* her second chance. To his private shame, Damien no longer was willing to give up everything that made life worth living to protect his Realm.

His mind was increasingly captured by the idea of the baby daughter who would soon be born. The other children that would follow... also implied by that curse or prophecy. The *family* that awaited his return.

Genevieve and Jason and Adam.

Lord Aldred and Ciriis.

Tim and Aryllis and Lena and... Genevieve.

Always and forever, Genevieve.

With determination, Damien turned his attention to the books that seemed most useful out of that profusion: the *Encyclopædia* and the books about banishing demons. After all, he didn't really need to know how to summon the creatures or control them. Or even bind them, as Azella's Master had bound the stair-demons. *Un*binding demons might be useful, though only if he could then also banish them.

He spent some time with Denisa.

The girl had few illusions about her fate. The Mistress was preparing for a demon-summoning, and she was the offering. She wasn't even bitter about Damien's refusal to deflower her. She wanted to live longer, but she was still her Mistress' creature and claimed she felt honored to serve the Mistress' will.

Damien shuddered and asked what she would have done if she had been able to persuade young Rob to do as she asked. Rob, he knew, had harbored notions of spiriting her away.

Denisa, however, knew that she was Bound by her true-name. She could not leave without Azella's permission. She had merely hoped to be rendered unfit to be a demon-offering, and then to serve the Mistress in some longer-term capacity.

"And if you could be free entirely?" Damien asked. He had some notion now of what might be done about the Binding Power of a true-name.

Denisa looked at him with a blank expression. "You mean... with no one to own me? To go where I will and do as I choose?"

The sorcerer-king nodded. "What would you do?"

She was brighter than he had guessed at first on the ship. He'd sketched out a chess-board on her floor and made up counters for the pieces and she'd picked up the idea quickly. She was also more Powerful than Mikhail, more Powerful than – as he'd told the boy – most of the freeborn people who earned their living through use of their magick.

More Powerful by nature, in truth, than all but the highest nobility of his Realm – whose families seemed to have risen to their position though their unknown but natural gift for magick.

"Why..." Denisa's light hazel-green eyes seemed to glow. "I have learned but little from the Mistress, but enough, I think to be able to make my way in the world."

Damien began to relax. He was ready to tell her that Rob would near certainly be willing to make a home with her, but she continued.

"I know how to extract enough magick to extend my life, if not my youth. I would hide myself well and collect what knowledge I could until I could restore my youth and build me my own keep. And then I would be Powerful enough to protect myself and claim my own demesne."

Damien's heart fell. "What about... using your Power to help others? To build a happy life? To support yourself while you make a home and a family?"

She had no model for these things, after all. Her origins were, like Mikhail's, from those same breeding programs.

The girl tossed her braid back over her shoulder, the rich mahogany of her hair a contrast to the un-dyed wool of her fine woolen dress. "Rob spoke of these things also. A small cottage. Babes. Work from morn till night, cooking and cleaning and caring for squalling things. I have been down to the village, milord. I have seen how the women there live. They are servants, even if they are each a mistress of their own cottage, enslaved by the needs of their 'families' and their own mortality. Why should I dream of such a thing if I am to dream of impossibilities?"

"For love," Damien tried to explain. "For the touch of someone else's hand that is neither forced nor coerced. For *choices* of your own that do not destroy the choices of others."

She looked at him disbelievingly. "I have seen much of labor and little of this 'love' you speak of. I would rather dream of a long life and luxury. And if that means I live in the shadow of the Mistress and work her will, I would be most pleased. If it meant I might *become* as the Mistress, that might be even better, but she holds my true-name, so it is not like to happen."

She was the same as Mikhail.

Damien had tried to show each of them another path.

And failed.

Azella had been amused by his efforts – duly reported by both young people. But she had banned him – using her Bound demons – from visiting the boys again, especially the younger ones. He guessed that she thought *they* might be more open to his word-pictures of a future outside of the influence of evil.

Damien had learned the way to free a person of the tyranny of their true-name.

And he did not dare use it to free Mikhail or Denisa – or any of the older boys – lest he loose a plague of young Evil Wizards upon Farivera and Sindala. And eventually upon Ilseador and other Realms.

At least his studies of the banishment of demons – and the various types of demons – were going well, though he needed to study in the night by lantern-light lest the spells on the books put him to sleep. Those wonderful clerestory windows were an effective protection against getting anything accomplished during the day.

Damien didn't mind the reversal in his days and nights – it meant he usually had Azella's bed all to himself, and after all the south-facing windows never brought much light into the room anyways.

But the change irritated the sorceress. Finally, she gave up remonstrating with him, and trying to wake him from his deep mid-day sleep, and switched herself around to the same schedule. With a smirk, she told him that she was coming close to the date for her planned demon summoning and it was as well to make herself comfortable with being awake at night.

"You don't really believe I will summon a demon, do you, my sorcerer-king?" Azella said with gentle mockery one morning as they were settling to sleep. She toyed with his hair, but made no other move to touch him.

Damien propped his head up on one arm to look at her. "I believe you entirely."

"Then why seek to spend so much time with Denisa? You know by now that she will be my offering. You will only make yourself more miserable when you see the fate to which she goes."

"I hadn't really planned to *watch*," he said dryly. "It seems rather too dangerous for a casual observer."

To put it mildly.

Azella smiled in that lazy, superior way she still affected. "But as my Apprentice, your place is at my side. Most *especially* for a demon summoning."

Damien shook his head. "I may be your colleague in magick, milady, but I am most assuredly *not* your Apprentice."

The pale sorceress traced a finger down his bare chest. "Of course. And you are here *entirely* by choice." She smirked. "You have not tested my wards and shields. You continue to sleep in my bed – even if that is *all* you will do here. And you have not made any fuss about the single suit of clothes I have permitted you."

Her eyes went low-lidded, and her smile predatory. "Nor have you asked me for *help* in your studies of the summoning of demons. I think you know who is in control here."

"I have not questioned your control over this keep," the dark-haired man said slightly evasively. "And it would be rude to test your wards when I've no need to do so."

He ignored her comment about clothes and sleeping spaces. Both were irritants... but he had lived through far less comfort in the Royal Library in his youth and had no *great* complaints.

And knowing that he had choices... helped a great deal.

She looked at him knowingly.

"You don't seem to have any interest in me anymore," Damien went on. "Why don't you send me off to sleep somewhere else?"

Azella looked even more amused. "The Power raised by sex can also be enhanced by abstaining for a time."

He knew that. The soul-bond's hungry and impractical demands had made that excruciatingly clear.

"A demon-summoning demands all of my resources. Having you here beside me makes the *abstaining* more Powerful still." She paused. "I will be raising Power through pain again before I perform the rituals as well."

Her eyes seemed old and – not *wise,* but *cruel* – as she waited to gauge his reaction.

Damien went very still. "The same as you did before?"

She regarded him coolly. "There are other ways. But that one seemed unexpectedly effective... especially when you added *your* emotional pain to the mix."

He swallowed. "I'm shielded now. You can't raise Power off of me without my explicit permission."

Azella's smile was coldly calculating. "You will give it to me by choice if you wish to Heal my victim. You cannot pretend to me that you do not still have a fondness for Mikhail."

No. He could not. Pray the Gods that she didn't realize he would react even more strongly – probably – if she chose to victimize one of the younger boys.

"At least you don't mince words," he said a little bitterly.

She shrugged. "Why bother? You are as much my chattel as any of these others, should I choose to exert my Powers, Damien. Unless you can master Demonology, I will always be your superior in strength and Power and since you will not *ask* for my help..."

Her blue-grey eyes had a look of triumph...

...and something clicked.

"The books in the library are nothing but decoys," Damien said slowly. "The only ones that truly show how to summon a demon are in your study. And under your spells of protection."

"Or my spells of pacification," she admitted casually. Azella rolled onto her back, brushing the thin sheet down below her small, proud breasts and looked at him seductively. "Change your mind about anything?"

He narrowed his eyes at her. "Maybe..."

She laughed a little nastily. "The offer is rescinded for now, my handsome lover. I am saving myself for the summoning."

"You mean saving yourself for the demon." Damien put it into words, though she'd hinted at it before. "How much suppressed lust does it take for you to be able to give yourself over like that, Azella?"

She smiled lazily. "Oh, Damien, *that* is hardly the issue. Demons can be lovers to – how did you put it – exceed high expectations that *'mere mortal lovers'* never could. And since that *is* how they transfer their Power to mortals... or at least the most *effective* way... it is more than worth it even were it not a pleasure in and of itself."

He blinked. That was *not* what he'd expected to hear her say.

"Of course, they can also *take* Power from mortals through sex as well," she added. "It depends entirely on the bargain that is struck and – what other offerings they may find acceptable."

He could imagine what that might mean. He wished he couldn't.

"But just because *I* am abstaining certainly doesn't mean that *you* need to," Azella continued wickedly. "You *would* like to give Mikhail something pleasant to remember before he becomes my victim and your patient once again, would you not?"

The beautiful youth entered as she said that, clearly summoned. How, Damien still did not know, since Mikhail could not hear Azella's voice in his head. It had been nearly two weeks since he had seen the young man, and the impact of his intense sexuality was greater for having been absent.

"Damien..." he said in a low, seductive voice, and the king was startled to realize that the boy was mixing his Power into the name... Damien's *true-name,* that he had inadvertently given him so many months earlier.

"Mikhail," he said reprovingly as he hastily readjusted his own layers of protection to prevent this trick from working. "You told me you would treat that as a gift."

The youth wilted slightly. Damien had used his 'disappointed swordmaster' voice – copied from Adam and Jason and even Genevieve... and a tone he had heard all too many times for himself.

But... "And I have also *told* you, Damien, that my Mistress' will is mine in all things."

The king's eyes slid over to the pale sorceress.

She shrugged. "He has the Power of your true-name, for you gave it to him. Why, I have no idea. I have given him the Power to use it – temporarily."

That at least explained what he'd felt when Mikhail had purred his name.

Azella believed there was no way to break the hold that a true-name held over a person. If Damien didn't respond to Mikhail's... *overtures,* she would know he had found a way around that, and he would lose a weapon that he might need later.

Reluctantly, the dark-haired king released his own protections – but slowly, as if they were crumbling under the continued assault.

And he waited until Mikhail purred his name again before allowing them to open entirely.

It was a *choice* he was making, he told himself. The better to lose this battle and win the war. That was what this entire time had been – four months he had been here now – a series of skirmishes to position himself to win the war.

If only Kandy had lived. She and her Raphael would be the monarchs of Ilseador now, and he would merely be an exceptionally talented Healer. It was all he *wanted* to be.

Well, a Healer and Duke-Consort of Elaarwen at Genevieve's side.

His Genevieve...

Damien closed his eyes and surrendered his body to the beautiful youth's blandishments.

And if either Mikhail or Azella noticed the tears trickling down his cheeks, neither one of them mentioned it.

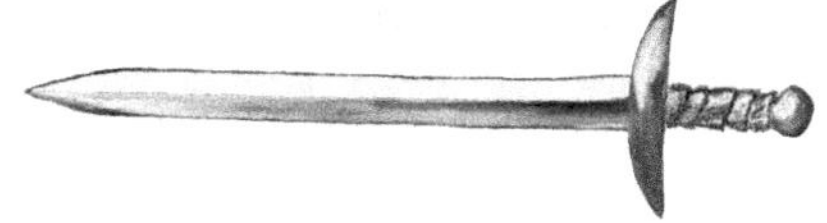

# Chapter NINETEEN

# *Discovered Check*

THE WORST PART OF THIS, in many ways, Damien reflected, as he lay awake and still beside the sated, sleeping youth and his entirely and intentionally *un*satisfied, sleeping Mistress, was that this captivity was so luxurious.

There were inconveniences, certainly, but he was comfortable. Well-fed, now that Azella wasn't using semi-starvation to confuse and control him. Intellectually occupied with his studies. Entertained with playing chess. Exercised by arms-practice and... this.

And *this* was certainly not unpleasant in any physical sense. Rather completely the opposite.

It was all too easy to understand Denisa and Mikhail, who had known nothing else and seen just enough of the struggles of normal people to know that normal life was not this luxurious. If Damien himself had been some peasant or smallholder, he could imagine being quite as tempted as they.

Tempted? Say it straight, at least to himself. They *embraced* their roles.

And how much of his own ability to withstand resulted from the knowledge that he would be returning to his own luxurious life as a king? Was it moral strength that he possessed or merely less temptation?

And, he asked himself wryly, noticing his fingers stroking Mikhail's unnaturally golden braids as the youth slept soundly in the curve of his shoulder, was it even reasonable to think he *had* any moral strength after everything he had done here? Could the ends – of protecting his Realm, his wife, his child – ever justify the means he had taken to reach that point?

Why, for example, was he still here at all?

Azella believed he was waiting for the knowledge he now believed she would never grant him; the demon Summoning and Binding rituals that he was now aware were secreted within her study on those untouchable shelves. When she admitted it and tried to entice him with her body again, he had pretended to be reconsidering her offer.

But in reality, Damien knew he had what he needed. She had discounted the value of the books (and scrolls) on Banishment and Unbinding, having herself little use for such things. Like as not, that information was replicated in the books in her study and she knew the techniques; it would make sense as a safety precaution and a hold over the fell creatures she Summoned that she could also Banish them. Damien's studies suggested that it took very little Power to Summon a demon – though rather more effort and better offerings to Summon, or rather Invite, particular demons of greater Power or station. The Power Azella was so carefully harvesting and husbanding was to enable her to retain *control* over the Summoned demon... to Banish it if she so chose.

He'd read about – and thereby memorized – every type of demon, and every Banishment ritual and technique. Once he'd decided to focus on just those things, her vast library of Demonology had become much more manageable and he'd been able to start combining the knowledge and concepts as he did with everything else.

The Sorcerer-King of Ilseador had no question that he could stand successfully against Azella the Unpitying and her demons if she should seek to test him again.

So why was he still here...? And why was he allowing her to think he was her captive – her *chattel* as she had called him?

Why not just walk out of here and go home?

He should...

Mikhail stirred slightly in his sleep and snuggled in a little deeper to Damien's shoulder, drawing a gentle smile out of the dark-haired man.

He stopped playing with the youth's hair and wrapped his arm around the young man's shoulders, amused by the contrast of his winter-pale skin against Mikhail's rich mahogany. If the youth ever had a chance to spend time outside, would he turn darker still? Damien found himself caught up in a fantasy of teaching Mik to ride a horse...

And there it was.

He was staying for *Mikhail*.

Perhaps it was something about the lad that reminded him of himself... or perhaps he had fallen slightly in love with the youth. He'd spent too much time with Mikhail, both intimately and teaching him chess and swordsmanship. If Jason were here to *Look* with his Seeing Eye, doubtless he'd note that the youth was covered with those cobwebby Bindings that apparently decorated everyone Damien loved.

His eyes strayed to the sleeping sorceress and shook his head.

Not her, though. A month earlier... perhaps.

And Damien still believed that there *was* hope for her, that a *soul* lurked deep beneath that layered, hurting shell that was the Evil Wizard part of her.

But it was *very* deep and Damien no longer believed that *he* might have the keys to free her.

Whether he had the keys to free Mikhail was another question entirely.

The king had to admit it looked fairly hopeless.

The young man – the *boy* for all that Damien had not allowed himself to think of Mikhail as such – had proven his attachment to Azella and his ambition to serve her or follow in her footsteps at every turn.

Damien could free him from the tyranny of his true-name, but what then? Could he reasonably expect to bring the lad home with him? Aside from the embarrassment... Jason and Adam – and Genevieve – would take one look at Mikhail and know exactly what they had been to each other. Aside from that, Mikhail was Powerfully Talented, ruthless, and if he had a conscience, it was severely underdeveloped.

And then there was Denisa, whom he had promised Darvin and Franz he would do his best for as well...

Damien closed his eyes, and the Realm began to claim his attention. He was getting almost no sleep these days. At least, the Realm gave back in energy what it took from him in focus – and gave him the Healing which he had never been able to adequately do for himself. It was being quite solicitous of him these days, as if nearly losing him had made it aware in its inhuman way that he was precious to it.

The pieces of the puzzle were all staring at him. He just couldn't fit them all together yet. Mikhail and Denisa and the Realm... and Genevieve... and Jason... and... Tomas Elsevier?

The king frowned. Surely Tomas had returned to Siovale with his family once the city was freed of ice and Genevieve and Jason – and Adam – had things in hand.

But Damien couldn't get the image of Tomas Elsevier out of his head.

Tomas Elsevier.

And Queen Estelle of Deltheren.

Though he didn't have an image of Estelle to picture, besides the painting that had been sent him. Well, it had been sent his grandfather on the ascension of the young Queen, some thirty years earlier. And about the same time that Countess Miraly's mother and predecessor had taken Elendria over to Deltheren's rule. For tax incentives, Adam had said, his father being the former Countess' brother.

Deltheren and Queen Estelle. Tomas. Jason. Genevieve. Mikhail. Denisa. And his own Realm.

Why not Farivera? He was *in* Farivera right now. What had happened to the noble families of the province anyways? This was the first of the Lost Provinces, but they had no diplomatic relations with Sindala, to the south, to whom Farivera now looked, or so they'd thought.

There was something *wrong* here – beyond the fact that the keep of an Evil Wizard had sat at the mouth of the Tree of Life River from time immemorial.

Deltheren and Tomas Elsevier kept crowding into Damien's thoughts. And Mikhail.

Deltheren... from where Azella's allies had sent the ice-storm...

His Realm was trying to tell him something. Without either Sword or Throne, he couldn't make the deeper contact he needed to get more than vague impressions.

The pieces slid up, down, sideways, backwards in his mind.

"There's a missing piece," Damien muttered irritably to himself...

...and froze.

That was *exactly* what Genevieve had said, as they were preparing for the battle with the pirates.

Who had benefited from that ice-storm anyways?

Or rather who *should* have benefited from it? If Damien hadn't been able to sense it coming down upon them all, if he hadn't tried to fight it by using the hurricane brought in from the sea and accidentally strengthened and broadened and sped it up... it would have taken another day to reach Emeralsee.

He'd only called that last Council of Peers the day after Jason and Adam's wedding because the soul-bond had made it impossible for him to focus in the week preceding... which surely no one outside of their small circle could have predicted. Damien had always been the soul of courtesy with regards to his nobles and never imposed on their travel plans or demanded they attend upon his whims.

If not for that concatenation of unanticipated events... most of his nobles would have been on their way home. The storm had been much narrower – mentally, he traced the path it would have taken on the map he had memorized long before his Binding to the Realm had made it an intrinsic part of him.

The ice storm would have destroyed Dalzialest, Brindlewell, Cedarwen... a litany of other counties and baronies and smaller holdings ran through his mind. And Emeralsee.

The shape of the land: Reyensweir would have largely been spared, but Duke Quillian's second capitol just east of Cedarwen along the Emerald River....

Tomas Elsevier and his duchess and his children had been planning to stay on for a little to visit with the king and queen, but Quillian and Duchess Tariana of Embervest would have been traveling together on that path. And possibly Duchess Laura of Alpinsward as well. And Rosa and Zachary and their baby girls...

They might all have been within walls when the storm struck... but it was just as likely that they wouldn't have been, some of them anyways. It had borne down with no warning and crossed the Realm within hours. What chance for men and women – and children – on horses and in carriages to find shelter in the broad, open plains with no more notice than the wind picking up and the sky darkening ahead of them?

Elaarwen would have largely been spared, but Genevieve was Bound to the Realm as Queen. As the *soul-bonded Queen* to a King Bound to a Realm that had just suffered a devastating storm. It would have been just the two of them and their usual retainers in the Castle to face the pirates and Azella and the ice-stricken city.

Jason was supposed to be a temporary Heir to the Throne. A placeholder. He was the son of a minor Countess and there was nothing outstanding about him save his swordsmanship and a reputation for absolute honesty and incorruptibility.

No one would have guessed, so much as a week earlier, he was a great-grandson of King Reginald with a hidden Talent for magick and that the Monarch's Blade would 'speak' for him. He'd held the damned Sword before, after all.

No one else at *all* knew that Genevieve and Adam were supports in that way. Or could have guessed that Damien would weaken his position with regards to his Court by waking the magick in the entire nobility of the Realm.

The King would have been alone in his magick and all too easily overwhelmed.

The Queen would have been dead at his side.

The Crown Prince – a 'useless placeholder' – would have been left holding the reins of government, with only Duke Tomas of Siovale – out of all the Peers of the Realm – left alive and in ice-bound Emeralsee to support him.

And all that would be left standing, what was just across the mountains from Farivera...

Siovale.

# Alsterling Family Tree

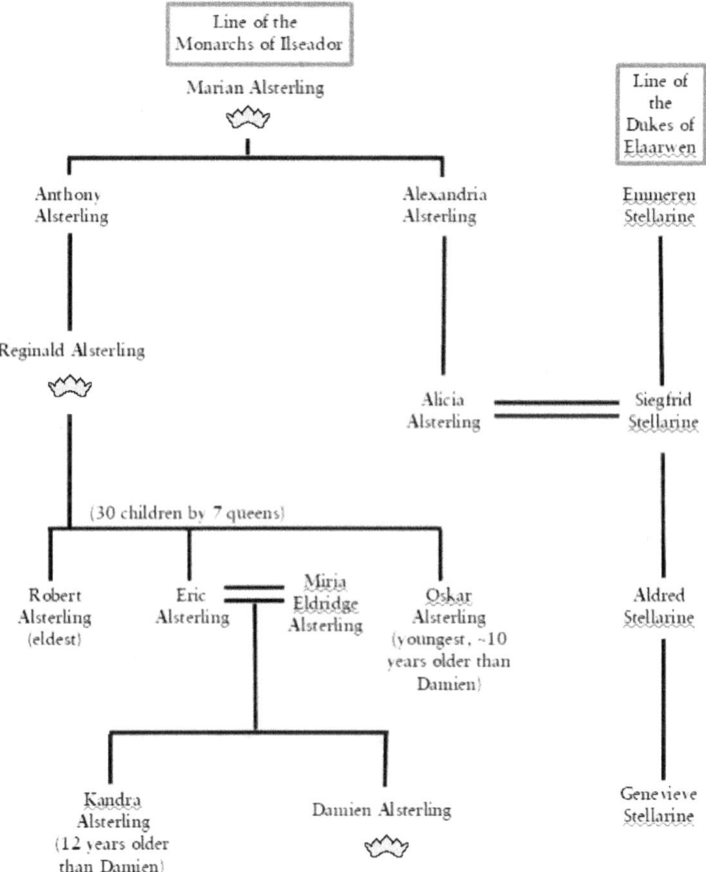

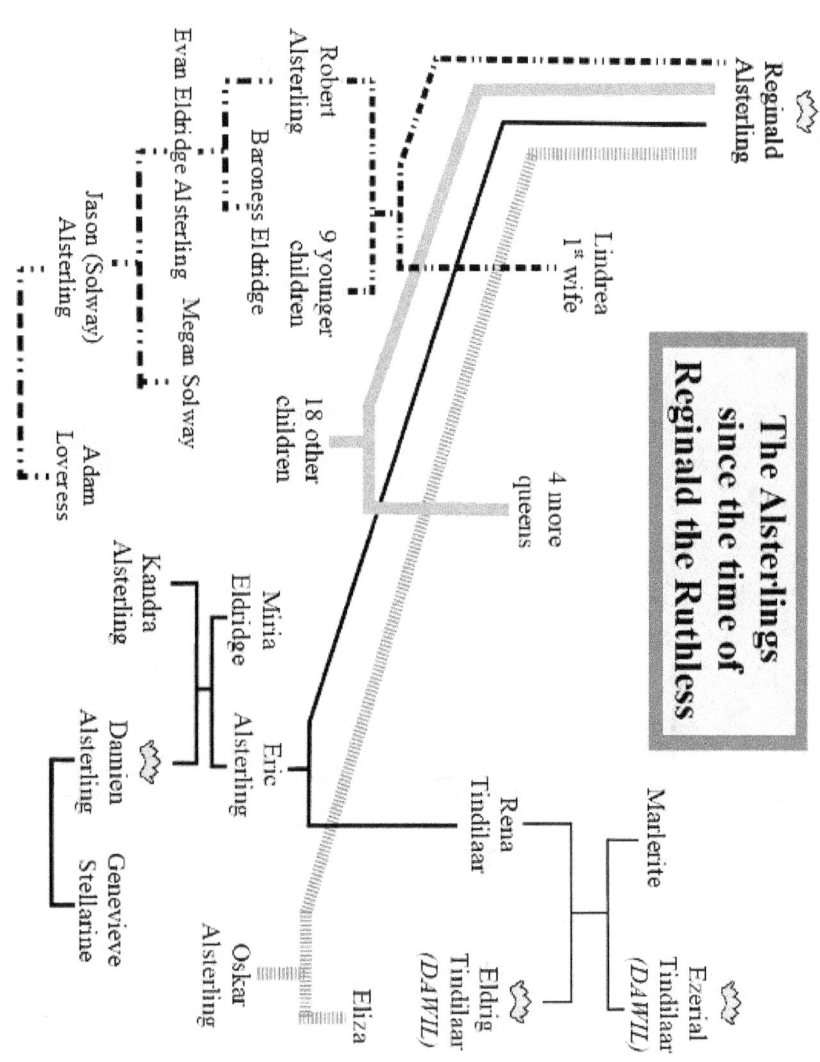
The Alsterlings since the time of Reginald the Ruthless
Reginald Alsterling
Robert Alsterling
Evan Eldridge Alsterling
Baroness Eldridge
9 younger children
Jason (Solway) Alsterling
Megan Solway
Adam Loveress
18 other children
Lindrea 1st wife
4 more queens
Kandra Alsterling
Miria Eldridge
Eric Alsterling
Damien Alsterling
Genevieve Stellarine
Rena Tindilaar
Oskar Alsterling
Eliza
Marlerite
Ezerial Tindilaar (DAWIL)
Eldrig Tindilaar (DAWIL)

# Index of Characters

Characters that appear in this book are <u>underlined.</u>
(Characters that are referenced, but do not actually appear are in plain type. Some additional characters are included who are not mentioned in this book to clarify relationships.)
Deceased characters are in *italics*.
Characters with speaking roles in this book are in **bold**.

The grandchildren of a reigning king or queen are officially grand dukes and grand duchesses in Ilseador, but are also referred to as princes and princesses when the question of their position in the line of succession is not in question.
Damien was Crown Prince after Oskar died.

**Contents of the Index:**
- Royal Family of Ilseador
- Provinces of Ilseador in order of precedence and relevant ruling family members
- Emeralsee contains the following fiefs named in the story: Seasbourne, Cedarwen, Eldyrwyld,Lynncrag, Elmirscroft, Ravenscroft
- Elaarwen contains the following fiefs named in the story: Brindlewell, Cloudcroft
- Siovale
- Reyensweir contains the following fiefs named in the story: Zialest
- Embervest contains the following fiefs named in the story: Minglemere, Everfields
- Alpinsward contains the following fiefs named in the story: Dalizell
- Dalzialest, duchy
- The Lost Provinces: Alpinsward, Minglemere, Elendria, Farivera, Everfields

***Royal Family of Ilseador***
*(and noted individuals in the Royal City and Province)*

- <u>**Damien Alsterling,**</u> King of Ilseador
    - <u>**Queen Genevieve (Stellarine) Alsterling**</u>, Duchess of Elaarwen
      (a.k.a. 'the Rebel Duchess'), King Damien's wife
    - <u>***Queen Marian Alsterling***</u> (a.k.a. 'Marian the merciful'), King
      Damien and Queen Genevieve's great-great-grandmother
      (common ancestress)
    - <u>**Crown Prince Jason (Solway) Alsterling,**</u> Duke of Emeralsee, son
      of Evan Eldridge Alsterling
    - <u>**Prince Adam (Loveress) Alsterling,**</u> husband of Prince Jason
        - *Eric Alsterling,* son of old king *Reginald Alsterling,*
          former Crown Prince, King Damien's father
            - » *Queen Rena (Tindilaar) Alsterling,* a princess from
              Dawil; mother of Prince Eric Alsterling; grandmother
              of King Damien; sister to *King Eldrig Tindilaar*
            - » *Miria (Eldridge) Alsterling,* King Damien's and
              *Princess Kandra's* mother; wife of *Prince Eric;*
              daughter of a minor noble family in the countryside
              of Emeralsee Province; oldest of seven children
                - * *Miria's father, David Eldridge,* was a failed
                  squire, son of the former Baron of Elderwyld
                - * *Miria's mother, Alexa,* was a blacksmith's daughter
            - » *Grand Duchess (or Princess) Kandra 'Kandy' Alsterling,*
              King Damien's sister; Prince Eric and Lady Miria's
              daughter joined the army as a common foot- soldier at 18,
              worked her way up. Was to have married Lord Raphael
              Anvliyar of Cedarwen (love-match) and helped her
              parents and brother escape to the Rebellion in Elaarwen

        - *King Reginald Alsterling* (aka 'the old king' or 'Reginald
          the Ruthless'); King Damien's grandfather
            - » *'Lord' Prydeen,* his Apprentice Evil Wizard
            - » *7 wives*
            - » *1st Princess Lindrea Alsterling (died before he was crowned)*
            - » *2nd*
            - » *3rd*
            - » *4th*

» *5th*
» *6th Queen Rena (Tindilaar) Alsterling* of Dawil, *Prince Eric's* mother, King Damien's grandmother
» *7th Eliza Alsterling* (Oskar's mother, married to *King Reginald* simultaneously with *Queen Rena*)
» *Oskar Alsterling*, the youngest son of Reginald.
  * <u>Sir Jason Solway</u>,  *Prince Oskar's* bodyguard before he was Heir, his Champion while he was Heir
  * <u>Sir Edmund Railston</u>, *Prince Oskar's* Champion and bodyguard at the time Ring was taken from *Prince Oskar* (also Adam Loveress' first lover)
» 30 legitimate children (all dead), including the following:
» *Crown Prince Robert Alsterling (son of Princess Lindrea)*
» *Princess Selda Alsterling*
» *Crown Prince Eric Alsterling (son of Queen Rena)*
» *Crown Prince Oskar Alsterling (son of Queen Eliza)*
» Some 100 grandchildren (all dead besides Damien and Evan) including the following:
  * *Alric Alsterling*
  * *Grand Duke Salleen Alsterling*
  * *Grand Duchess Kandra Alsterling*
  * Grand Duke Evan Eldridge Alsterling (son of Prince Robert)
  * Crown Prince Damien Alsterling
- **King Damien's Royal Guards**
» **Champion: <u>Sir Adam Loveress</u>**  (shield is puce with a rose, argent, crossed by a black sword), a close advisor of King Damien
  * **Captain and Knight Commander of the Royal Guard: <u>Sir Timothy Ancellius</u>** (a.k.a. 'Tim'), Second-in-Command of the Royal Guard when Damien is crowned, marries Secret Cadre member Aryllis after Damien is crowned, has son Enrico (a.k.a. Rico)
» **Original Guards**
  * **Champion: <u>Sir Jason Solway</u>** (mother is Countess Alexa Solway), a close advisor of King Damien's.
  * **Captain and Knight Commander of the Royal Guard: <u>Sir Adam Loveress</u>**
  * **<u>Sir Timothy Ancellius</u>**

* Sir Leverett Childress (a.k.a. 'Lev'), marries
  Secret Cadre member Terellie
* Sir Otto
* Sir Randolph
* (plus seven others not named)

- **Newer Guards members** (five years into Damien's reign)
  » <u>**Sir Timothy Ancellius,** (Captain and Knight-Commander)</u>
  » <u>Sir Marcus</u> (Second-in-Command)
  » Sir Mikal 'Mik'
  » <u>Sir Rodney</u>
  » Sir Everett Ladler
  » Sir Drake Milbourne
  » <u>**Sir Angelos Eldridge**</u>
  » (and five others not named)

- **The Secret Cadre of Royal Guards**
  » **Original twelve King's Ladies:** the Secret Cadre of Royal
    Guards (all but Lena and Ciriis marry one of Damien's
    original Royal Guards following his coronation)
    * Ciriis Celavell: Mistress of Protocol and
      Spymistress, Commander of the Secret Cadre
      under Adam Loveress, later King's Advisor
      and then Assistant to Duke Aldred
    * Lena Devergnon: Poisoner/anti-poisoner,
      later Assistant Royal Librarian
    * <u>Aryllis Ieldore</u>: marries Royal Guardsman Tim
      Ancellius; mother of Enrico Ancellius (a.k.a. Rico);
      becomes Mistress of Protocol and Spymistress and
      commander of the Secret Cadre under Adam Loveress
    * Felena
    * Terellie: marries Royal Guardsman Leverett Childress
    * Sasha
    * Elsa
    * Emerie

* Thielda
* Nalda
* Kamauri
* Licia
* Mirabelle
» **Newer Secret Cadre** (five years into Damien's reign)
* <u>Lady Alanna</u>
* Lady Lisa
* Lord Aaron
* Lord Devin
* Master Xavier

- **Castle Personnel**
  » <u>Elista</u>, senior maid, later Chatelaine. Began work the day *Prince Eric* and *Lady Miria* were killed, fed Damien until *Lady Theresa* discovered her. Married to *Robert*, Captain of the Castle Guard during the Usurpation
  » *Captain Robert* of the Castle Guard, married to Elista, died during the Usurpation
  » <u>Maree</u>, knife sharpener for the kitchen, had a huge infatuation with Damien

## *Provinces of Ilseador*

in order of precedence and relevant ruling family members

- *Emeralsee,* duchy – Alsterling family, gold and turquoise (guards wear dark blue and black)
  - <u>Duke Jason (Solway) Alsterling,</u> Crown Prince of the Realm
  - <u>Duke-Consort Adam (Loveress) Alsterling,</u> husband of Jason
  - <u>Damien Alsterling</u> former duke
  - <u>Genevieve (Stellarine) Alsterling,</u> wife of Damien
  - <u>*Ghost of Queen Marian Alsterling*</u>, great-grandmother of Damien and Genevieve and great-great-grandmother of Jason
  - *Dead-and-gone:*
    - *Prince Anthony Alsterling,* eldest child of Queen Marian
    - *King Reginald Alsterling,* eldest child of Prince Anthony (see 'King Damien Alsterling' at top for details of *King Reginald's* offspring)

- *Other siblings of King Reginald* (and their families and Alsterling cousins)
- *Other siblings and half-siblings of Prince Anthony*
- *Princess Alexandria Alsterling,* youngest child of *Queen Marian* (fled Emeralsee with the Monarch's Blade shortly before *Queen Marian* was assassinated by Prince Reginald; played the role of 'Erawan the Kind Robber' while hiding out in the mountains of Elaarwen)
- *Grand Duchess Alicia Alsterling,* only child of *Princess Alexandria;* married *Siegfrid Stellarine,* Heir to the Province of Elaarwen, had one child, Aldred Stellarine

- **Others of note within Emeralsee** (see under 'King Damien Alsterling' at top)


- *Fiefs within Emeralsee*
  - *Seasbourne,* county – family Laidly
  - *Cedarwen, barony* – Anvliyar family
    » Baron Raphael Anvliyar (intended husband of King Damien's sister, Princess Kandra)
    * *Dowager Baroness Theresa Anvliyar,* mother of Baron Raphael, former Royal Librarian and guardian of King Damien as a child after his parents were slain; died a traitor's death for having conspired to betray *Crown Prince Eric, Lady Miria,* and *Princess Kandra,* as well as for Conspiracy Against the Crown due to her role during the Usurpation of *Harald Elsevier*
  - *Elderwyld,* barony – Eldridge family
    (Note: names in the Eldridge family aside from *Miria, Alexa,* Angelos, Eugenio, and Evan have not been given in the story yet; they are included here to make the family connections clear)
    » **Baron Eugenio Eldridge**
    * **Sir Angelos Eldridge,** one of Baron Eugenio's sons
    * *Previous Baron Eldridge,* grandfather of the current Baron (Eugenio), father of *Baroness Dara* and *David*

* *Baroness Dara Eldridge*, mother of Baron Eugenio
* *David Eldridge,* Lord of Ravenscroft (gifted to *Prince Eric* and *Lady Miria* and deeded to her parents), younger son of the *former Baron,* a failed squire, husband of Alexa, father of seven (*Lady Miria* was his eldest)
* *Alexa Eldridge, David's* wife; a blacksmith's daughter, mother of seven
* *Lady Miria (Eldridge) Alsterling,* Damien's mother, eldest child of *David* and *Alexa Eldridge*

» Unknown fate
* Evan Eldridge, a cousin of *Lady Miria's,* son of *Baroness Dara Eldridge,* half-brother of Baron Eugenio

- **Lynncrag,** baronetcy – Loveress family
  » <u>**Baronetta Linda Loveress**</u>
    * Lord George Loveress, husband of Baronetta Linda
    * Their children (ages given for the 5th year of King Damien's reign)
    * <u>**Sir Adam Loveress**</u> – 34yo, Captain of the Royal Guard
    * Charles (a.k.a. 'Charley') Loveress – 32yo – a forest ranger
    * Lorenzo (a.k.a. 'Lorry') Loveress – 30yo – married and divorced twice
    * Desirée Loveress – 28yo
      * Desirée's 2 little boys (8yo and 10y o)
    * Fontaine Loveress – 24yo – priestess novitiate (but left before final vows)
    * Martin Loveress – 20yo - healer
    * <u>**Marianna Loveress**</u> – 18yo – lady-in-waiting applicant (Secret Cadre)
- *Elmirscroft,* property
- *Ravenscroft,* property
  » *David Eldridge,* grandfather of King Damien
    * *Alexa Eldridge,* grandmother of King Damien, wife of David

- *Elaarwen,* duchy – Stellarine family, violet and silver
  - <u>Duchess Genevieve (Stellarine) Alsterling</u>
    - <u>**Duke-Consort Damien Alsterling,**</u> husband of Genevieve
    - Lord Aldred Stellarine, widowed husband of Duchess-Consort *Giendra (Topasirre) Stellarine,* father of Duchess Genevieve, only child of Duke Siegfrid Stellarine and *Grand Duchess Alicia Alsterling*
    - *Duke Siegfrid Stellarine,* father of Duke Aldred, husband of *Grand Duchess Alicia Alsterling,* son of Duke Emmeren
      - » *Grand Duchess Alicia Alsterling,* wife of Duke Siegfrid Stellarine, mother of Duke Aldred
    - *Duke Emmeren Stellarine,* father of *Duke Siegfrid*
    - *Duchess Shalla (Elemandros) Stelarine,* wife of Duke Emmeren
    - **Others of note in the duchy:**
      - » Lord Adsel Topasirre, Chatelaine and Regent of Elaarwen, from Genevieve's mother's family

  - *Fiefs within Elaarwen*
    - *Brindlewell,* county – Solway family
      - » Countess Alexa Solway, mother of Megan and Jason
        - * <u>**Lady Megan Solway**</u>, Heir to Brindlewell, oldest child of Countess Alexa, wife of David
        - * <u>**Lord David Solway**</u> (a.k.a. Captain Daffyd Metreedi), husband of Lady Megan
        - * their children (ages given for the 5th year of King Damien's reign)
          - * <u>Elaina Solway</u> – 22yo
          - * *Rudolph Solway* (deceased) (would have been 19yo)
          - * Roger Solway – 13yo
          - * Esmerelda Solway – 11yo
        - * <u>**Sir Jason Solway**</u>, younger child of Countess Alexa
    - *Cloudcroft,* property – Stellarine family
      - » Lord Aldred Stellarine
        - * Lady Ciriis Celavell, Aldred's mistress

- *Siovale,* duchy – Elsevier family, forest green and silver (guards wear dark green and black)
    - <u>Duke Tomas Elsevier</u>
        - » Duchess-Consort Sildra (Miramar) Elsevier
        - » Their six children (ages given for the 5th year of Damien's reign, not all of their names have been given in the story as of yet)
            - * Mark Elsevier - 20yo
            - * Arabella Elsevier – 17yo
            - * Lorinda – 14yo
            - * Denis Elsevier – 12yo
            - * Gemma Elsevier – 10yo
            - * Gary Elsevier – 7yo
        - » *Duke Hector Elsevier,* father of Tomas, husband of *Lydia*
        - » *Dowager Duchess-Consort Lydia Elsevier,* mother of *Harald* and Tomas, died a traitor's death for Conspiracy Against the Crown for her role in the Usurpation by her son *Harald*
        - » *Harald Elsevier,* cuckoo's child of *Duchess Lydia* by *King Reginald,* died a traitor's death for Usurping the Throne after Damien was crowned... Genevieve Stellarine Alsterling's first husband

- *Reyensweir,* duchy – family Mirion
    - <u>Duke Quillian Mirion</u>

    - *Fiefs within Reyensweir*
        - *Zialest,* county – Teraseel family (adjacent to Dalizell, across some challenging mountain passes from Elaarwen; HOWEVER see also DALZIALEST below)
            - » <u>Countess Rosa Teraseel</u>
                - * *Gavin Teraseel,* Rosa's brother; he was to marry Ciriis Celavell

- *Embervest* duchy – family Eledor
  - <u>Duchess Tariana Eledor</u>
    - *Duke Istvan Eledor,* father of Tariana
    - Lord Robard Eledor, Tariana's older brother

  - *Fiefs within Embervest* The Lost Provinces of Minglemere (returned) and Everfields (still Lost to Vindalia) are part of Embervest
    - *Minglemere,* barony – family Krakenroost
      » Baron Densal Krakenroost
      » Lost to Vindalia some seventeen years
        before King Damien was Crowned
      » Regained in the 4th year of King Damien's reign
    - *Everfields*
      » Lost to Vindalia some fifty years before
        King Damien was crowned

- *Alpinsward,* duchy – family Marseill
  - The last of the Lost Provinces to defect (in their case to Mercasia after *Crown Prince Robert Alsterling's* negotiations failed following his murder by 'bandits')
  - The first of the Lost Provinces to return, following King Damien's coronation and negotiations with Queen Genevieve
  - <u>Duchess Laura Marseill</u>

  - *Fiefs within Alpinsward*
    - *Dalizell,* county – Miramar family; HOWEVER see also DALZIALEST below
      » <u>Count Zachary Miramar</u>
        * Sildra (Miramar) Elsevier, Zachary's next elder sister, was already married to Tomas Elsevier when *parents* and *Elsa* died
        * Zachary's *parents* (died of flux)
        * *Elsa,* eldest child and former Heir to Dallizell; Zachary and Sildra's older sister; died of the same flux as their parents

- ***DALZIALEST*, duchy,**
  combined of Dalizell and Zialest when Rosa Teraseel and Zachary Miramar married just after King Damien's coronation – the Miramar family was granted the promotion to a Duchy in recognition of their loyalty to the new king (the counties had been asking for royal permission to merge for several generations)
  - <u>**Duchess Rosa (Teraseel) Miramar**</u>
  - <u>**Duke Zachary Miramar**</u>
    - 2 children in the 5th year of King Damien's reign
      * Talia Miramar (a.k.a Tally), 3yo
      * Betha Miramar, newborn

- The Lost Provinces
  1. Alpinsward, duchy – family Marseill
     Duchess Laura Marseill
     - Lost to Mercasia some five years before King Damien was crowned
     - Regained in the 3rd year of King Damien's reign
  2. Minglemere, barony – family Krakenroost
     Baron Densal
     - Returned to Duchy Embervest
     - Lost to Vindalia some seventeen years before King Damien was Crowned
     - Regained in the 4th year of King Damien's reign
  3. Elendria, county – formerly part of Duchy Alpinsward
     Countess Miraly
     - Lost to Deltheran some twenty-five years before King Damien was crowned
     - negotiations begun to Restore Elendria to Ilseador in the 5th year of King Damien's reign
  4. Farivera – formerly part of Duchy Siovale
     - Lost to… Sindalla? Some forty years before King Damien was crowned
  5. Everfields – formerly part of Duchy Embervest
     - Lost to Vindalia some fifty years before King Damien was crowned

# MAPS

## *Ilseador*

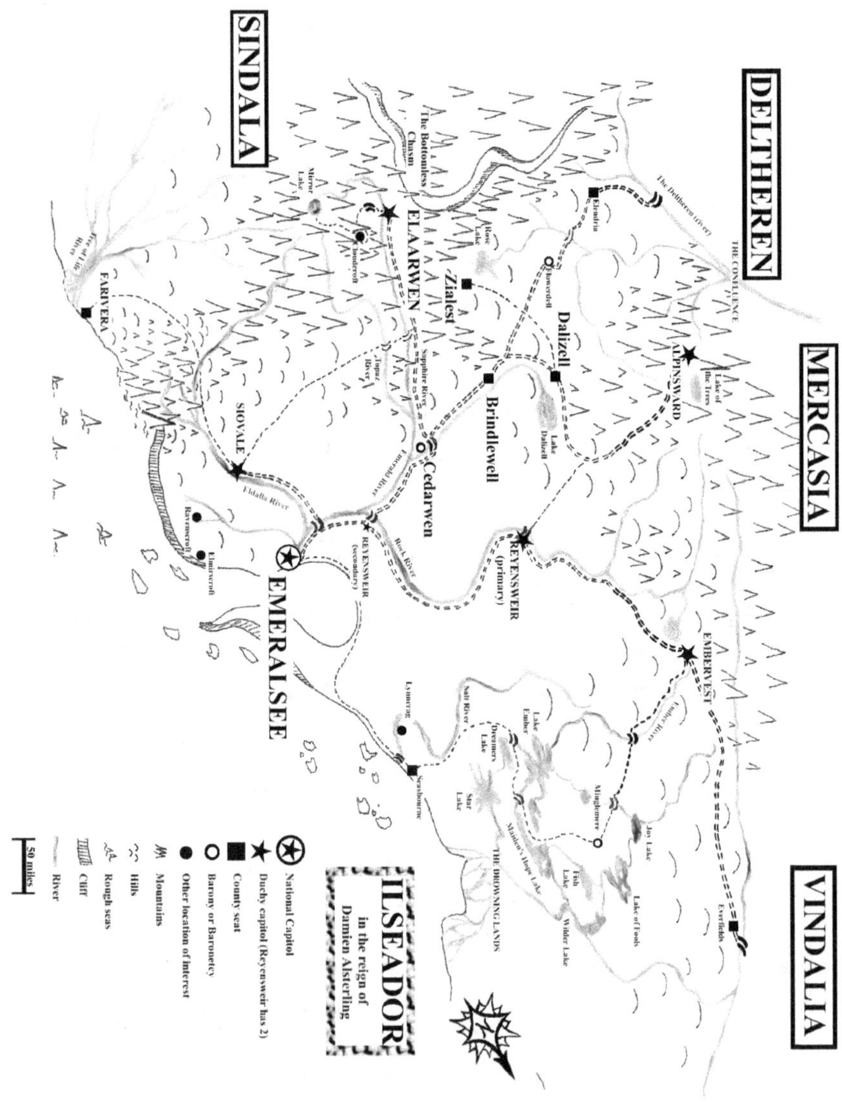

# *LANDS Around the MERUTIAN SEA*

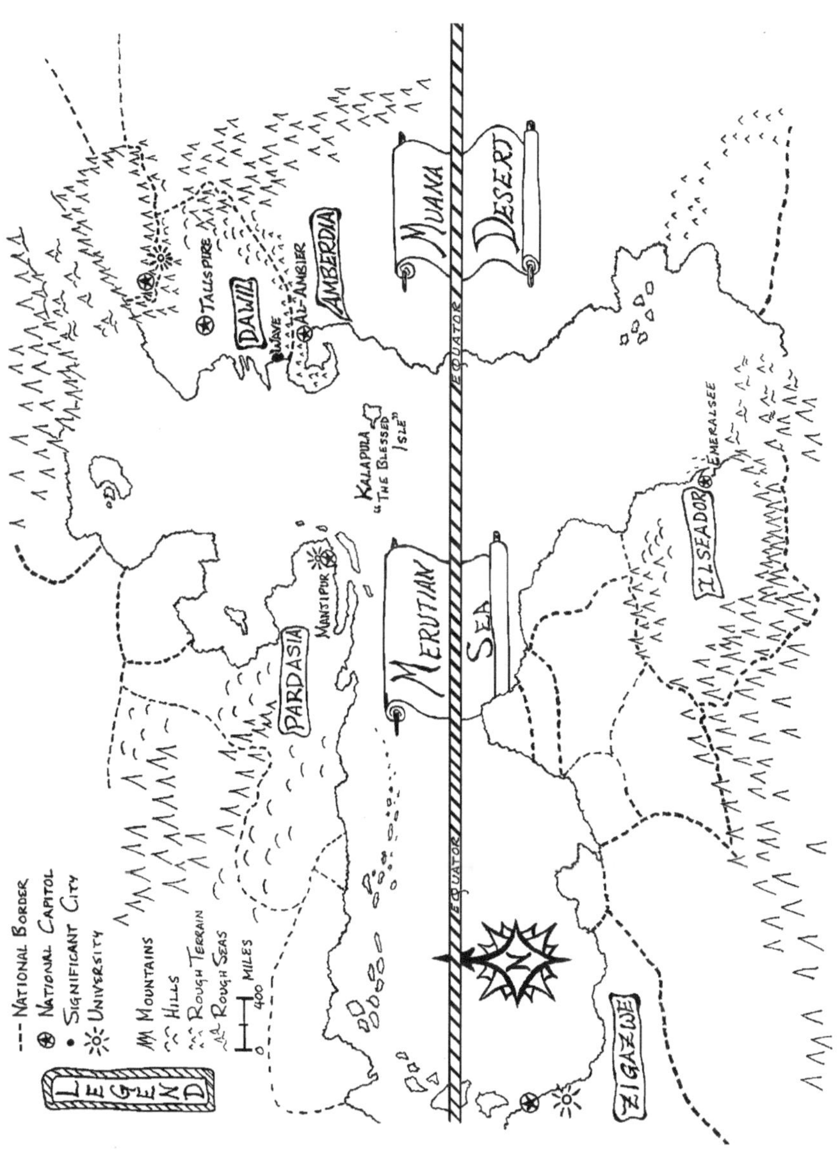

*And now, for your delectation...*
*an excerpt from...*

# Chapter ONE

## *Caught!*

GENEVIEVE HAD NOT FORGOTTEN THE old king's pet sorcerer. She *had*, however, assumed he would not be a problem. This was clearly not the case.

She ducked into a rubbish-strewn alley and prayed that one of the doors leading off of it would open to somewhere that was not a dead-end. Unlike the alleyway itself. Genevieve really wasn't familiar enough with the layout of the capitol to be doing this sort of thing. As her advisors had repeatedly told her. Her chagrined memory replayed the scene of her tossing her head as she assured them that "the Rebel Duchess" could handle anything.

Not that she had *planned* to have to handle anything at all. She was just going to come in as part of the crowds hoping to get a glimpse of the new young king, on this last day of the coronation festivities. Just another gawker from the countryside. She still had no idea how Lord Prydeen had identified her.

The second door on the right opened at her frantic tug, and Genevieve hurried into darkness, pulling the door tightly shut behind her. She could hear people talking somewhere off to her right and the darkness seemed a little less dark in that direction. Perhaps there was a way through the building and back to the main street she had veered off of so abruptly. She needed to get back to the streets to complete her mission. The inhabitants of

the room ahead would be startled, but if she could get past them quickly –
before they decided to hold her for a thief – she might make it.

Just as the young woman started towards the sounds, the door behind
her crashed open and the sorcerer stepped through.

Lord Prydeen was a master of dramatic effect, some odd corner of her
mind noted absently. He stood framed in the doorway, too deeply cowled to
see his face, his ankle-length black cloak flapping and curling about him in
the sudden cross-currents of air between building and outside. The alley was
brighter than the room – so perhaps he merely paused to let his eyes adjust
– but in that moment he was more silhouette than shape, more demon than
man.

Genevieve could not – *could not* – lead him towards those unsuspecting
innocents in the room beyond. Perhaps the completely unexpected would
gain her – well, *some*thing.

She took a deep breath, but carefully did not think too hard about what
she was doing – though whether it was because Lord Prydeen was rumored
to be able to pull one's thoughts from the air itself or because she wouldn't
have the nerve if she did–

She spun on her heel and charged directly at the sorcerer, startling him
sufficiently that she shoved past him and back out into the dead-end alley.
Then to her left and back out to the main street – perhaps she could lose him
in the crowd. She had to try.

In her haste, however, Genevieve's own hood was pushed back, exposing
her signature red-gold hair – and confirming what had surely only been
Lord Prydeen's guess about the identity of his quarry.

Fool that she was for not having dyed it.

Thrice a fool for deciding to skulk about the coronation festivities – like
any small child playing "Erawan the Kind Robber" – instead of listening
to the reports of her spies as the mature, careful, strategic leader of the
rebellion should do. That stupid, romantic title – "Rebel Duchess" – really
*had* gone to her head, as Rosa had accused her. She would do the Cause
no good by being taken by the king's sorcerer. Even if the new young King
Damien lived up to his month-old reputation for fairness, Lord Prydeen
would never give her a chance to find out.

No time for this.

Genevieve jerked her hood back up and tried to blend into the crowded
market square, trying to outguess Lord Prydeen. Which direction would
the sorcerer be unlikely to go? – or which way would he be unlikely to
follow? Surely the feared and hated Royal Sorcerer could not make his way

through the crowd without causing an uproar that would let her dodge away... though he had before, when she first caught him following her. Could there be *any* safety for her here in the capitol, just six days after Damien's crowning? Surely the old guard was still in place and *no one* (not even the young king?) would dare to gainsay Lord Prydeen.

Abruptly, and entirely on instinct, not daring to look back to measure her pursuit, Genevieve swerved and tore for the royal viewing stand. Damien, if the stories were right – the stories that she had not believed and had come in person to verify – would merely have her executed for a traitor. Lord Prydeen – as she had reason to know – would sell her soul to demons and wring every last memory and secret from her shrieking heart.

The fine bright day taunted her travails, small poofy clouds ambling across a sky as blue as her own eyes. The market square – packed with a crowd of pleasantly frolicking merchants and peasants – impeded her swift progress. The swarms of children playing games of tag nearly tripped her up. The very *joy* of it all nearly derailed her thoughts, for such gaiety could never have been shown in the old king's rule, and part of her could not leave off trying to determine if there was still the undercurrent of desperation that she expected from her previous, and more successfully clandestine, visits to the capitol city.

But the Rebel Duchess knew exactly where the royal platform stood, both due to having marked it well when first she arrived and for the fact that it stood as tall any of the half-timbered two-story buildings surrounding the square. She had hoped to catch a glimpse of the young king from afar when first she arrived, and the royal platform had seemed like the right place to start. She had perhaps stayed still too long, staring too intently at the brilliantly bunting- and flower-clad structure, trying to discern which, if any, of the milling nobles on its three ornately decorated levels was the young king. Then, as now, the top level was empty, save for a matched pair of guards.

Part of her – the part that had insisted on this mad mission against all rational thought and advice – was certain that, if she could but look into his eyes, she would know if Damien was all that the reports claimed... or if he had been corrupted by his grandfather and Lord Prydeen.

Part of her – if she dared admit it – wanted to believe, even if it seemed beyond belief, that he could have been untouched. That the Cause was won, the need for a Rebel Duchess was done. That the Rebellion could quietly fold itself up and her folk could slip back to their homes, to their lives...

though perhaps not the Rebel Duchess herself, recognizable as she was as a symbol...

Yet – how could those two old, evil men *not* have insured that the crown prince was a "fit successor" to the king who had controlled a creature such as Lord Prydeen?

Genevieve had met the prince once, when they were both children. He had barely been of an age for his first pony, and she – a few years older – had just graduated to a mild-mannered horse... and her father's half-tamed, firebreathing mare that Duke Aldred had no idea she would even attempt to ride. Her father had brought her to Court to make her curtsy to the old king and see her named his Heir. Damien had been but one of a pack of the old king's grandchildren – a nondescript royal child, good-looking as they all had been, but special in no particular way. They had spent perhaps minutes in each other's presence, on separate ends of the audience hall that had seemed miles-long to her then.

Now those other siblings and cousins, aunts and uncles, were all gone and Damien – unremarked offspring of an unremarkable parent – had been named Crown Prince, and now King. For him to have inherited would seem to signal that he had done something to earn the old king's approval – perhaps by being ruthless enough to have ensured no other contenders were available. Certainly, he had made no mark by protesting his grandfather's policies while the old king lived, no mark of any kind, in fact. Despite all the time Genevieve had spent at Court, she did not recall ever noticing him again.

Yet she could still remember a certain clear-eyed gaze from that long-ago child. A gaze that seemed to recognize and promise to right all the wrongs that existed in the world. A gaze that had haunted her dreams since she had heard he had been crowned, and had kept her skepticism from becoming outright denial when rumors of the new king's beneficence came to her. And so, she had come to see for herself...

She had reached the royal platform at last, and hunted for a spot to clamber up. Not an easy endeavor, as it was so heavily be-ribboned – in every color, not merely royal gold and turquoise – with bright buntings stretched between triple rosettes made of actual rose petals. An elegantly illuminated sign noted that these were the coronation gifts of the Weavers' and Florists' Guilds – but the small barrel that the sign rested upon was of more interest to her, as it gave her a leg up to the first level, which was filled with younger noblemen. These young men were here to satisfy fathers and mothers who wanted them close to the source of power. They eyed her with interest – her cloak had of necessity been pushed aside to climb and she was dressed in hunting leathers fit tight to her athletic frame – and she in turn ignored them, using the spigoted ale kegs at which they were amusing themselves to give her a step up to the recessed second level.

The older noblemen and -women – and their maiden daughters – on this level looked at her quite askance. Genevieve hoped her hood shadowed her face enough to keep any of them from recognizing her, for she knew no few of them, though she did not recognize the barely-grown girls, nor more than a handful of the hardly-older lads below. These nobles had toadied up to the old king while Genevieve – and her father before her – had sought to protect their people. She knew all too well that they would as soon sell her out to Lord Prydeen as look at her. Even now they were trying to toady up to King Damien, bringing their marriageable daughters to parade before him – an array of maidens scarcely past puberty, for their elder ones had been taken to serve the old king and Lord Prydeen in years gone by, many never to be seen again. They, too, must surely be hoping for better from Damien, yet she saw nothing but avarice in the faces of even the children.

A good-looking young man – unusual only for being the only *young* man on this level of the platform, did someone think the new king's taste ran to boys? – with very dark hair and clear grey eyes offered her a hand onto the level. Genevieve was not too proud to accept help, even from a scion of one of *these* families. They exchanged a startled look and nearly let go of each other as an electric spark seemed to jump between their hands. Surely it wasn't dry enough today for such things, and so close to the harbor besides.

Putting such irrelevant details aside, Genevieve brushed off her hands on her breeches as she looked up towards the highest level of the reviewing stand, but saw only the pair of Royal Guards – two blondely handsome men so perfectly matched as almost to be twins – decorating that august space. Knights chosen for their beauty, just as were the horses that pulled the royal carriage. She wondered who they were – might they have enough real skill at arms to have faced her in the Battle of Siovale seven years earlier? She'd caught no more than a glimpse of either of them so far, as they turned, watchfully, eyes raking the crowds. Perhaps they were more than merely decorative.

Hopefully the king himself was sitting down and merely out of view. Genevieve needed for him to be there, before Lord Prydeen caught up with her. It was a wild gambit – praise all the Gods at once that Rosa really could handle the Rebellion, since it looked like she was going to have to. Rosa – would never forgive her for getting herself captured and killed. The

Rebel Countess – surely that sounded just as impressive. They had known it couldn't last – this would free Rosa to wed and produce the Heir that she needed. Genevieve's own proper title – Lady Stellarine, Duchess of Elaarwen (she dared not think "Princess of the Realm", though her bloodlines were as good as the king's) – would pass to a collateral line...

No matter. The issue at hand was to get up there to the top level and there was no obvious stair or ladder.

Genevieve dropped her useless disguise of a cloak before it could hinder her further in climbing higher, ignoring the massed gasp from the gathered nobles, and looked for a convenient way to boost herself to the king's level. The balustrade of the king's level – still festooned with those slippery buntings and banners – was more than head-high to her. It was higher than she could hoist herself on arm-strength alone.

That young man was still watching her – looking slightly amused, damn him. Or maybe that was *be*mused. Surely, he had little idea what to make of her and her sudden arrival. But he seemed to come to a decision and wrenched a ring with a large grey pearl on it off his finger, thrusting it towards her. It was the sort of thing a nobleman might offer a noblewoman to indicate interest – a sort of "let's get to know each other" offer, not quite a tryst, but more than an offer of acquaintance. The ring would have a house sigil on it, perhaps even a personal seal – enough information for her to find him again later on. A crazy thing to hand to the highly recognizable Rebel Duchess as she attempted to single-handedly besiege the new king's festival viewing platform. The young man must be completely daft.

And then he bent and cupped his hands as a stablehand might do to help someone into the saddle. The sparkle in his eyes suggested he was prepared to toss her high enough to pull herself up over that balustrade.

Again, the gathered nobles gasped, but this time there were also mutters and a fearful eagerness... and she guessed someone had spotted Lord Prydeen approaching.

There was no time for this. Genevieve stuffed the ring onto her finger – her beltpouch would take too long to open – put her foot in his hands and leapt up in concert with his toss.

And got the – third? fourth? – shock of the day as her reaching hands were grasped from above and an all too familiar voice gruffly said "Young miss, this is the king's place, you can't be climbing... up... her–" The voice cut off as and the hands fumbled and nearly dropped her back down, as their owner peered over the edge and then grabbed her more securely and helped her over the balustrade.

The Royal Guard was looking at her in exasperation and some of the same confusion Genevieve was feeling. It was the strangest and least appropriate timing on anything ever – but the touch of his hands had inflamed her with desire. *Not now, not now!* The Rebel Duchess thought frantically. She'd heard of this, but thought it a fairytale... Rosa, *Rosa* was her love...

"Jason Solway?" she managed to gasp out.

"Genny?" He was as flabbergasted as he was, and if the blush rising in those perfect cheeks was anything to judge, he was suffering from the same reaction. Suffering...

"Here now," said the other Royal Guard, coming forward from his ceremonial position. "Jase, what's this all about?"

She looked almost gratefully at the other man, just as gratefully *not* recognizing him as yet another childhood friend. But his familiar behavior towards Jason – were they lovers? Why did that thought make her heart – or something lower than her heart – do flips? And why, oh, why, *was this all happening at once?*

"Stand back, gentlemen," growled a low, cultured voice.

Lord Prydeen.

Apparently, she wouldn't have to sort any of this out after all.

The two Guards obediently stepped aside, though she rather thought that Jason only reluctantly let go of her hands, and she could see that the sorcerer had come up a set of stairs at the back of the reviewing stand. A brief surge of wind whipped the cowled hood from off Lord Prydeen's spotty, balding head, and tossed his long, drooping mustaches. He had not aged well since the old king's death; his hair had been thinning, but was still full when last she had gotten a good look at him, some months earlier, and the lines around his mouth were graven deeply, where once they had been entirely masked by his whiskers. Genevieve had heard tell that evil sorcerers cast vile spells to keep themselves young – by sacrificing true youths and maidens to demons, some said. She had scoffed, even as she wondered. The old king had lived long past his age, and Lord Prydeen, some said, had not aged at all, even as those noble daughters came to serve them both and were rarely seen again.

"Lady Genevieve." Lord Prydeen greeted her, coldly, but not correctly. He needed nothing besides himself to emphasize his authority, but he had brought a squad of his personal guards up with him. They fanned out behind him, blocking the path, even to headstrong young women who might push past a sorcerer.

She tilted her chin up – her nose was too snub to properly glare down it, but she was tall enough to try... and the arrogance might mask the tremble that the tumult in her stomach had settled into. "The proper title is '*Your Grace*', messir." She was actually in line for the throne herself, with all of Damien's family gone, and 'Lord' Prydeen was, after all, a sorcerer of no particular breeding.

And if she told herself that a few more times, perhaps she could dare to face him.

A wintry smile passed over Lord Prydeen's lips – gone as quickly as snow in the Summer. "No longer, I fear. My former master stripped you of your titles for your treasonous activities."

Genevieve inclined her head. "So, I have heard. But even a Royal Decree does not make a thing reality. Even His – belated – Majesty never put it to the test in *Elaarwen*."

Something sparked in the sorcerer's eyes. Anger, perhaps? Could such a one as he even feel something as tender as grief? He gestured to his men. "Bind her and bring her."

Jason bestirred himself to protest, "My lord–!" but the other Guard pulled him back and Genevieve found herself being roughly seized and turned around by hands that made no pretense of not enjoying their task. Even the king's own Royal Guards, it seemed, dared not speak against the sorcerer. Not yet anyways. If only she had waited to see if the young king could consolidate his power; if, indeed, he would continue in the way he had begun!

"My Lord Prydeen! What passes here?" The mild voice interrupted from the direction of the stairs, but was no one Genevieve recognized. She had been turned to face outwards towards the square whilst they bound her, and could not see the speaker.

Lord Prydeen's voice was a curious mix of ingratiating and dismissive. "Nothing you need trouble yourself over, my lord. Some rabble found her way up here, clearly to cause some trouble to you. It is my task and my privilege to safeguard Your Highness. We'll be away momentarily."

Gentle hands cleared away the thongs that had begun to lash her wrists. "Surely you are mistaken, my Lord Prydeen. This is no rabble, but Her Grace, the Duchess Genevieve Stellarine of Elaarwen."

"Yes, my Lord, the so-called 'Rebel Duchess'," Lord Prydeen's voice was growing impatient. "I am taking her to the castle dungeons to have out of her what she knows. You can make an example of her later on – you must not detract from your coronation festivities."

"Nonsense, Lord Prydeen," the mild voice replied. "That isn't how we treat visiting royalty... not to mention that the people would rise in protest and not even you could put them *all* down at once."

He came around to Genevieve's right side, and before she could register that this was the same young man who had cupped his hands for her boot like any stableboy, he gave her that same enigmatic smile, and faced the crowd – who had begun to turn as they saw their king. Damien lifted Genevieve's right hand in his left, holding them high above their heads and called out, "I give you Genevieve Stellarine, the Rebel Duchess!"

It was the sort of moment a Duke's Heir is trained for and – bemused as she was at the turn of events – Genevieve flattened her palm against the king's and stood tall before the crowds, the errant breeze tossing her red-gold curls like a mane. She smiled fiercely, trying to think if this would be taken as some sort of inadvertent admission of surrender.

Even as the people roared their approval – and Lord Prydeen fumed behind them – a sudden, strange crackling noise erupted and ribbons of white fire fountained up between their pressed fingers. It wreathed down to wrap their hands and curl around their arms.

For all that she was the reigning duchess of a province, the leader of a rebellion against an unjust king and an evil sorcerer, and had spent most of her life in that struggle... Genevieve was tempted to faint right then and there. This was absolutely the *last* thing she had expected. If she hadn't seen this happen before, she would have thought it was some new and clever attack by Lord Prydeen.

But she *had* seen this before. And, likely, so had every member of the crowd below.

At least young King Damien looked nearly as befuddled as she felt.

He, however, recovered more quickly than she.

"And your future Queen!" he announced in what sounded like a calm voice.

He pulled her in and kissed her.

And the crowds went absolutely wild.

***Read the rest of this exciting story of rebellion and romance!***
***The Rebel Duchess***
***now at your favorite online ebookseller in print or ebook!***

# *Also by Mangala McNamara*

Fantasy in the World of the Living Gods:

The Chronicles of Ilseador
> *The Rebel Duchess: Book One*
> *The King's Champion: Book Two*
> *The Pirate-King: Book Three*
> *The Pale Sorceress: Book Four*

The Prankster Prince
> *Thony and the Much-Anticipated Adventure: Book One of The Prankster Prince*
> *Thony Goes Astray! (in the Deep, Dark, and Dangerous Fairy Wood): Book Two of The Prankster Prince*
> *So You Want to Be a Hero? Book Three of the Prankster Prince*
> *How Thony Stopped a War (and Fixed a Friendship): Book Four*

Knightess of the Realm
> *A Not-So-Sacrificial Maiden*
> *Out of the Woods… Hopefully (a Prequel Novella)*
> *Turns of a Page (A Prequel Story Collection)*
> *A Not-So-Simple Mission: Book One of the Heir's Journey*
> *An Entirely-Unexpected Revelation: Book Two of the Heir's Journey*
> *An All-Too-Surprising Homecoming: Book Three of the Heir's Journey*

More Fantasy coming soon…
> *An Altogether-Curious Altercation: Book ONE of the SECRET OF DRAGON MOUNTAIN (A Knightess of the Realm Novel) (September 2024)*
> *Diary of a ~~Runaway Prince~~ Bold Questing Hero: Book Five of the Prankster Prince(October 2024)*
> *The Un-Captive King: Book Five of the Chronicles of Ilseador (last in the Prydeen Prophecy Cycle (November 2024)*

# Author's Note

This story was a particularly challenging one for me to write. It helped that a few years back I wrote a story about our favorite Evil Sorceress that takes place a bit farther into the future.

And yes, Azella the Unpitying's story will be published eventually... Keep an eye on my website or join my newsletter to find out when. I'll only say that her tale is even harder to tell, and since she absolutely insisted on telling it in the first-person... well...

It was emotionally easier to see things from Damien's perspective.

It was also a great deal of fun to write about him fencing with Darvin, Franz, and even Rob and Mikhail – especially while the 2024 Summer Olympics were going on and Team USA Fencing did such a great job.

I'm a fencer myself. I began with foil when I was sixteen – so I know whereof I speak when I talk about picking up a sword for the first time at about that age! More recently I've taken up epée (with the occasional bout of saber). It's something I do for fun with my three sons (Big Red Driving Hoodie, The DungeonMaster, and Little Red Biking Hoodie), though none of us are competing in tournaments for now.

I highly recommend trying out fencing if you haven't (or going back again if you have). It's a great, full-body sport, incredibly safe, works for everyone from 10-year-olds to 80+-year-olds, and – heck, you're swordfighting. It immediately makes you the coolest person you know, and you are totally justified in quoting Inigo Montoya from The Princess-Bride until your friends and family beg you to stop.

On a more serious note... the next book in the Chronicles of Ilseador: The UnCaptive King will bring what I am now calling the Prydeen Prophecy Cycle to a close.

Fear not, however, Dear Reader! Damien and Genevieve's adventures (along with Jason, Adam, and the children) are definitely not coming to an end.

Ilseador is still healing.

Deltheren – and its treacherous Queen Estelle – is still holding on to Elendria.

Giendra Marlerite needs to be born and grow up and – if you were paying attention – she's going to have some younger siblings. At least one of whom is going to wreak a great deal of havoc and break his poor parents' hearts.

Not to mention that as unusual a situation as the Alsterlings have ended up in has got to have some odd ramifications in a country that just barely acknowledges same-gendered marriages.

And… a story that has been shouting to get written down is probably kicking itself out for Valentine's Day. I'll have some more details in the Author's Note for The UnCaptive King. (At least right now in my head it's a 'story.' These things have a way of getting away from me and turning into full-fledged books… and messing with my planned publication schedule… because, yeah, I have 2025 and 2026 planned out!)

Let me know if you fence!

Maybe we can have a bout sometime – allez!

Mangala

August '24

(Email me at RisingDragonBooks@gmail.com to join my newsletter and find out immediately when new things come out – or scan the QR code to get to my website at https://www.RisingDragonBooks.com)

# *About the Author*

MANGALA MCNAMARA LIVES IN FLYOVER Country (the far northern end of the US South) with her husband, The Professor, and four of her six children. The remaining children are in college – you can blame the oldest for the excessive amounts of math showing up in Mangala's fantasy novels, the second one for better attention to staging of scenes, the third for all the economics, and the fourth for great attention to history – and all of them for a focus on political science! Mangala is a former professional bellydance instructor, and used to enjoy knitting, crotchet and embroidering Temari balls but now is much more boring as she rarely does anything but write… although she also fences (the sport) and plays D&D with her kids. She owes her love of books and reading to her mother, who was a professional folklorist and could recite – from memory – stories from every nation in the United Nations.

*Her Knightess of the Realm and Prankster Prince series occur in the same world as Damien and Genevieve's stories.*

Learn about Mangala's upcoming projects (fiction and nonfiction both) and sign up for email updates at
https://www.RisingDragonBooks.com